IT WAS ALWAYS YOU

A RIDGEWATER HIGH NOVEL

CHERRY
BLOSSOM
ROMANCE

JUDY CORRY

Cover Illustration by Wastoki

Edited by Precy Larkins

Also By Judy Corry

Eden Falls Academy Series:

The Charade (Ava and Carter)

The Facade (Cambrielle and Mack)

The Ruse (Elyse and Asher)

The Confidant (Scarlett and Hunter)

The Confession (Kiara and Nash)

Kings of Eden Falls:

Hide Away With You (Addie and Evan)

Rich and Famous Series:

Assisting My Brother's Best Friend (Kate and Drew)

Hollywood and Ivy (Ivy and Justin)

Her Football Star Ex (Emerson and Vincent)

Friend Zone to End Zone (Arianna and Cole)

Stolen Kisses from a Rock Star (Maya and Landon)

Ridgewater High Series:

When We Began (Cassie and Liam)

Meet Me There (Ashlyn and Luke)

Don't Forget Me (Eliana and Jess)

It Was Always You (Lexi and Noah)

My Second Chance (Juliette and Easton)

My Mistletoe Mix-Up (Raven and Logan)

Forever Yours (Alyssa and Jace)

Standalones:

Protect My Heart (Emma and Arie)

Kissing The Boy Next Door (Lauren and Wes)

For my son Jonah

PLAYLIST

"Perfect" by One Direction
"Legends" by Kelsea Ballerini
"Take Me There" by Rascal Flatts
"Machine Heart" by Kelsea Ballerini

1

LEXI

CONGRATS ON GETTING *first chair again.*

I tried the words out in my head, attempting to figure out the perfect line to finally get a conversation started between me and my long-time crush, Harrison Carter.

When Mrs. Willis moved me up to second chair trumpet this morning, you would have thought I'd won the lottery with how excited I was. I knew I'd had no chance at getting first chair, since Harrison was *amazing,* but second chair was just as good because it meant I got to sit by *him.* My hands had been shaking ever since I'd caught a whiff of his cologne, and I'd been trying to think of reasons to scoot my chair a smidge closer to him.

I like your new haircut.

I shook my head. That was stupid. He'd think I was totally oblivious since he'd gotten the haircut sometime between Monday morning band and Tuesday at lunch where I'd stared at him and wished I could run my fingers through his blond spikes and smooth them down to the soft curls he'd had the day before. He looked good with the new haircut—it was hard to ruin perfection—but I missed the cute head flick he used to do to keep his hair out of his eyes.

Harrison finished putting his trumpet back in the case and was latching it shut. I needed to hurry and say something now or I'd miss my chance until next week.

Say something.

Anything.

I opened my mouth, but nothing came out.

His gaze, which had been on his trumpet case, lifted to my face at the exact moment that I was sitting there like a fool with my mouth hanging open.

"Any fun plans for the weekend?" he asked me in his ultra-smooth voice.

Now would be a good time to look like you have a brain, Lexi.

I managed to close my mouth but still stared blankly at him like I didn't know how to talk.

His Adam's apple bobbed as he swallowed. He probably regretted saying anything to me.

What had he asked me again? I'd gotten too lost in his blue eyes to comprehend his question.

Oh right. Weekend plans.

Was he asking because he wanted to ask me out? My hands felt sweaty with the thought. I didn't go on dates. My dad barely let me talk to my brother's best friend Noah without making me feel like I was committing some sort of crime. If my dad ever found out I was thinking about dating actual guys instead of just crushing on them from a distance, I was sure he'd lock me up, or at least put a tracking bracelet on me to make sure I didn't end up like my sister.

"I don't have any plans set in stone yet," I finally managed to say, my voice only coming out slightly breathy.

If you ask me on a date and make all my dreams come true, I'll definitely say yes!

"Cool."

I waited for him to ask me his next question, but instead he took the band folder off the music stand we now shared and shoved it under his arm as if he was about to leave.

Desperation crashed through my veins. I couldn't let him leave me yet. Not when this was the longest conversation I'd had with him all year.

I cleared my throat. "W-what about you? Any fun plans?"

He shrugged. "I was thinking about going to the new Justin Banks movie tonight."

Justin Banks movie? I jogged my memory, trying to figure out which one he was talking about.

"Is that the one where the alien saves a small town from his alien family?" I adjusted my glasses—a nervous tick I needed to get rid of.

"Have you seen it?" Harrison's eyes lit up, and it felt like hitting the jackpot because *I* had made his eyes do that.

"N-not yet." The trailer I'd watched last week looked stupid. But I would totally sit through it if Harrison invited me.

He glanced at the band room exit before meeting my gaze again. "Cool, well, have a good rest of the day." He gave me one of his heart-stopping smiles before putting his music stand and chair away. My gaze followed his back the whole way across the room until he walked out the door.

I slunk back in my seat, feeling dizzy after our short interaction. If Harrison was going to the movies tonight, I was going to be at that theater. I pulled out my phone to see what time the movie started. Seven o'clock. Harrison didn't know it yet, but he was going to be watching the latest Justin Banks movie with me. I was going to finally make this thing happen.

IT WAS SNOWING when I walked outside after school, the early December weather finally deciding it was winter after all in Ridgewater, New York. I zipped up my gray parka and lifted the furry hood over my long brown hair as I zigzagged through the crazy traffic jam of students, on my way to meet my brother, Easton, and his best friend, Noah Taylor. I was the first to make it to Noah's car, a silver Mazda 6, so I leaned against it to wait.

Noah was the first to come out of the school. He clicked the unlock button on his key fob once he was within range, and I was able to open the door and climb in the back. We both sat in silence as we waited for my brother to arrive.

Noah and Easton had been friends since middle school, but he and I never really had much to say to each other...probably because we were on completely different social ladders. He was the cool, football and lacrosse player who only had to smile at a girl to get her to bow down at his feet and beg him to kiss her. I was the weird girl who played the trumpet and liked to read comic books—someone he'd only seen as the dorky little sister of his best friend. I was definitely not the kind of girl who wanted to kiss him...not anymore, at least.

Yep, Noah and I were about as opposite as two people could get. Which was why I was more than happy to crush on Harrison these days.

I pulled out my phone to scroll through my Insta-feed so I wouldn't have to make small talk with Noah.

Easton opened the passenger door a couple of minutes later.

"So, what's going on with that?" Noah asked when my brother sank into his seat.

"Going on with what?" Easton asked innocently as he brushed the snow from his hair.

Noah laughed. "I was watching you talking to Mercedes Atkins."

Easton shrugged. "I asked her out."

"What?" I leaned forward, not believing what I was hearing. Easton had actually asked a girl out?

"Don't act all shocked," he said, turning his face to me. "I *have* asked a girl out before."

"Yeah, but that was only for a school dance." He'd never been on a regular date. He must *really* like Mercedes. "What are you doing for your date?"

His eyes widened, a deer-in-the-headlights look. "I don't know. I hadn't thought that far ahead since I didn't really think she'd say yes."

I laughed but then remembered my plan to try and spend time with Harrison tonight. "You could take her to the movies. I was kind of hoping you could give me a ride there around six forty-five, since dad has drill tonight and your car should be out of the shop."

My brother sputtered. "Yeah, like I'm totally going to let my little sister tag along when I finally bag a date with the hottest girl in school."

Oh no. This was not going to happen. I *had to* show up at that movie tonight. I was finally going to make good on my promise to my best friend Juliette to not be the loner band geek anymore. I was going to finally put myself out there tonight.

"I promise I'll leave you alone," I hurried to say. "I just need a ride since...you see, I kind of have a date tonight too." I rushed those last few words out quickly, as if saying them faster would make them sound truer. I *really* needed that ride.

My brother turned all the way around in his seat at my comment. "*You* have a date?"

I should've probably been offended at the surprise on both Easton and Noah's faces at that moment. But it was a pretty shocking thing to say, considering I'd never been on a date before. Aside from not being gorgeous and popular, my reputation for having an overprotective father wasn't very encouraging when it came to guys.

"I'm going with Harrison Carter," I blurted into their stunned silence. "We're watching the new Justin Banks movie."

Technically, not a real date, but the latter part of it could be true—if we were in the same movie theater, then we would be watching it together. But there was no way I was telling Easton and Noah that Harrison didn't even know I was planning to meet him there.

"I thought you hated Justin Banks," Noah said, looking at me with surprise in his big brown eyes.

I tilted my head to the side and played with the zipper on my coat. "This one looked okay. I mean, it's not every day that you get to watch an alien show, right?" And since when did Noah ever pay attention to what I did and didn't like?

"Do you think Mercedes would like that show, too?" Easton asked, looking at me and then to Noah.

Noah lifted his hands. "Don't ask me. I'm not the girl in here."

I shrugged. "I don't know, she's pretty mainstream so she'd probably prefer the new Zac Efron movie."

"What do you mean by 'mainstream?'" My brother pulled his head back as if offended that I could say such a thing about his date.

"I don't know. She's just one of those normal, every-day, vanilla-kind of girls."

Noah raised an eyebrow at me. "You say that like being mainstream is bad."

Of course *he* wouldn't understand. He'd dated the most mainstream girl there was all last year. Ashlyn Brooks was the epitome of every guy's fantasy—tall, blonde, blue-eyed, outgoing, and popular. Pretty much everything that I wasn't, with my brown hair that would be considered mousy at best and plain old hazel eyes that needed correcting with my thick black-rimmed glasses.

"I'm just trying to say that if you're into a girl who will fawn all over you and make you feel like a stud for making a touchdown at the football game, then Mercedes is one of those kinds of girls."

"And what guy wouldn't want that? Am I right, bro?" Noah nudged Easton in the shoulder.

"Yeah, well, this is a no-brainer then. Looks like I'm going to the Zac Efron movie tonight." Easton glanced back at me like I was clueless to think a guy would ever want a girl with a different flavor than Mercedes and Ashlyn. "But hey, I can give you a ride. Just promise to keep it quiet in the backseat. I can't have you offending my mainstream girl with your band-geek ways."

"Hey, I'll have you know that being the band geek is exactly why I have this date with Harrison tonight."

Or, a pretend date, at least.

"You make it sound like you're not sure it's really a date." Noah narrowed his eyes as if he could read the lie in my face.

I sat up taller, hoping to appear more confident than I felt. "Just because you don't think I'm pretty and intriguing doesn't mean that other guys feel the same."

Noah's face went from jovial to serious in half a nanosecond. "Hey, I never said that about you."

I rolled my eyes and shrugged, urging the blush to stay away from my cheeks at his comment. And then, to prove to him that I didn't really care what his opinion of me was, I said, "Well, it's not like it matters, anyway."

Noah shifted forward, his back to me. "Well, I guess we better get going so you two can get ready for your hot dates." He turned the key in the ignition, and I tried not to dissect his last few sentences too much.

There was no way he would ever think of me as anything more than the annoying girl he was stuck spending time with because of our mutual relationship with my brother. So, instead of thinking about all the years I'd spent watching Noah and Easton play in their sports together, all the times he'd looked over me as he went to flirt with another girl who wasn't two years younger than him, and all the times he'd come to my house wearing a tux so he and Easton could pick up their dates to the dances, I crossed my arms and looked out the window.

Noah and I lived in two different worlds. But tonight, everything would change. I was going to meet Harrison at the movie. And if I had my way, Justin Banks and aliens would be the furthest things from his mind.

2

NOAH

"PAUL, Brielle, and I are going to dinner at Friendly's tonight. You want to come?" Mom asked when I came down from my bedroom upstairs.

I didn't know why she asked. She knew just as well as I did that hanging out with Paul, my stepdad, was about the last thing I'd want to do. But I resisted the urge to roll my eyes because I knew better than to treat my mom with disrespect. She already had enough of that in her life, and the bruises from last time were just finally beginning to heal. "Not really."

"You sure?" She looked at me over her shoulder as she put a dangly earring in her ear. Paul liked her to dress up when they went out.

"I'll grab something on my way back to Easton's." Now that football season was over, I tried to spend as much time at his house as I could.

I didn't realize until a second later that I couldn't hang out with Easton tonight because he'd be on his date. Man, I needed a girlfriend again. I needed something to get me out of here and away from Paul when Easton was busy.

If only Ashlyn was still available and I hadn't completely killed any opportunity I might've had with her. But as much as I hated that Luke had stolen my ex-girlfriend, I knew she was probably a lot happier with him. I'd let my stepdad and the way he treated my mom get to me too much while we were dating, and I learned my lesson too late.

Oh well, that's just the way my life was meant to be.

I looked at the clock on the wall. Paul would be home from work in fifteen minutes. Time to head out again.

I went out the door and climbed into the car my dad bought me out of guilt for replacing me with his new family. Ten minutes later, I went through the slush-covered drive-thru at Wendy's and ate my burger and fries as I drove around absent-mindedly.

I was pulling into the parking lot to the movie theater before I realized I'd driven there. Ashlyn's family owned the place, so I'd spent a lot of Friday nights over here last year. Apparently, my conversation with Easton and Lexi today had my subconscious guiding me to the theater.

Since I was already here and had nothing else to do, I scanned the list of movies on the big sign out front. There was a kid movie, a horror movie, the alien action movie Lexi had talked about, and the latest Zac Efron romantic movie.

Looks like I'll get to watch Lexi on her "date" with her crush. That should be entertaining.

I got in line to get my ticket and concessions. The lobby was full, as typical for a Friday night. I felt a little weird going to a movie by myself, but if anyone from school saw me and had a problem with that, they could suck it.

I shoved my hands into my pockets and let my gaze wander around the room. Easton and his date were nowhere to be found, but after a good look around, I spotted Lexi standing with a bunch of guys from the grade below me. She hunched her shoulders, and if I didn't know any better, I'd say she was super uncomfortable. Maybe her date hadn't arrived yet?

But then I saw the guy who was supposed to be Lexi's date, Harrison Carter. He'd been in one of my classes last year. And next to him was a leggy blonde, his arm around her waist.

Either Lexi had been embellishing her story about having a date with him tonight, or he'd asked two girls out. From the way he was looking at the blonde and ignoring Lexi, I got the feeling that he wasn't there for Lexi at all.

Poor girl. She really did like the guy. I was sure I'd overheard her and her friend giggling about Harrison last summer when I was at her house.

"Who invited the nerdy sophomore to hang out with us tonight?" a female voice sounded from behind me.

My ears perked up. Were they talking about Lexi?

Another voice spoke. "Harrison said he told her about going to the movie. Pretty sure she's stalking him."

"What a loser," the first girl said.

I clenched my hands into fists at my sides and looked back over to where Lexi stood. She was still in the same spot, but now she was gazing around the room as if looking for some excuse to leave the group.

The line ahead of me cleared out. I stepped forward, formulating a plan in my mind.

"I'd like one ticket for *Whispers from Another Galaxy*." The girl at the counter tapped on her screen then turned it around for me to pick my seat. I chose one then asked, "Can I also get your biggest popcorn and two drinks?".

She nodded and put in my order. "What would you like to drink?"

I strummed my fingers on the counter, trying to remember what Lexi usually got. Then I remembered—we always ordered the same drink. "Two Cokes."

After I paid, I awkwardly gathered the popcorn in my arms and carried it with the two drinks over to Lexi. I swallowed and hoped she wouldn't punch me for what I was about to do. I never could be sure with Lexi.

I squeezed into the space between her and the lanky redhead to her left. "Sorry, it took so long to get the drinks. You wanted Coke, right?" I offered her the soda, hoping she'd play along.

At first, she startled, but then her face went through a range of emotions: shock to confusion to relief.

Her lips quirked up into a smile, and she took the soda-filled cup from my hand. "Thank you. I was worried we'd miss the previews, and I know how much you love those."

"Are you two here on a date?" a guy next to us asked, his eyebrows raised.

I looked at Lexi, giving her the opportunity to answer that question however she wanted.

She linked her arm through mine and gave the guy a broad smile. "Yeah, of course. Did you think I came here by myself?" She winked at me, and I worked hard to hold in my chuckle. I'd committed to this when I first came over here; I wouldn't blow it now.

The guy had the insight not to look too surprised, which I had to give him credit for. I knew my reputation around the school. I wasn't exactly known for hanging out with Lexi's crowd—usually going more for the drill team and cheerleaders. But who was to say I wouldn't ever branch away from my typical type? Me taking Lexi on a date couldn't be that far-fetched. She was two years younger than me, and yeah, she was kind of nerdy and could talk circles around me when it came to music and science, but she had always been fun to hang around. And despite what she'd said earlier in my car, she was kind of cute in her big glasses. And I liked that she was short enough that I could wrap her under my arm if I wanted to. Not that I'd thought about that before...

"Should we go find our seats?" I asked, not wanting to make small talk with a bunch of people I didn't know very well.

She sighed and gave my arm a gentle squeeze. "Yes. You know how much I love Justin Banks."

"And you know how much I love previews." It was a super corny thing to say, but I actually did like watching the previews and seeing which movies were coming out next.

We handed our tickets to the guy at the ticket podium then headed to theater four. It wasn't until we were looking at our seat numbers that I realized we wouldn't be able to actually sit by each other.

"What's wrong?" she asked when she noticed my troubled expression.

I held up my ticket. "I'm sitting in seat 4I." Then I pointed to hers. "And you're sitting in seat 15J."

Understanding replaced her look of confusion, and she bit her lip. "I guess that is a problem."

"There was still a seat open next to mine when I bought the ticket. Do you want me to see if I could trade yours? Or do you want to still sit with your friends?"

"And let them know that I totally lied to them?" Her eyes were wide. "I'll wait here with the drinks and popcorn while you go check."

I walked her to a bench and then left her with my armload of junk food. A few minutes later I was back. I held up the new ticket. "Looks like you get to cuddle with me tonight after all."

Her cheeks flushed at my joke. "We're not cuddling."

"Fine." I shrugged. "I'm just saying that if you really want to sell this to your friends in there, you might need to get a little closer."

She smacked my arm and gave me a warning look. "Stop messing with me, Noah. I'm already nervous enough as it is."

I laughed. "Come on. It's not like we've never watched a movie together before."

"Yes. But you know as well as I do that I've never been on a date before, so yeah, cuddling is definitely out of my comfort zone. Even if it's fake."

Would she count this as her first date then? That wasn't an unpleasant thought.

"Well, since this is your first date, I promise to be a complete gentleman and follow your lead."

She smiled and seemed to breathe a sigh of relief. "Thank you."

"Though, if you do decide that you wanted your first date to end in a first kiss, I can get on board with that, too." I winked. I couldn't help myself, and the look of terror in her eyes was totally worth it.

"I'm going to pretend you didn't say that. Let's go find our seats, okay?" She turned on her heel and left me to carry the popcorn and both of our drinks.

3

LEXI

I DON'T KNOW why I thought that showing up to the movie theater to try and get Harrison to notice me was a good idea. I really must have left my brain at home today. I wanted to die as I stood there by him and his friends, pretending like I was supposed to be there. And I'd wanted to go completely invisible when his girlfriend, who I didn't even know existed up until that point, showed up. Guys who dated girls from other schools should have some sort of label on them, so girls like me, who crushed on said guys, wouldn't look stupid trying to make something happen.

I wished Juliette wasn't in Paris doing her semester abroad. If she'd been around, she would have talked some sense into me before I showed up at the movie theater today.

I literally could have kissed Noah when he came up to me with the sodas, looking all dashing with his shaggy auburn hair pushed just far enough away that I could see the golden flecks in his big brown eyes. I was pretty sure that if I looked up "knight in shining armor" on the Internet, his picture would have earned him the top spot after saving me today.

Well, until he started teasing me about cuddling, that is.

"Do you think you'll like this movie then?" Noah asked as he shrugged out of his letterman jacket and let it rest behind him in the seat.

I pulled my arms out of my coat as well, deciding to get comfortable. "I've never seen Justin in an alien movie before, so maybe this one will be fine."

Noah peeked over his shoulder briefly before leaning closer to my ear, speaking in a low voice, "Looks like your friends are right behind us. Wanna give them a good show?"

"A good show?" I asked, not understanding. We were all here to watch the same movie.

He leaned closer and whispered conspiratorially. "I figured you might want to cuddle up with me like we talked about earlier."

Why did he have to keep saying stuff like that? Didn't he know that I'd dreamed of doing that for so many years? Imagined his soft, pouty lips brushing against mine and telling me he liked me, too?

But if he didn't know it, I was certainly not going to give him a reason to start thinking it now, so I pretended the thought of cuddling with him didn't affect me at all. "Do you want me to regret going on a fake date with you? I thought you were here to help me out, not tease me all night."

The wicked smile was back on his lips. "Who says I can't do both?"

"Me. Just—" I gestured to the screen in front of us. "Just watch the movie. Let me worry about the people behind us."

Afterwards, Noah was a lot more tolerable. He did lean in closely a few times to whisper things in my ear. And I might have noticed that he smelled really good tonight. But he didn't attempt to put his arm around me or hold my hand, so I didn't get too anxious. About halfway through the movie, the storyline was so dumb that I could barely stand the idea of sitting through another forty-five minutes of aliens blowing up while Justin Banks' character miraculously managed to come out of the scene unscathed.

"This movie is ridiculous," I said under my breath.

Noah leaned close, his warm breath on my ear doing weird things to my stomach. "But I thought you loved Justin Banks."

"Not in this movie."

"Well, you could've always chosen the Zac Efron movie."

"Yeah, even that one would probably be better than this."

Shock formed on his face and he grabbed my arm. I tried not to notice how my skin warmed under his calloused hand. "Are you going mainstream on me, Lexi?"

"Psssh. Hardly. This movie is just terrible."

"Terrible enough to leave?" he offered.

"What would we do?" I asked, wanting to see what I was getting myself into before I agreed.

He shrugged. "I don't know, we can do whatever you want. It's your first date after all. Make it a night to remember."

Was I really going to count this as my first date? The thirteen-year-old girl inside wanted me to definitely count this as a first date, since she'd always hoped for a date with Noah. But the sixteen-year-old and much less naïve version of me knew it was fake. Noah didn't date girls like me. He dated prom queens.

I checked behind me to see what Harrison and his dumb girlfriend were doing. Of course, his tongue was totally stuck halfway down her throat. Why did I think he was so cool? He was just like all the other guys whose hormones went into overdrive at the first sight of a hot girl.

His girlfriend probably didn't even know the little things about him. Like how his blue eyes had tiny flecks of gray and green. Or how he always pinched his lips together in a super cute way before pulling his trumpet to his mouth.

She didn't deserve him.

I looked up at the screen and sighed. This whole night was getting worse and worse. "Let's just go. Now."

Noah nodded, seeming to take in my depressed mood. "Okay."

Once we were in the hall that led to the lobby, we tossed our empty cups and popcorn bowl in the trash and shrugged into our coats.

"Do you need to tell Easton that you're leaving?" Noah asked.

I zipped up my coat. "No, I was planning to bum a ride home with someone here, so I told him not to worry about me." It was embarrassing the lengths I had gone to today. I was thankful Noah seemed to be in a more generous mood tonight. Any other day and he'd probably give me an even harder time than he already had.

"Okay, so where to next?" he asked.

"I don't know. You're the one who asked me on this date."

"Oh, so it *is* a date." He wiggled his eyebrows.

I shrugged. "It's whatever it is. You saving me from utter humiliation. A date. Pretty much the same thing."

"So, from what I gathered back there, I'm guessing Harrison didn't know that tonight was a date."

I scrunched up my face, embarrassed. "Yeah, pretty sure I was just stalking him and hoping something magical would happen."

"His loss."

"I kind of think he's happy with that supermodel of a girl-friend he has back there."

"Well, she is hot." And there he was again. Noah had managed to act kind of like a gentleman for the last hour. But, alas, it was short-lived.

Two girls, Sarah and Ava, who I'd seen hanging out with Harrison earlier turned the corner and were walking toward us. They eyed Noah and me in our coats as we got ready to leave.

"That was a fast date. I knew the world would right itself soon enough." Ava, the girl with long, straight blonde hair, looked at me with disapproval.

"What are you talking about?" Noah asked, his tone more irritated than it had been a moment earlier.

Sarah answered his question. "We knew you overheard us talking in the line and that was the only reason you went up to Lexi. We figured you were doing your best friend's little sister a favor by faking a date since her brother wasn't around to save her from her stupidity."

How dare they say any of that! They didn't even know me!

It was either insanity or anger or both that made me do what I did next. But I was not about to end an already bad night on an even worse note. So I stepped closer to Noah and linked my arm through his possessively.

"Yes, please tell everyone it was just a favor. I really don't want Easton or anyone else finding out that we've been secretly dating behind my brother's back for months."

They didn't look convinced. "If you're secretly dating, why are you leaving early?" Ava asked.

My mind went blank, but Noah pulled me even closer, overpowering my senses with his too-heavenly cologne. He gave me a suggestive look that made me blush all over. "We wanted to find somewhere more private. Easton never leaves us alone and we can't pass up this chance."

My insides did a little flip at his words. Was he suggesting we were going to make-out? Make-out with Noah? I would probably hyperventilate if he actually tried.

And Easton would most definitely kill Noah...if my dad didn't get to him first. The backseat of a car was exactly where my cute nephew, Grant, got his start, and ever since my dad found out he was going to be a grandpa at thirty-seven years old, he'd been paranoid that I'd follow in my sister's footsteps. So, thanks to my sister Maddie, I was the one who got the super strict rules and the purity ring with the promise that my dad would pay for my college if I kept it on.

But these girls didn't have to know about any of that, so I pulled on Noah's arm and said, "We only have an hour, Noah. Let's get to the overlook before we miss our chance."

To his credit, Noah didn't even laugh at my ridiculous suggestion. Instead, he winked at the girls, leaving them standing there with their mouths hanging open and their minds in a daze. Then he pulled me toward the back exit.

We burst up laughing as soon as the doors shut behind us.

"That was priceless!" I said when I finally stopped to catch my breath.

"The look on their faces!" Noah bent over and slapped his knee. "You're hilarious, Lexi. I wonder how many people they've told already."

That sobered me right up. "You think they're going to tell people?" If my dad caught wind of something like that, I would be so dead.

"I can take you to the overlook right now if you're worried about people following us." He raised an eyebrow. I was surprised he didn't seem to mind the repercussions that rumors about him dating a lowly sophomore would have on his reputation. Did he really not care what people thought about him?

"Yeah, no. You know I'm going to need all the college funds I can get from my dad if I want to go to Yale. So, like pretty much everything else I've said tonight, that was a lie."

"I'm crushed." He held his hand to his chest dramatically. "I was really hoping things were going somewhere between us."

"Somehow I think you'll get over it." I shook my head. "I don't know what's happening to me today. I've never lied so much in my life."

The lights on his car flashed when he pressed the button to

unlock it. "Well, if you change your mind, you know where to find me."

I looked at him pointedly. "And my *dad* knows where to find *you*, too."

His eyes got big at my mention of my dad.

"Okay, yeah. I'll take you home. We'll try parking at the overlook some other time."

4

NOAH

EASTON: **My date was awesome! Do anything fun last night?**

So, Lexi hadn't told him about our fake date. That was probably good...since it was fake, after all. I could only imagine what he'd do if he found out and thought it was real. There was some sort of unwritten guy code that says you don't date your best friend's little sister.

But I texted him back just to be up front about everything. I didn't trust those two girls we'd run into to keep their mouths shut for a second.

Noah: **I ran into Lexi at the theater last night. We both thought the movie sucked so I took her home.**

Easton: **I thought she was on a date?**

Oh, oops.

Noah: **You should probably ask her about that.**

Easton: **You getting your college applications done today?**

Noah: **Yup. Just about finished.**

Easton: **Me too. College is going to be awesome!**

Yeah…it probably would be awesome for Easton. He was a good student. As for me, I'd be lucky to get into Ridgewater Community College with my grades. I really should have tried harder to study more during my first few years of high school. According to the school counselor, suddenly getting my act together my senior year probably wasn't going to work the miracles I was hoping it would. But hopefully, the lacrosse teams at Syracuse University or Cortland State would be watching me later this year and be willing to overlook the past three years and give me a spot on the team.

I sent off my application to Yale—a last-ditch effort—and tried to read the boring *Pride and Prejudice* book my English teacher assigned me as her latest form of punishment. As my eyes traveled over the words, my mind wandered off. I thought of how weird it was that teachers always talked about how reading was the single most important indicator of success in education, only to assign this old crap that might as well have been written in a foreign language. I mean, I'd probably enjoy reading a heck of a lot better if I actually got to pick the book. But since *ESPN Magazine* didn't count as approved reading material, I was stuck with one of the books Ashlyn had always raved about.

The ornery Mr. Darcy guy was insulting the Elizabeth girl when I heard the yelling coming from downstairs. I listened for a minute to get a gauge on its intensity. At the moment, it was just a low rumble. If it stayed that way, I wouldn't have to go down and interfere.

The door to my room opened, and my eight-year-old half-sister, Brielle, stepped inside, fear etched all over her face.

"I'm scared, Noah." She rushed over and wrapped her arms around my torso. "I don't want to go to that shelter again."

I pulled her closer and kissed the top of her head. "I won't let you go there again." They'd only spent three days at the women's shelter the last time Paul's temper got out of control, but three days was more than the length any little girl should ever have to hide from her dad.

We were quiet for a moment, listening to the argument below. When I noticed Brielle was shaking, I pulled her onto my lap. "Sorry you have to hear this," I said under my breath.

She nodded and burrowed her head against my chest. A huge part of me wanted to go downstairs right then and bring Paul up so he could see what his rage was doing to his little girl. And another part of me wanted to bring my mom up too, so she could see how staying with her unpredictable husband was affecting her daughter.

"Is it really that hard to put the dishes in the dishwasher instead of the sink?" Paul's voice bellowed up the stairs, louder than it had been before.

"I'm sorry. We were rushing to get Brielle to her basketball practice. I was going to put them away when we got home."

"You should wake up when I do if you don't want to be rushed. Is it so much to ask that my wife get some common sense?"

I clenched my hands into fists at Paul's rant. How dare he talk to my mom that way.

"I-I'm sorry. I was just so tired after last night..." my mom's voice drifted off. I hated how scared and small she sounded. She was a grown woman. She shouldn't be treated like she was a naughty child.

"That's no excuse. I bust my butt every day, sucking up to my idiot of a boss. The least you can do for me is keep this house clean!" His voice roared even louder, causing my insides to vibrate with the intensity.

My heart pounded in my temples. I needed to stop this before he hurt her again.

I shifted Brielle off my lap, setting her down on my bed. "I'm going to check on things. Stay here where it's safe, okay?"

Her big, brown eyes showed fear, but she nodded.

I rushed down the hall and stopped on the staircase once I had a view of where they stood in the hall downstairs. Paul was waving his hands in anger as he went on and on about what he *deserved* and how my mom was failing at everything.

My chest hurt to see my mom cowering under such a domineering man.

"You need to calm down, Paul," Mom said after Paul finally shut his mouth for a second.

That sentence seemed to flip the switch because he immediately grabbed her by the shoulders and slammed her against the wall.

"Don't tell me to calm down. You know what happens when you talk back to me."

I was down the stairs two seconds later and shoving him away from my mom. "Keep your hands off her!" I yelled.

He stumbled back, knocking a black vase to the tile floor. Anger flashed in his eyes, and before I knew what was happening, his fist collided with my face.

"Get out of the way, Noah."

Pain shot through me, but I stood in front of my mom, not about to let him touch her again. My neck prickled as I felt her cowering behind me.

Paul's eyes went cold as stone. "This is my house. And I'll take care of things as I see best."

I touched my lip and my fingers came away with blood. I wiped it on my pants.

When I looked up again, Paul was standing inches away. He wasn't a small man, but neither was I. "That's the last time you'll do something like that, Noah." Then he glared at my mom still hiding behind me. "When I get back from Angelo's house, your son better be gone. I won't have that kind of disrespect in my home."

What? He was kicking me out?

A moment later, Paul disappeared out the front door.

My mom immediately went down the hall and came back with a cold washcloth in her hands. "Maybe you should go stay at your dad's house for a few days, just until Paul calms down." She gently patted my lip with the cloth.

I looked down at my mother, not believing what she was saying. "You want me to go?"

"Just for a few days. You two feed off each other."

I shook my head, still not believing her words. I took the washcloth from her. "He was about to hurt you again."

"I had things under control. You didn't need to step in. You just made things worse."

"So you wanted me to stand by and let that jerk hit you?" I scoffed. Was she seriously saying that right now?

"He's just stressed. Something happened at work, so he's a little irritable."

He had my mom brainwashed so badly it made my blood boil. How could she fail to see that this wasn't healthy behavior? "That's not *a little* irritable. If I hadn't been in the way, you'd be the one with the bloody lip. And in case you forgot what happened last time, he probably wouldn't have stopped there."

She looked away and wrung her hands. "As soon as he gets his big promotion next week, everything will be better. Just give him a break."

"Give him a break? Are you hearing yourself right now? This is not how a healthy person thinks."

I regretted my last sentence almost immediately. I knew better than to say things like that to her.

Her gaze hardened. "So you're going to start insulting my intelligence, too?"

I groaned, and my shoulders sagged. "I didn't mean it. I'm sorry, Mom." I ran a hand through my hair. "I just can't stand how you let him treat you so badly. What is it that keeps you here?"

But she wasn't listening. She was already busy cleaning up the broken pieces of the vase on the floor. "I think you should spend the next week at your father's house." She didn't look at me when she said it.

This was insane. She let Paul treat her the way he did but would kick me out because he told her to? Her own son?

I didn't say anything. It was pointless to talk to someone who wasn't willing to listen. This wouldn't be the first time this year that I had to find somewhere to stay because of Paul's temper.

I went upstairs to pack my bag. When I got to my room, Brielle was standing in the doorway with tears in her eyes. "Do you really have to leave?"

I brushed past her and pulled my duffel bag off the top shelf in my closet. "Your dad said to get out, so looks like I have to leave for a few days."

She followed behind me as I started packing. I threw a couple of pairs of jeans in my bag along with my favorite hoodie and a few pairs of underwear and socks, and a couple of t-shirts. Plus my toothbrush and shampoo, and then I figured that was about all I needed.

"I don't want you to go, Noah. I don't want to be here alone if something happens."

My heart broke for my little sister. It wasn't fair that she had to deal with any of this. She was so young.

I sighed and sat on my bed. She wiped at her tears with the back of her hand as her bottom lip trembled. I pulled her into a hug. "Mom thinks things will be better if I leave for a few days."

She clung to me. "But what if something happens again?"

I held her close, rubbing a hand down her curls. "You can message or call me on your watch if you ever feel scared and I'll come right home, okay?" I pulled back and held her at arm's length, so I could see her face.

She nodded and wiped at another tear trickling down her cheek. "Okay."

With another sigh, I stood and finished packing the rest of my things in the duffel. Then I slung it over one shoulder and my backpack over another.

I gave my sister one last hug before making my way downstairs.

Mom was waiting for me in the living room. "I'll call you when Paul calms down. Just give him a week, okay?"

I hitched my duffel bag higher on my shoulder and huffed. "Just make sure he keeps his fists away from you and Brielle. If anything happens, you have to leave."

She nodded slowly. "I will. But everything will be fine. He'll get the promotion, and everything will be great."

For my mother and my sister's sake, I hoped she was right.

I DROVE to my dad's house on the hill—a massive brick home—where he lived with his new family. Just when I was about to knock, my half-siblings burst out the front door, startling me. Mason, who was ten, and his six-year-old sister Paige dashed toward the family's big SUV parked at the end of the driveway. I didn't think they even noticed me.

My stepmom, Tracey, was rushing down the hall with her fancy purse slung over her arm and her blonde hair flying behind her. She speed-walked to the door in her high heels. Tracey had been a model before she met my dad, and I didn't think I'd ever seen her without heels on.

"Oh! Hi, Noah. Sorry we're in such a hurry. Mason has a karate test today and we're running late."

"Is my dad here?"

She nodded as she sidestepped past me and continued on to the car. "He's just inside putting on his shoes," she called over her shoulder.

"Can I go in and talk to him?" I yelled after her. She was already halfway down the path that led to their driveway.

"Make it quick." She waved her hand at me in dismissal before opening the passenger door and climbing in.

I shoved my hands in my pockets and stepped inside, wondering where I should go first.

My dad came down the staircase a minute later, fastening his Rolex to his arm as he did so. "Hi, Noah." He peeked up from his watch for a moment but didn't really look at me.

"Hey, Dad." I chewed on my lip, not knowing what to say. "Um—can I talk to you for a minute?"

He was at the bottom of the stairs now, pulling his coat out of the entryway closet and shrugging into it.

"I'm actually in a huge hurry right now, Noah. Mason has this karate thing and we're going to be late if we don't leave now."

"I just need somewhere to stay for a few days. Mom and Paul kicked me out."

He went still and really looked at me for the first time. Then, after taking in my face, his eyes hardened. "Looks like you're getting into trouble again."

Of course, he would blame my swollen lip on me being up to no good, instead of asking what really happened.

"This—" I pointed to my face. "—is not my fault."

"Sure, Noah." He nodded, like he thought I was full of crap. "I thought it was because of football, but football is over. Are you in a gang of some sort?" He shook his head and took a few steps toward the door. "I can't have you around Mason and Paige when you're getting into fights. It's not good for them. I can't have you bringing that sort of stuff into my house."

"Really? You can't have your own son be around your new kids?" I scoffed. This was just the same as it always was. I was the bad kid, always getting into trouble. His other kids were the perfect little angels who he didn't want anywhere near my bad influence.

"I really don't have time to talk about this right now. And I won't have your friends targeting me for drug money."

He thought I was into drugs? What the heck did he think I was doing with my life?

He glanced at his watch to check the time. "The *sensei* gets upset when families walk in late. Come back later tonight and we'll talk after the kids have gone to bed."

And that was how it always was with my dad now that he had his new perfect family. Any other day or time was more convenient for me to come over than when I actually needed him to be a parent.

My temper flared and I didn't try to hide it. "You know what? Never mind. I can see that you're too busy with your perfect replacement family to care about the one you started with."

He reached out to grab my shoulder, but I shrugged his hand off. He drew in a deep breath and gave me an annoyed expression —something he always did when he had to actually do some parenting. "Noah, you know I didn't replace you when your mom and I divorced."

"Yeah, whatever. I've heard the joke you always tell. 'Kids are like pancakes, if you mess up the first one you can always just throw it out and start over.'"

I didn't wait to see his reaction. Instead, I turned and stomped out into the cold evening air.

I didn't know why I'd even attempted to come here in the first place. Nothing had changed. Nothing was ever going to change. My dad had gotten a fresh start in life; he had tried to buy me off with a new car and a monthly allowance in my checking account.

But when it came to actual parenting, he had washed his hands clean of that years ago.

It had just taken me ten years to finally get the hint.

But I was done with that man. I was done with everything.

I got in my car and drove to the last place I could think of. I pulled in front of Easton's house and checked myself in the visor mirror. I should have thought to put ice on my lip before driving off. It wasn't pretty, but experience had taught me that it would look a lot better by Monday. I drew in a deep breath and climbed out of my car.

Lexi answered their front door when I knocked.

"Is Easton here?" I asked, keeping my head tilted down so she couldn't get a good look at my face. Lucky it was already pretty dark outside.

She shook her head. "He's at work right now. He doesn't get off until ten."

Right. He'd been complaining all week about having to work the closing shift at Emrie's.

Lexi's inquiring gaze meant she knew something was up. She always noticed stuff like that.

I sighed heavily, turning to go. "Okay, um, well. I guess just tell him I came by."

Where was I going to stay? It was winter. My weather app showed snow and freezing temperatures tonight.

"Noah? Is everything okay?" Lexi asked, taking a step closer behind me. I tensed, feeling tears prick at my eyes at her question.

"I'm fine." I sniffled. I hoped she'd assume my nose was just running from the cold and not because I was on the verge of a breakdown.

Where was I going to stay tonight?

"Are you sure?" She grabbed onto the hem of my letterman jacket.

I stepped away from her touch. "I'm fine. Just..." I looked down the street. I needed to get out of there before she saw me crying like a baby. "Just tell Easton that I came by."

"Is it something important?"

"Nothing important." My voice came out more gruff than usual, but at least it didn't break with a sob. I kept walking down the path toward my parked car, and once I was a good distance away I called over my shoulder, "I'll see you at school on Monday."

I tried not to break down as I pulled onto the road.

I was out of options.

I had nowhere else to go.

So, I did what I'd done last month when my mom and sister went to the women's shelter and I wasn't allowed to go in because I was an eighteen-year-old male and my presence would make the women there feel unsafe. I drove to a camping spot in the forest and pulled out of the trunk the sleeping bag, pillow, and blanket that had been there since October. Then I leaned the passenger seat back as far as it could go and hoped it wouldn't get below zero tonight.

5

LEXI

MY HEART RACED as I walked up the path to the school Monday morning, gripping my trumpet case handle.

I hadn't been able to relax all weekend as my mind kept wondering if everyone had already heard about my Friday night disaster. I really hoped they weren't waiting to laugh me out of school. I'd already been worried enough that my dad or Easton would suddenly barge into my room after somehow hearing that I'd been secretly dating Noah for months.

There was a reason I hadn't ever been on a date yet, and it wasn't just because I was a nerd. I was pretty sure if any guy ever did try to take me on a date, he'd change his mind once he met my dad. At six-foot-two and two hundred twenty pounds of muscle, my dad was intimidating. A guy would need nerves of steel just to walk in my house with the intention of taking Dad's little girl anywhere. So if my dad even *thought* I was sneaking around with Noah, who had a reputation for being a bad boy, that would be the end of everything.

I made it to the band room without too many stares coming

my way and sighed with relief. Maybe everything would be okay.
Maybe no one had heard about my fake date with Noah.

I set my trumpet down and grabbed a stand before sitting in
my new "second chair" spot by Harrison.

I startled when Harrison spoke to me. "You and Noah left the
movie early on Friday. Did you not like it?"

Wait, he'd noticed that we'd left?

That was all it took for my heart to start racing. Stupid heart.
Harrison had a girlfriend.

I cleared my throat and tried to appear calm. "We didn't
really like it."

He pressed his lips together as he set the music folder on the
stand. "Sarah and Ava said you two were sneaking out for some
alone time."

Ok, so he hadn't noticed us leave. He'd just been told about it.

Which meant Sarah and Ava were talking about us.

Oh crap!

What was I supposed to do now? Was it time for me to come
clean and tell him that I'd followed him to the movie theater like
some sort of delusional lovesick puppy?

I cleared my throat again. "We figured we could entertain
ourselves better than the movie could."

The words were out before I realized how bad they sounded.

"Not that we were doing that much," I hurried to say.

Harrison furrowed his brow. "I'm not sure I know what you're
talking about."

"At the overlook. We didn't..." Why had I opened my big
mouth? I should just run out the door right now and hide somewhere until I learned to talk without making myself look like an
idiot.

Harrison, still frowning, shook his head slowly. "It's none of
my business what you and Noah do when you're alone."

Oh no! He totally thought we were hooking up. Did he not

see the huge purity ring on my left hand? I mean, it wasn't that big really, but it felt huge with all the meaning behind it. College tuition was a big incentive for keeping that ring on my finger.

Plus, Noah would probably never talk to me again if people thought we were hooking up.

My mind scrambled for something to say that could make everything all right. "What I'm trying to say is that Noah has always been a complete gentleman with me."

Harrison's face flushed. "I don't think I need to know about that."

My whole body felt like I was sitting in a sauna. I pulled my shirt away from my now sweaty skin and started to fan myself with it.

This was getting out of control.

"There really isn't anything to tell. We're, uh..." I looked around the room. Where was Mrs. Willis? I needed her to start class now, so I could stop digging my grave even deeper.

But of course she was late on the one day that I needed her to distract someone from my socially inept mouth. Harrison was staring at me like I was a freak, so I hurried and held up my left hand. "I'm still wearing my purity ring. I'm not hooking up with Noah. I'm not hooking up with any guy anytime soon. I wouldn't even hook up with you." I clamped a hand over my mouth, and when I glanced at the row in front of me, I realized just how loud I'd said that last sentence. The whole saxophone section was looking at me with wide eyes.

Was it possible to die from humiliation? Because the Grim Reaper had to be around here somewhere. Please, just put me out of my misery already.

Harrison held up his hands, turning to the onlookers. "I wasn't planning to hook up with you, Lexi. I have a girlfriend, remember?"

"Of course I know you have a girlfriend." But it certainly

would have come in handy to know that information last week. I rubbed my fingers over my eyes and then down my cheeks. "I was just saying that Noah and I aren't doing anything bad together."

"So it's true that you and Noah Taylor are secretly dating?" Chrissa Fatone asked from the chair beside me.

Was everyone listening to us?

"That's what Ava told me this morning," Nate Baker said.

I felt dizzy. This was not happening. How many people did she tell? "She wasn't supposed to say anything!"

"And you believed her?" Harrison asked, his voice incredulous.

"Can I have your attention please, class?" Mrs. Willis's voice cut through the hysteria threatening to take over my mind.

Everyone who had been staring at me and Harrison now turned to face our band teacher. And I was left with my mind scrambling to figure out a way how to make myself just disappear.

I ALTERNATED between speed-walking and going at a regular pace as I headed toward the lunch room. And here I'd been anxious all weekend about the possible rumors that might have been started, but that anxiety had nothing on me now. I was in full-blown panic mode after what happened in band.

I needed to talk to Noah. I needed to make sure he knew what was being said about him, and what people were now thinking we were doing since I'd opened my big stupid mouth.

I rushed to the lunchroom as soon as the bell rang and found Noah sitting at his usual table. But since the universe seemed to have a grudge against me, of course he was already sitting with one of the cheerleaders, Raven Rodgers, and she was practically hanging all over him. Her chair was so close to his, her hand perched on his shoulder as she leaned in. Her long, black hair cascaded down her back. She'd been friends with Easton and Noah since the beginning of the school year, and it was pretty obvious that she was impatient for Noah to finally get over his ex-girlfriend Ashlyn so she could move in.

But what I needed to say to him couldn't wait, so I adjusted my glasses and stood as tall as my five-foot-three-inch frame could allow and walked over to them.

"Hey, Noah," I said, my voice breathy with nerves. I still had no idea how I was going to tell him what everyone was bound to be talking about already.

He turned to look at me. When his eyes reached mine, they didn't hold the usual amusement I was used to seeing. Had he heard then? Was he mad?

He was probably regretting the moment he'd stepped in to save me.

"Hey, Lexi." His voice sounded not just tired when he spoke but completely drained of its usual life.

"H-how are you doing?" I rocked back and forth on my toes.

"I've been better."

"So you heard then?"

His brow knitted together. "Heard what?"

I hesitated for a moment, trying to figure out what to say.

"Just spit it out, Lexi." Raven crossed her arms, obviously annoyed that I was distracting Noah from her. "We were having a very important conversation."

Noah moved his shoulder, so Raven had to lean back from her perch, and looked up at me with question in his eyes. "What is it?"

I looked around to see if anyone was watching or listening. Of course, eyes from tables all around were staring right at us.

This was bad. My heart thundered in my chest. This was really, really bad.

But if he hadn't heard about what I'd said in band, why was he looking so depressed?

Images of him standing on my front porch came to my mind. I'd almost forgotten about how strange he'd acted Saturday night, since I'd been so worried about my own mess.

"It's like she forgot how to talk," Raven said, following it up with her high-pitched mocking laugh.

Noah rolled his eyes. "Just let her talk, Raven."

I looked at them both, feeling even more flustered. Why did Raven always have to be around Noah at school?

"So, what did you need to talk to me about, Lexi?" He rested his elbow on the table and lifted his face at me, his shaggy hair falling across his eyes.

He really had no idea. Part of me wanted to just run now and not add to whatever was making his life hard at the moment. But I knew I needed to get this over with before I actually got physically sick.

So, I drew in a deep breath and bent over so I could whisper in his ear. "Did you hear all the rumors? A-about me and you?"

I pulled back so I could watch him. His eyes sparked to life and his lips quirked up into a half smile. "Are you telling me that those girls didn't keep our secret?"

I shook my head. "Pretty sure they told everyone." *And I only made it worse.* I held my breath, waiting for him to get mad about being lumped in with someone like me.

"What secret?" Raven crossed her arms and looked at us both expectantly.

Noah shrugged. "It sounds like people are gossiping about how Lexi and I are secretly dating."

Raven's jaw dropped in surprise, and then she laughed—more like cackled. "People actually think you two are dating?" She pushed on his shoulder gently with her hand and laughed again. "That's the most ridiculous rumor I've ever heard." Then she glanced back at me. "In what universe would Noah date someone like you? Football players don't date band geeks."

Her words hit me like a physical punch to the gut. And despite trying my hardest to keep my reaction out of my face, I felt tears instantly prick at the back of my eyes. This wasn't the first time someone had said something like that to me. The one time I did go to a party with Easton and Noah this fall, I'd sat in the corner all night and listened to people whispering about why I was there and how I was too socially awkward to realize when I wasn't really invited somewhere.

And then of course I'd just done the same thing on Friday night with Harrison. When would I ever learn my place? Cool kids didn't hang out with people like me. We belonged in different worlds.

After searching my eyes for a moment, as if he was seeing right through me, Noah raised an eyebrow at Raven. To my amazement, instead of laughing with her, he said, "Shut up, Raven. You don't know what you're talking about."

Her black eyebrows squished together. "You're not actually saying that you two...?" She waved her hand in our direction. "You're not actually *dating?*"

It sounded like she gagged trying to get that last sentence out.

Then Noah did something that I'd never expected. He stood, winked at me so only I could see it, and then put his arm around my shoulders. "We've been trying to keep it a secret because of Easton. But, yeah, we're dating."

He met my stupefied gaze, and I knew my face had to show how shocked I felt. He was stepping in and saving me from humiliation once again.

But then I remembered something. He probably hadn't heard the new rumors from this morning. Which meant, he had no idea what all the people who had heard the gossip were thinking we were doing when we were alone.

I stood on my tippy toes and leaned closer to him to speak, catching a whiff of his too-good-smelling cologne. "I-I don't think you understand what people are saying about us."

He looked around, seeming to notice for the first time that we had an audience. He winked at the freshmen sitting at the next table, staring at us with their mouths hanging open. Noah *actually* winked at them as if they were all in on some sort of plan together. Then he looked back to me and spoke in a dramatic voice. "I don't care what people say. I only care about you and me."

Okay, now he was just putting on a show.

Then he turned to face me and weaved the fingers of his right hand through my hair. His eyes dipped down to my lips.

Excitement and terror exploded inside me at the same time. What was he going to do? Was he going to kiss me? Right here in front of everyone?

I'd barely had time to register that I didn't know the first thing about kissing or whether I even wanted him to do it, when my brother's voice boomed from behind me.

"What's going on here?" Easton came to stand by us. "When I heard the rumors, I laughed at them. But..." His blue eyes inspected us, taking in the way Noah was holding me. Then his hands clenched into fists at his sides. "Are you sneaking around behind my back?"

I extricated myself from Noah's arms, rubbing my sweaty palms on my jeans. "Noah's just joking around. O-of course there's nothing going on between us."

From behind Noah, Raven's brow furrowed. "It's just a joke? I knew it!"

Noah instantly pulled me against his side again. "Of course it's not a joke."

Easton raised his eyebrows. "That's my sister! I know how you are with girls, Noah. How could you even think this would be okay?" He crossed his arms. "And Lexi, what do you expect Dad to say when he finds out?"

My heart pounded harder at the mention of Dad who definitely couldn't find out about this.

"Noah's just pretending. We're not dating." I slipped away from Noah again.

But Noah wasn't listening. Instead, he put his hand on my arm. "Lexi, seriously. You don't need to hide it anymore."

I looked at him, so confused. Why was he pushing this?

I cleared my throat. "Can we go talk in the hall? I think I need to tell you something before this goes any further."

"Sure." He winked. "We can go *talk*."

Easton perked up at that. "I'm coming, too."

I almost expected Raven to say she was joining us as well, but she stabbed a piece of pineapple with her fork instead. "Oh fine. Just leave me to eat my lunch alone."

Noah looked over his shoulder at Raven before leading me out of the lunchroom. "We'll be back in a few minutes."

We found a private spot outside in the hallway. Easton crossed his arms and demanded, "So what's really going on? Because, so help me, I will beat you up if you're really messing around with my sister." His jaw clenched, and he'd never looked so much like my dad before. He wasn't quite as big as Noah, but from the protective glint in his eyes I wouldn't put it past him to get a few good punches in before Noah stopped it.

"Calm down, Easton, and let me talk." Noah leaned against the cinderblock wall behind him, not seeming nervous at all. "It's kind of a crazy story..."

Noah told Easton all about how he'd pretended to be my secret boyfriend on Friday night.

When Noah finished, the fire that had been in Easton's eyes before completely extinguished. "So you're not really trying to date my sister?"

Noah scoffed. "Of course not."

The incredulity in his voice stung, especially after everything Raven had said.

"He was just helping me save face in a really embarrassing situation."

Easton pursed his lips. "But this doesn't explain why everyone was talking about you taking my sister's virtue. What did you do to get *that* rumor going around?"

"They think we hooked up?" Noah turned to me with a mixture of shock and confusion on his face.

I looked at my Chuck Taylors, feeling myself blush. "I um..." I bit my lip. How was I supposed to tell him that *I* had started that rumor?

Noah stepped away from the wall and tilted his head toward mine. "Who told people that we hooked up? Was it Sarah and Ava?"

I shook my head and forced myself to meet his intense gaze. "I accidentally said something this morning that got twisted into something about that. And before I knew it, the whole band class thought we were..." I let my voice drift off, not daring to say the actual word out loud.

"They think we're having s—"

I covered his mouth with my hand before he could finish his sentence. "Shh. Don't say that out loud."

I slowly removed my hand from his lips. I could tell the moment when he realized exactly what was happening, because he got this shocked and dazed look in his eyes. Then he appeared nervous for the first time.

He held his hands up in surrender at Easton. "I swear I didn't lay a finger on your sister. I didn't even kiss her."

Easton folded his arms across his chest. "I would hope not."

Noah pointed his thumb over his shoulder. "Is that what all those people in there think we're doing?"

I nodded. "I think so."

He ran a hand through his tousled hair and blew out a long breath. "Wow. That's uh..." He scratched behind his ear and stared at me like he really didn't know what to say. "'That's not what I was expecting to come from this."

"Yeah, me neither." I shuffled my feet and looked down, wanting to turn invisible.

"I know I don't have the best reputation, but they should know that that's the last thing I would do," Noah said.

"Hey," I said, feeling offended that the thought of being with me would be the *last* thing he'd ever do. Was I really that gross to him?

He shook his head. "You know I don't mean it like that, Lexi. I'm just saying that I know all about the purity ring and college thing, and I'd hate any guy who would take that from you."

"So now that we've got that all cleared up," Easton said awkwardly, rocking back on his heels. "Let's all just focus on the real win for today."

"And that is?" Noah asked.

Easton clapped Noah on the back. "I didn't have to beat up my best friend for hitting on my sister."

Noah laughed. "Like you could even hurt me."

Easton laughed, too. "I know." Then after he'd laughed some more, he asked, "So are you going to keep this lie going?"

"No!" I said.

"Why not?" Noah said at the same time.

What?

"You want to let people think that we're actually dating?"

He shrugged. "I don't know. I mean, it would actually help me out right now."

I pulled my head back, not believing my ears. "How would this help you out?" While it would boost my reputation, being lumped with a lowly sophomore would cause a serious hit to his social status. Not to mention all the girls who wanted to date him, like Raven, would have to sit on the back burner for a while.

Easton checked the time on his phone then put one hand on mine and Noah's shoulder. "I'm gonna grab some lunch and let you two figure out what you're doing. But just remember, if you don't treat her well in this weird scheme of yours, I *will* hurt you."

"You have nothing to worry about," Noah said.

Once Easton was gone, I stepped closer to Noah and leaned my shoulder against the wall. I still didn't understand what was happening here.

"So what do you gain from pretending to date me?"

A half smile lifted his lip. "Well, I don't know if you've noticed, but I'm pretty sure Raven has a thing for me. And while I've been trying to get her to take a hint that I'm not interested in her, she's not getting it. If anything, she's been even more persistent since Ashlyn and Luke started dating."

Ahhh. It all made sense now. "And you're still not over Ashlyn?"

He looked away for a moment, as if that fact made him anxious. "I'm not saying that. I'm just not ready to jump into a relationship at the moment. I kind of have a lot going on in my life right now."

I knew he didn't really like his stepdad, and that him and his bio dad didn't get along very well, but what else could Noah have going on that I wouldn't know about?

"So you think pretending that we're dating would help?"

"It would definitely help get Raven off my back. Plus, if you really like that Harrison guy, you could always use this as a way to get him to dump his girlfriend for you."

Okay, now I knew Noah was talking crazy. "How would me dating you accomplish that?" And did I even want that anymore?

"Guys are all the same. We want what we can't have." The

way he looked at me when he said that made goosebumps erupt on my arms.

But there was no way he would ever think of me in that way. I was not someone he couldn't have. I was the girl who'd been standing on the sideline for years, just waiting for him to notice her.

I swallowed the lump his gaze had caused to form in my throat. "Okay. But what if my dad finds out? No offense, but you as Easton's friend is one thing. Us dating is another."

"Your dad doesn't need to know. It's not like we'll be actually dating. It'll only be at school or activities where we'd be seen together. I doubt your dad checks into high school gossip." Noah said it like there was nothing to worry about. And it did sound like a reasonable thought process.

I nodded. "Okay."

"So you're going to help me out?"

I sighed. "I guess. I mean, you kind of did the same thing for me already on Friday. Might as well return the favor."

Noah smiled. "Great. And once we both have what we want, we can just stage a big break-up and go back to normal."

I swallowed, feeling a nervous pit in my stomach at the thought of what we were about to do. "Sure."

This was probably the dumbest thing I'd ever done.

And that was saying something, especially after what I'd already done this morning.

But if it helped me save face, and helped Noah out at the same time, it might just be worth it.

I followed Noah to the double doors that led back into the cafeteria. Before he pushed them open, something occurred to me.

I grabbed his arm to stop him. "Wait."

"What?"

"What about the whole *other* part of the rumor?" I raised my

eyebrows, hoping he'd get what I was talking about without actually having to say the words out loud.

Understanding dawned on his face. "You mean the part about
us having s—"

I clamped my hand over his mouth once more. "Stop trying to
say that word."

He laughed. "It's just a word, Lexi."

My cheeks grew hot. "I know. I just don't like to say it."

"So you're worried that people will think we're having—" He
paused, trying to think of another way to say it. "Forbidden
relations?"

I nodded, unable to speak.

He reached for my hand, lifting it so I could see my purity
ring. His hand was warm and calloused, and my skin burned
where he touched me. "As long as you keep this on, your reputation should be safe."

I swallowed. "You think so?"

"Yes. Now, don't go spreading this around or anything, but I
never did that stuff with Ashlyn, either." He swallowed and let
my hand drop. "So, if anyone gives you trouble over it, you can let
me deal with them."

He really had never hooked up with Ashlyn? I tried not to let
the shock show on my face over his revelation. I thought for sure
he did that with every girl he dated. Which had been another one
of the reasons why I'd decided we could never be anything more
than people who were stuck together because of my brother.

But was it really possible that Noah, the ultimate bad boy
who was the kind of guy my dad had nightmares about me dating,
really didn't expect that from every girl he was with?

That was such a mind-altering thing to think about.

Noah draped his arm around my shoulder, making my legs go
weak. "Now that that's settled, let's give the students of Ridgewater High the show of their lives."

6

NOAH

I KEPT my arm around Lexi the whole walk through the cafeteria, hoping those Sarah and Ava girls would get their view and get all worked up over the fact that the rumors they were spreading really did seem true. Instead of finding them, I caught the gaze of that Harrison kid Lexi liked so much.

I knew the moment Lexi had noticed him too, because in the same instant she stepped away just enough that I had to drop my arm.

She looked up at me, anxiety written all over her face. "Maybe this isn't such a great idea."

"Why?" I was doing this for her. Well, okay, maybe I'd told her I was doing this to get Raven off my back. And sure, part of me also really wanted a distraction from the fact that I was kicked out of my house and sleeping in my car. If we were fake dating, it would give me a reason to hang out at her house even when Easton was working. The less time I spent in my car, the better.

And maybe a tiny part of me also wanted Ashlyn and Luke to see that I had moved on from wanting my ex back.

But this had all started out as a favor to Lexi.

She stepped forward as the line moved. "When you helped me out on Friday, I had no idea how fast it would get out of control."

"Are you embarrassed by me?" I asked.

"Of course not! Why would you think that?"

The surprise on her face did good things for my ego. "I just wanted to make sure I'm not below your usual standard for date-able material." Seriously, what was so awesome about that Harrison guy, anyway?

She shook her head. "Yeah, that's not going to be an issue here."

I grinned and couldn't help myself. "Does that mean you've had a secret crush on me for years and that I'm making all your wildest dreams come true?" I nudged her playfully in the side with my elbow.

Her jaw dropped, and she punched my arm. "Get over yourself, Noah. I-I..." She shook her head, so flustered she couldn't finish her sentence.

I laughed, loving how red her cheeks were getting. She had always been so fun to tease.

"Hey," I said, holding my hands up. "I'm just saying it's not too crazy of an idea. I mean, Brielle is totally in love with Easton."

"Brielle is only eight. I'm twice that." She said it like the only way she'd get caught on a date with me was if it was fake.

Ironic, I know.

"I was just joking with you, Lexi. No need to bring me down a notch."

"Sorry, I just..." She sighed and lowered her voice. "You know as well as I do why we got *involved* in the first place." She raised her eyebrows as if to communicate something to me that she couldn't say in front of the students surrounding us in the lunch line.

"Because you can't resist this chiseled jaw and magnificent physique of mine?" I gestured to myself, standing as tall as my six-foot-three-inch frame allowed.

She rolled her eyes. "Sure, Noah. Who can resist that."

Her tone told me that she was exactly the type of girl who could resist that. It shouldn't have stung, since we were just pretending to date, but it kind of stung, anyway.

She seemed to notice that she'd offended my man-pride, so she stepped closer and tentatively slipped her hand up to squeeze the inside of my bicep. My skin felt warm where she touched me.

"I was thinking more along the lines of how anyone could resist that shaggy brown hair and million-dollar smile." She winked at me through her black-rimmed glasses. And I never would have believed it if I hadn't seen it, but her cheeks got even darker. Could there be some truth to what she'd just said?

We reached the front of the lunch line and grabbed our trays. I'd been starving all morning, having been in a rush to get to school early enough to shower in the locker room while the drill team practiced. And then I'd been too embarrassed to get breakfast at the cafeteria because someone was bound to ask why I hadn't eaten at home like I usually did.

So I loaded up my tray with food, grabbing the biggest slice of pizza they had and the biggest helpings of the other sides.

Lexi eyed my tray as she scooted hers down the row. She had chosen the chef salad and fruit cup. Was she going to fake dump me because I didn't eat as healthily as her?

"Hungry today?" she asked.

Not wanting to go into why I was hungry, I just said, "Yup."

The lunch cashier added up our food and charged our accounts. When we were back in the commons area, Lexi stopped, as if unsure of where to go.

"You should probably sit at my table today," I suggested.

"You think so?"

"Of course. You're my *girlfriend*, right?"

She sighed, like she was relieved I'd been the one to suggest it. "Thanks. I've been table swapping ever since Juliette went to Paris."

"You should have said something sooner. Easton and I would have let you sit with us." I led her through the maze of tables to where Easton and Raven were arguing over some vampire show they both watched but could never agree on. I offered Lexi the chair I'd sat in earlier and stole an empty one from the table behind ours.

We ate quietly for a while, listening to Raven go on and on about how the main characters were clearly meant for each other and that the head vampire was just sabotaging everything for them. I tuned her out and took a bite of my pizza.

"Don't look now, but I'm pretty sure Ashlyn and Luke are staring at us." Lexi's voice broke me out of my trance.

"What? Where?" I darted my gaze around until I found them sitting at their usual table with Eliana and Jess. And they were indeed looking our way and seemed to be saying something about us.

"Do you think they're talking about us?" Lexi dabbed her mouth with a napkin, looking uncomfortable under their scrutiny.

I glanced at them again. They weren't looking at us anymore. I knew Ashlyn and Luke weren't the type of people to gossip, but what could they be saying? Were they surprised to see me dating Lexi? Ashlyn had hung out with Lexi, Easton, and me a few times at their house while we dated, so I wondered if she could tell that this was fake. I had certainly not taken much notice of Lexi in the past.

But who's to say that something couldn't have changed between us? People started dating people they already knew all the time. Wasn't that what happened to them? One moment

Ashlyn and I had been together, and then the next, she was falling for my rival on the football team.

I scooted closer to Lexi and draped my arm across the back of her chair. "If they're hoping for a show, we can give them one."

Lexi raised her eyebrows and leaned closer; the fruity smell that I was coming to know as her personal scent wafted to my nose. "So you really aren't over Ashlyn then?" she whispered in my ear. To an onlooker it would seem like we were having an intimate conversation where she was whispering sweet nothings to me.

So I decided to take her lead and whispered back, "Just because I care that they're watching doesn't mean that I'm not over her."

She shivered involuntarily, like she'd enjoyed being so close. But then she pulled back to give me a look that told me she wasn't buying my load of crap. "That may be, but the way you grit your teeth every time you see them together tells me otherwise."

I automatically clenched my jaw. I was not still in love with Ashlyn.

At least I was trying really hard not to be. I'd messed things up while we were dating. That ship had sailed. I wasn't just going to wait around and hope Luke suddenly sprouted warts all over. We had already called our truce.

So I decided to turn it back on Lexi.

"Okay, since you're this all-knowing psychologist, what would you have to say about someone who noticed all those things about me? Do you think a psychologist might wonder if *you* were the one with the real crush?"

Her jaw dropped, and she shoved me away. "Just because I'm observant doesn't mean that I'm in love with you."

I shrugged and winked, just because I knew it would make her mad. "Whatever you say, sweetie."

She stabbed her salad with her fork and refused to look at me.

Mission accomplished.

"Is this how it's always going to be then?" Raven said, staring at me and Lexi. She must have finished trying to convince Easton to come to her side of the argument.

"What do you mean?" I sat up straighter.

Raven rolled her eyes and screwed the lid back on her water bottle. "I don't know. You guys are just so weird together. It's distracting."

"Jealousy is not a good look for you, Raven," I retorted, feeling irritated that she couldn't just get off our case.

Raven gasped. "I am not jealous."

I raised my eyebrows in a challenge. "Then, what's that look on your face you're giving us?"

She huffed. "I just wanted you two to know that not everyone is comfortable being around that much PDA."

Yeah, since she hadn't just been crawling all over me at the beginning of lunch period.

I took a drink from my water bottle and set it down on the table. "I'll keep that in mind." I was totally going to play up the PDA in front of Raven now. Yeah, she was hot and there was that one time we made out at Jake Haley's party. But if I hadn't been mad at Paul for hitting me, or if I hadn't been trying to forget how I'd been rude to Ashlyn when she showed up in her pajamas, I would have been in a better frame of mind and never kissed her.

Raven stirred her pudding with her spoon. "So, how long have you two been dating then?"

"Yes, I'm just dying to know how long you two have been sneaking around behind my back." Easton smirked.

I shook my head at Easton. A stab of guilt coursed through me when I noticed Raven's eyes were glistening. Had she really thought that night meant something to me?

Instead of answering, I turned to Lexi, not having it in me to pound in the final nail.

Lexi shifted in her seat, as if startled that I'd let her take the lead on this.

"Well..." She glanced at me, her gaze searching mine for some kind of indication on what to say. I nodded my encouragement, so she cleared her throat and looked back to Raven. "I guess it's kind of been going on for a while. Probably since the middle of football season when I noticed Noah couldn't seem to keep his eyes off me as I sat in the pep band."

I almost snorted when the image of her in a polo shirt that was two sizes too big came to my mind.

Yeah, that pep band shirt was about as attractive as a circus tent would be on her.

Lexi continued, "Anyway, he practically begged me to give him a chance after that. And I guess you could say things have been pretty serious for about a month."

I nodded, squeezing her closer to my side. "Yep. I just can't get enough of this girl. And I'm just glad we don't have to hide it anymore."

Raven narrowed her gaze, like she still didn't quite believe us. But she didn't say anything. Instead, she started stacking the remnants of her lunch back on her tray and stood. "Well, if you'll excuse me, I have a test I need to study for."

I CALLED my mom after dropping Easton and Lexi off at their house. I needed to see if I was welcome to come home yet. Sleeping in my car was much colder now than it had been in October. Winter in New York was not going easy on me.

My mom's voice cut through the line. "If you could stay at your dad's house for just a few more days, maybe until Saturday, that would be nice."

"Saturday?" That was five more days of sleeping in the

freezing cold. I'd have to buy myself a second sleeping bag if I was going to last that long in my car.

"That's only a week, Noah. It'll be good for you and your dad to have that time together, anyway."

Yeah, if only my dad cared enough to have me stay there, instead of thinking I was some punk kid who was always getting into trouble.

But I decided to just let her keep assuming that I was sleeping at my dad's house. Ignorance really was bliss, wasn't it?

"How is Paul treating you? Has he done anything since I left?" I asked. Then I perked up my ears to make sure I heard her tone right when she answered.

"He hasn't done anything again. He's still really stressed, but I think things should get better."

"That doesn't sound very promising, Mom. I don't want him hurting you again."

"We'll be fine."

"Is Brielle okay?"

"She's fine. Everything is fine." And she sounded like she really believed the lie she'd been telling herself for years. "Don't worry about us. Let's just wait to hear back about Paul's promotion and then you can come home."

I sighed and leaned back in my seat. "Okay. But make sure to let me know if things change. I don't want a repeat of last time."

"I appreciate your concern, Noah. But you don't need to worry about us. Paul said he was sorry for that night. It won't happen again."

I really hoped that was true. For everyone's sake.

I hung up the phone and tried to figure out what to do. There were still six hours left before my body would be anywhere near ready to call it a night. And since Easton had work, and Lexi didn't need me for any extra fake-boyfriend duties after school, I decided to use the money my dad had put in my checking account and buy myself another sleeping bag that was better for winter.

It was *almost* like he was giving me a warm place to sleep this week.

7

LEXI

"I STILL CAN'T BELIEVE that you're dating Noah Taylor!" Juliette raised her dark eyebrows at me. I'd messaged her as soon as lunch got over, and she'd immediately made me promise to FaceTime her as soon as I got home.

I sank down onto my bed next to the Yale poster on my wall —the poster that my dad bought as an incentive and a reminder to not get knocked up like Maddie. This room had been hers and my nephew Grant's before they moved out this summer, and Dad had been paranoid that this room might carry some sort of curse. So the very first things to go up once I switched rooms were the Yale posters and paraphernalia to ward off any teenage hormones that might get awakened through my sister's influence.

"We aren't really dating. Just putting on a show for everyone," I insisted.

"Yes, but you still get to cuddle with him. That's going to be real." Juliette applied a layer of lip gloss and smacked her lips together. While I was about as nerdy as you could get, she was all about fashion and makeup—which was why her semester abroad in Paris had been a once-in-a-lifetime opportunity that she couldn't pass up.

"Do you think I'm going to have to cuddle with him?" The thought of being so close to Noah sent a nervous jolt through my veins.

"Have to?" Her brown eyes went wide through my phone's screen. "I think 'get to' is a much more accurate description. Those muscles have been known to make girls hyperventilate before."

I shook my head and laughed at her ridiculousness. Yeah, Noah was ripped. And I was pretty sure I'd heard rumors of him being one of the top candidates for the senior class award for best physique, but that didn't mean I needed to pretend like I wanted to see his physique.

Or at least, I didn't need anyone knowing that I might have occasionally sneaked glimpses of him when he and Easton had their hot tub nights on the back deck.

"Do you think it's completely stupid for me to go along with this? I mean, I've never dated a guy before. How am I supposed to know how to fake it? What if he tries to kiss me or something?"

"Then let him kiss you!"

"Seriously? You're, like, absolutely no help here," I said.

Her head fell back as she laughed. "Fine. If you aren't comfortable with that, just invite him over and tell him you want to go over some rules or something. He plays sports, so tell him you want to have a game-planning session."

I sighed. "You think that'll work?"

She smiled. "It's worth a shot. And make sure you tell him kissing is mandatory. At all times."

"Juliette!" I scolded.

She laughed again. "Okay, do whatever you're comfortable with. But try to be open to possibilities. I mean, it's not every day that you have an opportunity like this. Make it count."

"Okay, I'll try that." She may have only been six months older than me, but that whole year she had ahead of me in school really had given her a lot more experience with guys than I had.

"And make sure to keep this going as long as you can. I want to see this show of yours when I get home in two weeks. Okay?"

I laughed. "I'll do my best."

"*Au revoir.*" She blew me a kiss through the phone.

"*A bientôt,*" I replied, happy I'd get to see her soon.

AFTER ENDING my call with Juliette, I paced around my room for fifteen full minutes, trying to summon the courage to text Noah about "game planning" this new arrangement of ours.

I should be a lot cooler about this, since it was fake, but every time he said something about my crush on him in the past, I was scared he'd be able to see just how true his words were. I *had* crushed on him growing up. Five long years' worth of crushing on Noah. But I had finally bit that bad habit in the bud and had moved on a year ago.

I couldn't have him figure out that it was ever true, or that a tiny piece of me might still be just a little attracted to him.

Yeah, he definitely couldn't find that out or he was sure to make our fake-dating scheme a whole-lotta painful for me and a whole-lotta fun for him.

But we still needed to talk somewhere private, where we wouldn't have any prying eyes and ears discovering what was really going on.

So I clicked send on my message.

Me: **Can you come over? I think we need to set up some ground rules.**

Noah: **Ground rules? Those don't sound like any fun.**

Of course. Rules were like a bad word to guys like Noah. He was all about breaking them.

Me: **Ground guidelines then?**

I could just picture him laughing at this. He had a nice laugh. It was deep and full and did funny things to my insides.

I waited for him to respond, but when I didn't see any conversation dots, I texted him again.

Me: **My dad is making meatloaf, potatoes, and carrots for dinner. We can eat first.**

He was like a bottomless pit. I probably should have offered food in my original message.

My phone chimed almost instantly.

Noah: **What time is dinner?**

Yep, I should have definitely mentioned food first. I'd know better for next time.

Me: **6:30**

Noah: **I'll be there.**

"SO WHERE WOULD you like to *talk?*" Noah stood close to me as I loaded the last of the dishes in the dishwasher after dinner. And I didn't know how he did it, but he managed to make the word "talk" sound like we were going to be doing something against the law.

I looked around to make sure my dad wasn't watching. I absolutely could not have him thinking anything was going on between us. He'd skin me alive...after he was finished with Noah, of course.

Dinner had already been stressful enough with Noah

there. Yes, he'd eaten with us a million times before, but now that we had this secret between us, I felt like if I even looked across the table to him that my dad would know what was going on.

I added the detergent packet to the dishwasher. "We can talk downstairs if you want."

As I pushed the buttons to start the load, he leaned in closer and spoke into my hair. "I'll be waiting for—"

He stopped mid-sentence. I moved my focus from the dishwasher buttons to see what had startled him. My dad had just walked into the room.

He'd gotten his dark hair trimmed today, so he was back to looking like he had when he was a drill sergeant.

I didn't think he'd seen how close Noah had been standing to me, but that didn't keep my heart from letting me know it was still in there.

"H-hi Dad." I swallowed the thickness in my throat and hoped I didn't have sweat beading on my brow.

"Where's Easton?" Dad asked.

"He went downstairs to do his homework since he was busy working this afternoon."

My dad's blue eyes drifted to Noah, as if trying to figure out why he was still here.

"A-and, Noah and I have a school project that we were just about to work on."

"You two have a class together?" Dad's eyebrows furrowed.

I looked at Noah, hoping he could help me out because my mind was clearly not working at the moment. Of course we didn't have any classes together. He was two grades above me.

Noah stepped forward. "No, but she's helping me with this English project I'm doing."

My dad nodded, his shoulders relaxing. "Lexi's always been a reader."

Then, as if that settled everything, he continued through the kitchen and into the living room.

I rushed Noah down the stairs as soon as the coast was clear, knowing my heart couldn't handle any more scares like that today. I was sure to develop an ulcer or something if my world didn't calm down quick.

We sat on the brown sectional, and I pulled up the notepad app on my phone.

"So what English project am I supposedly helping you with?" I asked.

He pressed the button on the side to recline in the seat. "*Pride and Prejudice.*"

I coughed. "You do realize that I know next to nothing about *Pride and Prejudice* or anything by Jane Austen, right?"

"I thought all girls loved that book." He looked at me like I was a strange anomaly in the world of girls.

"No, that's Ashlyn. I haven't even watched the movie version."

A sheepish grin spread over his lips. "Dang it. I was actually kind of hoping that as my *girlfriend* you might be able to help me figure out that book. Or at least watch the movie with me sometime. The test is next week."

"Well, okay. I guess we can both suffer through that movie together sometime." I held up my phone. "Which brings us to our next item of business."

"You make it sound so formal."

"What would you rather I call it?"

He thought for a moment before saying, "Our second date."

I grabbed the throw pillow beside me and chucked it at him.

He blocked it with his hands and laughed. "Sorry. It was just right there. I had to say it." And he just kept on laughing.

"I'm glad you can at least amuse yourself," I said as seriously as I could muster. I couldn't let him know that I actually kind of enjoyed his teasing. Which was another stupid thing. It reminded me of something Raven was ranting about last week. She said that when a boy teases a girl and we dismiss it as harmless and just a show of affection, we're actually encouraging future domestic abuse by enabling this behavior and mentality.

But it was hard to think of Noah's teasing like that when my stomach did little flips every time he winked at me.

"Okay, sorry." His face sobered, and he looked repentant. "What are the guidelines that we need to set?"

I shifted in my seat, preparing myself to talk about possibly awkward things.

"I was thinking that since we're pretending to be dating, we'll probably end up in awkward situations. So I want to make sure that we set up some rules for each other, so we don't cross any lines of comfort."

That came out weird, but I hoped he got the gist of what I was saying.

"That sounds like a good plan." He nodded, and for the first time all day he actually looked serious.

"Good. And I figured I'd jot them all down here, so I can send them to you later."

"Is this like a binding contract? Are you going to send me to a fake-dating jail if I mess up?"

"Of course not."

"Good."

"So do you have any specific things you don't want me to say or do while we're in front of people?"

He cleared his throat and sat up taller. "Actually, today..." He shifted his gaze to the side, as if about to say something nerve-wracking. "Um, when you put your hand on my arm and told me I had a million-dollar smile, I felt really uncomfortable. Like, I really didn't like it."

For a moment, I sat there in silence, stunned that he would

actually feel that way. Of all the things that happened today, he thought *that* was bad?

"I'm sorry, Noah. I had no idea..."

And then, of course, his lips lifted up into that million-dollar-smile of his.

"I'm joking, Lexi. I really don't care what you say or do to me." He burst up laughing. "You should have seen your face, though."

I grabbed the pillow again and threw it at him, this time hitting him right in the face.

"Hey!" He rubbed his eyes, but I couldn't manage to feel one ounce of guilt for making them water.

"So this whole conversation's going to be pointless then?" I asked.

He held his hands up in surrender. "That was the last one. I promise for real this time."

"It'd better be."

"You won't even need to use this pillow again." He set it down on the floor, as if that would help prove he was suddenly trust-worthy. Then he pulled the recliner back to its seating position. "I'll even sit here like I'm in a business meeting with you."

"You really don't have to do that," I said.

He tilted his head and scrunched up one side of his face. "Actually, I probably do. I tend to get unruly when I'm relaxed."

"Unruly?"

"Yeah, that Jane Austen lady must be getting to me."

"Okay," I said, finally ready to move on to the reason why I'd invited him over in the first place. "I guess I just wanted to figure out what we'll do in certain situations at school. Like, how far are we going to take this?"

He pursed his bottom lip. "Well, I'm thinking since this is only fake, if we get sent into seven minutes of heaven at a party, we should only make-out for five minutes tops."

Panic rose in my chest. "D-do they play that game a lot at the parties you go to?" I thought they only did things like that in the movies.

He lifted a shoulder. "Well, you never know. I thought we were planning for *everything*."

"Do you think they'd know if we really made out or not?"

"You don't want to make-out with me, Lexi?" He put a hand over his chest as if I'd just offended him in the worst way.

But it was more like I was scared to death of ever being in that situation. I'd never even kissed a guy.

"I just don't think we should have to make-out because of a silly game."

"Fine. I can just mess up your hair a little with my hands and call it good."

I was sooo out of my element here. I might need to call Juliette again and have her talk me through this.

But no, I was a big girl. I could figure this fake dating thing out on my own.

"How about we just don't show up to those kinds of parties, okay?"

He sighed. "Okay."

"So let's talk about school. Do you want me to eat with you every day? Or do you like space from your girlfriends?"

Noah and Ashlyn had spent all their free time at school together when they were still dating. But I wanted to make sure he understood that I didn't expect things to be the same as they were with her.

"Yeah, let's eat together. Raven won't believe any of this if we don't. And, if you want, I could pick you up for school in the mornings."

My mind imagined what it would be like to show up to school in his car in the morning instead of being driven by my dad or Easton. It would be pretty amazing. Except for one thing.

"I'm pretty sure my dad would get suspicious. And I doubt he'd believe that it was for your English assignment."

"Good point," he said. "So, I know you don't want to kiss me or anything, but I'm pretty sure Raven will expect us to hold hands and cuddle. Would you be okay with that?"

My palms went sweaty at the thought. I'd never done that before either. Would he be able to tell the first time we held hands?

I wiped my fingers along my pants. "Yeah, we could hold hands."

"And cuddle?" He raised his perfect eyebrows. Was it weird that I thought he had amazing eyebrows?

"Sure," I squeaked. I'd never done any of these things with a guy before, just my cute two-year-old nephew Grant, but I wasn't about to tell him that now.

He gave me a half smile. "Looks like our relationship is progressing already. Just last weekend you were telling me we wouldn't be cuddling on our first date. And now I get to hold your hand and everything."

How could he be so nonchalant about this whole thing?

"Just holding hands and cuddling, right?" I confirmed as I finished typing the rules of our agreement into my phone.

"I promise not to kiss you unless you ask me to."

My heart spiked at his mention of kissing. But I cleared my throat and did my best to appear unfazed. "Sounds good. Just don't hold your breath, because I'm not the PDA kind of girl."

8

NOAH

I CHECKED my phone for the time. It was almost ten. Easton and I had decided to play video games in his basement after Lexi and I finished our game-planning session for the next days at school.

I wondered if I could just ask Easton to let me sleep here. It was late enough that he'd probably let me chill on his couch for the night.

Mr. Stevens' heavy footsteps sounded at the top of the staircase.

"Time to hit the lights, boys. You've got school tomorrow."

Easton groaned, but he paused the game. "Looks like you'll have to wait until tomorrow to decimate my city." He saved the game and then shut the system down.

I stood and stretched, trying to get up the nerve to ask if I could stay over.

Hey, it's late. Mind if I crash on your couch? I ran the words through my head. That didn't sound like a weird request, did it?

"Noah, it's time for you to head home now." Mr. Stevens' voice bellowed down the stairs.

So much for staying out of the cold tonight. My shoes suddenly felt like they were full of lead. They did not want to carry me up the stairs and out to my car. That was about the last thing I wanted to do.

But as much as I didn't want to go outside, I was still too stubborn to go crawling back to my dad's house again. And too prideful.

So I grabbed my letterman jacket from the couch and shrugged into it.

"I'll see you at school tomorrow." I nodded to Easton.

He yawned and stretched. "Have a good night."

I'll try.

I trudged up the stairs and met Mr. Stevens at the top.

"You be careful out there driving on the ice," he said. "I heard the roads are slick tonight."

I nodded and met his eyes. I was technically an inch taller than him, but I always felt small in the presence of this giant of a man. "I'll drive slow."

I went out the door and was instantly hit with a gust of wind and snow. I could barely see a few feet in front of me in the blizzard.

I turned on my car and let it warm up, shivering as my body adjusted to the cold. I blew on my hands. I really didn't feel like getting caught in a snowstorm tonight. So instead of heading off toward my usual camping spot, I drove a few houses down and settled in for the night.

WHEN MY ALARM woke me at six the next morning, my car was buried. I leaned over the center console and started the engine, hoping it would warm up quickly.

While my car was defrosting, I wriggled out of my sleeping

bag and pulled on my boots from the backseat. By the time I had them on and had slipped my arms into my coat, the car was warm enough that some of the ice that were stuck to the windows started to melt.

But I still had to climb out and scrape the thick pile of snow off the windshield. Winter sucked.

About ten minutes later, I could finally drive to school. If I didn't get there soon, all the drill team girls would see me sneaking into the boys' locker room. And I knew Ashlyn would most definitely be curious about why I was at school so early. Back in October, when my mom was in the women's shelter, Ashlyn had gotten suspicious, questioning me about where I had been staying. If she knew that I was sleeping in my car now, she might interfere. And she didn't need to worry about me anymore. I was no longer a problem for her.

I parked in the lot by the gym and snuck in through the back door. Thankfully, no one saw me before I slipped into the locker room. The hot shower felt amazing on my skin, and I spent a few extra minutes lathering up. Half of the night I'd been awake, alternating between shivering and turning on the car heater for a few minutes because it had gotten so cold. My new sleeping bag had made it better, but if we had another night like that, I might have to humble myself and ask my dad to let me in. I knew I could probably just tell my mom about what was happening, but I really didn't want to cause any more problems between her and Paul right now. She said to give them a few days, so I would do that.

"ARE you coming to the game today?" Raven sidled up to me as I walked from my third-period class to fourth.

"I hadn't really thought about it. But yeah I'll probably go."

Then realizing that she was probably asking because she wanted me to sit near her as she cheered, I added, "But I'll be sitting by Lexi and the pep band, now that we're public. She's been telling me all month how she's been dying for me to get over my fear of Easton beating me up and just come and sit by her."

Okay, so that was a huge lie, but Raven seemed to believe it since her expression fell.

But almost as soon as I saw her disappointment, she forced a smile onto her face. "I'm going to have to get used to that. I still can't believe you and Lexi are actually dating. That came out of nowhere."

"Yeah." I shrugged as guilt gnawed at my insides. I remembered how Raven and I had made out just the week before Lexi and I had *allegedly* started dating. "You never know what's gonna happen. But she is certainly one-of-a-kind." I probably should've come up with a more romantic-sounding compliment for Lexi. One that would make this whole thing more believable. But I wasn't the romantic type of guy who wrote sonnets or sang love songs to girls. I was more of the "Hey girl, wanna make-out?" kind of guy. I certainly hadn't treated Ashlyn like she wanted, and I wasn't interested in dating Raven like she wanted. So this fake-boyfriend thing with Lexi would be kind of perfect. At least it would keep me from making out with random girls and then feeling guilty when I realized I was on my way to breaking another heart.

"Well, I guess I might see you at the game then." Raven quickened her pace to leave me.

"Sure," I called after her. "I'll see you then."

I pulled out my phone when I got to my next class and quickly shot Lexi a text.

Me: **Can I sit by you at the game tonight? Is that allowed?**

It took her a moment to respond, and I was worried she'd say no—which was crazy, since we weren't really dating. But for some reason, my heart raced like it thought she really had the power to hurt me if she turned me down.

I sighed when my phone vibrated with her text.

Lexi: **You sure you don't mind sitting with the band nerds instead of your cool friends?**

Well, since one of my *cool* friends was hoping to be my girlfriend, I really didn't feel like sitting by her tonight. Plus, I was pretty sure Easton had plans to sit with Mercedes since things were going well for them after their first date.

Me: **I'd rather sit by you. And we can try to make your secret crush jealous while I'm there.**

Lexi: **My secret crush?**

Me: **Isn't Harrison in the pep-band too?**

Had she seriously forgotten about him already? Hadn't she just been trying to snag a date with him on Friday? Not that much could have changed since then. It was only, like, five days ago.

Lexi: **yeah, you can sit by me if you promise not to embarrass me too much.**

I laughed. That was going to be hard. So I sent her the most honest reply that I could.

Me: **I'll try my best.**

9

LEXI

THE PROSPECT of tonight's game was stressing me out. Not only would I be sitting by Harrison all night, on the bleachers, possibly just inches away from him, but Noah was going to be there too...pretending to be my boyfriend and probably laughing at how anxious I was around both guys.

By the time six o'clock rolled around, I'd already tried on three different pairs of shoes—since shoes were my only chance at looking cute tonight. That band polo really needed to be burned. My dad had thought he was being economical by buying me a size bigger during my freshman year, hoping I'd grow into it as I went through high school. But in the past year and a half, I had yet to grow even a centimeter. I wasn't going to reach the average height like my sister did. Instead, I was most likely going to stay five-foot-two forever.

Easton dropped me off at school thirty minutes early so I could grab my trumpet from the band room and have time to get my stand and music all set up before the game started.

"Don't make it too easy on Mercedes," I gave Easton some advice before he drove off to pick her up for the game. "According to Noah, people want what they can't have. So make sure you don't seem too eager to pick her up."

He shook his head. "That's, like, the worst dating advice I've ever heard."

"I'm just saying it since it seemed to work for Noah." He had all kinds of girls after him. And it had certainly been true in my case. I'd always wanted the guys I couldn't have. Harrison had a girlfriend. And Noah, well...that was just not ever going to happen. Not for real, anyway.

I stopped by the girls' restroom on my way to the band room, just to make sure the snow hadn't totally flattened my hair—not because I cared what Noah thought of it. I just wanted to look good for myself.

Everything checked out, so I grabbed my trumpet from the instrument storage room and then made my way down to the gym.

The JV game was just finishing up as I got my stuff all set up for the varsity game. I decided to sit on the end of the trumpet section, since Noah would be sitting by me. I still couldn't believe that he was choosing to sit with the pep band tonight. He must really be committed to this fake boyfriend/girlfriend thing. And I had no idea why. Most guys would love to date one of the cheerleaders. And sure, Raven wasn't exactly the nicest to me, but she definitely had all the qualities most guys looked for in a girl. She was the kind that guys would call "hot," while I was what they'd call "quirky."

Harrison joined me in the trumpet section a couple of minutes later, his trumpet case in his hand, his shirt messily tucked only halfway into his jeans. It was kind of adorable how disheveled he looked sometimes, like he was always in a hurry and getting dressed as he stepped out the door. It made me miss his hair. It was too short to look messy anymore.

"Do you mind if I share your stand?" he asked, standing at the end of the row.

I caught a whiff of his cologne. He may look messy, but he smelled amazing. I cleared my throat.

"Yeah," I said. "But could you sit on the other side? Noah wants to sit up here tonight, so I'm trying to sit on the end."

"Oh, okay." He seemed a little surprised that Noah would be joining us. Did he somehow know that this whole thing was fake? He probably did. I had never come out right and told Harrison that I liked him, but I was sure it was obvious to anyone who had watched me very closely. Things had been a little awkward this morning during band, after my horrifying display the day before. But he hadn't brought it up again, so I was at least thankful for that.

Harrison shuffled around me before squeezing into the spot to my right. It was a tight fit, since Chrissa was on the other side, but I could handle bumping knees with him and not going into cardiac arrest, right?

The game started, and I was just beginning to wonder if Noah had changed his mind when I saw him standing near the back entrance wearing his blue-and-white letterman jacket. He seemed to be studying the pep band, so I waved. A moment later our eyes caught, and he smiled and waved back. My pulse throbbed when he started walking toward me, passing the cheerleaders on the floor and only giving Raven a nod before stepping onto the bleachers and climbing up to sit by me.

"Sorry I'm late." He scooted next to me and shrugged out of his jacket, his cheeks rosy from the cold outside.

"I was beginning to wonder if you'd decided not to grace me with your presence after all," I said.

He rubbed his hands together to warm them. "Yeah, sorry. The line at Subway took forever."

"Do you ever eat at home?" I asked. Seriously, it seemed like he was always eating all the food out of my family's fridge, or I was finding take-out wrappers stashed in the backseat of his car whenever he gave me and Easton a ride home from school. Maybe his mom just didn't cook?

But his face became guarded, and it made me wonder if there was another reason for why he wasn't eating his meals at home.

"I was busy." He shrugged, like there was nothing wrong. "I just grabbed something on my way here, so I wouldn't be too late." He eyed Harrison on the other side of me, and then put his arm around my shoulders, squeezing me against his side. "Plus, I wanted to spend as much time as I could with you."

He winked, but as much as he was trying to make it seem like nothing was wrong, his smile didn't reach his eyes.

He barely spent any time at home from what I could tell. During football season I'd run down to the girls' locker room before a game and had overheard him say something to Ashlyn about someone not pressing charges and that he could move in with his dad if he wanted. I hadn't been able to hear any more, since Luke Davenport had angrily stomped up the stairs past me, forcing me to relinquish my hiding place before it became obvious that I was eavesdropping.

I hadn't been able to keep that snippet of conversation out of my head and had watched Noah for the next few weeks. But things seemed to be okay, aside from him being moody. And he never said anything to Easton about moving in with his dad.

But *was* everything okay? And who was not pressing charges against whom?

Was Noah in trouble?

The Drum Major stood on the floor when the other team called a time-out. She counted four beats, and I put my trumpet to my mouth to play the notes on the sheet music before me. By the time we were finished playing *Hawaii Five-O,* I was out of breath.

When I sat back down, Noah was looking at his phone.

He groaned. "It's supposed to get below zero tonight." He handed me his phone. The weather app showed that it was twenty degrees right now, but it would get down to negative two tonight.

"Is that the coldest it's been so far this year?" I handed his phone back, and my skin tingled and burned where our fingers touched in the exchange. I quickly put my hand in my lap, hoping he didn't notice my reaction to him.

"Yeah, I think so. It makes me cold just thinking about it."

"Thank goodness for insulation and heaters." I shrugged. Sure, it was cold during winter in New York, but as long as I didn't have to spend too much time outside, it wasn't that bad.

"And don't forget that warm, cozy bed," he said. I would have normally expected him to say it with some sort of innuendo attached, since he couldn't seem to turn off the teasing when he was around me. But instead, there was a darker tone in his voice, and I couldn't figure out why. Was his bed not warm and cozy?

What else could it be?

He sighed, and before I could ask him about why the cold bothered him so much, he pointed to my trumpet in my lap. "How do you play so many notes with just three buttons?"

I shrugged. "There are only three valves, but you can play them in multiple combinations."

I showed him the different finger combinations that I used when playing a scale. "And then you also tighten and loosen your lips to control the pitch of the music as well."

"Interesting." He took the instrument into his hands, running his fingers over the brass curves. Then he played with the valves, as if trying to discover all the different combinations he could. "You must have to do a lot of the tightening and loosening of your lips to play all the notes I just heard."

"You can try it if you want," I offered when he continued to play with my trumpet.

"Show me what I'm supposed to do with my lips first."

I took my mouthpiece out of the trumpet, not wanting to make too much noise when I wasn't supposed to be playing a song.

I held the mouthpiece up. "To make the lower tones, your lips have to be looser." I showed him and blew into the mouthpiece. "And with the higher notes, you tighten them up really tight."

As I demonstrated, I suddenly became self-conscious at the thought of him watching my mouth.

He seemed to realize what I was thinking because he gave me a half-smile. "I guess it's a good thing you're really talented with your lips then." He winked, and I felt myself blush.

And of course, he noticed my blushing. To make it worse, he said, "I'll let you show me just how good you are later. Maybe we can heat things up in my car without even turning the heater on."

If it was possible to burst into flames at that moment, I would have.

I looked around to see if anyone was listening to our conversation. Of course, the saxophones in the row ahead were eyeing us and whispering to each other. I glanced at Harrison and noticed him staring ahead intently, his jaw flexing. Did he not like that Noah was talking about kissing me? Was this plan of ours actually working?

I leaned closer to Noah. "People are going to start thinking all we do together is make-out." And if they thought that, they'd probably keep on thinking the stupid rumors I'd started were true, too.

He just grinned that wicked grin of his. "I'm okay with that. I mean, if the rumors are already there, why shouldn't we just make-out all the time?" He winked.

Ok, where was the fire extinguisher? My face was on fire.

Noah touched my forehead, his hand cool against my burning skin. "Are you feeling well, babe? You're looking overheated."

My skin sparked even more to life at his unexpected touch, and my mind couldn't get over the fact that Noah Taylor had just called *me* babe! But since I couldn't have him noticing my involuntary reaction to him, I removed his palm not so gently from my forehead. "Y-you know I'm healthy as a horse."

He grinned again. "Good, I would hate to get sick after tonight." He peeked at Harrison then whispered next to my ear. "Don't look now, but I'm pretty sure Harrison wants to punch me in the face."

"And that's a good thing?" I whispered back.

Noah shrugged. "He's definitely noticing you and feeling some strong emotions, so I'd say it's good."

I wanted to turn around to see for my own eyes what he was talking about, but that would only make it obvious that we were up to something. So I looked into Noah's dark brown eyes instead and spoke in as calm a voice as I could. "I'll text Easton to tell him not to worry about giving me a ride home tonight."

"YOU READY TO GO?" Noah asked when the game ended. Ridgewater High won, 45-40.

After his initial over-the-top flirting, Noah had actually kept things in check the rest of the time. The only other time I blushed again was when he noticed Raven glaring at us from her spot with the cheerleaders on the floor and Noah decided to lean in real close and whisper nonsense in my ear just to make her jealous.

And it was totally working because she seemed to be having a really hard time looking upbeat during her cheer routine.

But as for Harrison, aside from that one moment where his jaw had been tense, he didn't seem bothered much at all. Which had me thinking that his flexed jaw had nothing to do with Noah talking about kissing me. It would seem that Noah's theory about guys wanting what they can't have was totally untrue, just like Easton had said. Because instead of paying attention to us, Harrison spent most of the rest of the game either texting his girlfriend or doing his homework.

I had planned to do my homework during the game like I usually did but found myself getting caught up talking to Noah instead. He was super distracting when he wanted to be.

But the game was over, so now he could take me home and I could stay up late doing my homework, since we were most definitely not going to be making out like he wanted everyone around us to believe.

"I just have to put my trumpet and stand away, and then we can go." I grabbed the case from where I'd stashed it behind me and opened the latches.

Noah gripped the stand in his hand. "I can put this away for you."

"Really?" I asked, not expecting his help. Even when I shared a stand with someone, I was usually the one always putting it away.

He shrugged like it was no big deal. "What kind of a boyfriend would I be if I didn't offer?"

I watched him as he followed the other band kids to the storage area by the stairs. On his way back, Raven stopped him.

I tried to push away the jealousy bubbling inside when she leaned in, closer than a regular friend would, and said something into his ear.

I shouldn't be jealous. Noah wasn't my real boyfriend.

"What's going on with that?" Harrison startled me out of my envious stupor, gesturing to Noah and Raven with his hand.

I sighed and started latching my trumpet case. "They're friends. She's probably talking to him about a class or something."

Harrison raised an eyebrow like he didn't believe me. "Friends don't usually stand that close unless they want the friendship to change."

"What are you trying to say?" I asked, not liking what he was hinting at. "Are you trying to say that Noah is cheating on me?"

That would just be my luck, though: Noah pretending to date me only to actually be dating someone behind my back. Was that what this was? Was he just trying to create a new thrill for himself? Like the ultimate dating behind someone's back, without it technically being wrong?

Harrison dropped his books into his backpack. "No, I'm not saying that about Noah. I'm just saying you better watch out for that Raven girl. She doesn't seem to be the kind to care if her target is already spoken for."

My shoulders slumped as I watched them interact. He didn't seem to dislike the way she was coming onto him at all. Could he actually have been trying to use this fake relationship in a different way than he'd told me? Was he the one who was really playing hard to get so he could make Raven want him even more? Was that his real agenda?

I really hope not.

Not that I should care. We had our arrangement after all.

But I kind of cared anyway. Which was really, *really* stupid.

I clenched my hands into fists at my sides and was considering telling Noah to take Raven home instead of me, when he finally finished his conversation and joined my side again. The rest of the band kids had already cleared out, so we were the only ones left on the bleachers. Everybody else was talking on the floor below.

"What did Raven want?" I asked, hating how jealous-sounding my question came out.

Noah grabbed his letterman jacket from behind his seat. "She invited me to grab hot chocolate with some of our friends."

"So are you going with her?"

He frowned his bottom lip as he pushed his arms into his jacket. "No. I told her you and I already have plans."

He did?

Why did he? Was that to play hard to get a little more, or did he really not want to hang out with her?

Ugh, I hated that I was doubting his real intentions in this fake relationship of ours. I wasn't supposed to care about his intentions.

I pulled my coat on. "You don't have to take me home if you'd rather hang out with them. I'll just catch a ride with Easton."

"I think Easton and Mercedes were going with them."

I bit my lip, trying to figure something else out. "I guess I can walk home."

"Don't be crazy, Lexi. I'm going to take you home, just like we planned."

"But if you wanted to hang out with Raven, I totally get it. I know you're still friends even if you say you don't want to date her."

That made me sound like a totally non-jealous fake girl-friend, right?

"Did you want to get hot chocolate with them?"

"What? No." I shook my head. "I have tons of homework tonight."

"Okay, then let me take you home." He lifted my trumpet cased, like he was going to carry it out for me.

How was it possible that he didn't want to hang out with the gorgeous Raven Rodgers tonight? Every other guy I knew would jump at the chance. Did they have some sort of history I didn't know about?

When I didn't follow him, he put his hand behind my back and led me down the stairs with him. "I'm not interested in

Raven. You already know that." He spoke in a lowered voice so the people below us wouldn't hear.

I lowered my voice, too. "It just doesn't make sense. Most guys at our school would drop everything if they had Raven looking and talking to them like that."

"Well, that's good for them."

My eyebrows squished together. "So why don't you want a real relationship? Don't get me wrong, I'm thankful that you're helping me save face and all, but most guys would call you crazy for doing it when you could date someone like Raven."

He narrowed his eyes at me. "Do you really think I'm the kind of guy to just drop my *girlfriend* because a cheerleader is after me?"

"Kind of." Why would I have a reason to think otherwise? He had a reputation for being a player. Why would that suddenly change now?

He laughed. "Well, I'm trying not to be that guy anymore."

"What kind of a guy are you trying to be then?"

We made it to the bottom of the stairs. He looked around. There were still a few people milling around the basketball court, but they didn't seem to be paying any attention to us.

"I'm just trying to be a good guy," Noah said. Then he leaned in closer and spoke into my hair, causing shivers to go down my spine. "And a good boyfriend."

He pulled back, his mouth spread into a huge smile. I wanted to shove him but didn't, because he actually seemed to like it when I whacked him. So instead I matched his smile and tried not to look like I really wanted his words to be true. "Well, I guess you better take me home then, *Boyfriend*, because I still have all that homework to do."

"Then let's go." He held his hand out to me.

I stared. He wanted to hold hands?

My heartbeat spiked. I'd never held a guy's hand before.

What if I did it completely wrong? What if he could tell that I had no idea what I was doing?

"I promise that I wash my hands every time I go to the bathroom," he joked.

I laughed awkwardly. Why was I so awkward? "It's not that."

Just grab his hand, Lexi. Put your trembling little hand into his big, strong, manly-looking hand.

It was just there, reaching out to me like it was the most normal thing in the world. At least it probably looked normal to everyone around me who actually knew a thing or two about hand-holding. But I wasn't one of those girls. I'd never seen people holding hands much in real life since my mom had left when I was little, and my siblings had never dared bring anyone around my dad.

Was I supposed to just slap my hand on his and give it a squeeze? Or was he expecting me to do that interlocking-fingers thing?

My palms started to sweat, which was just the worst timing. I didn't want him to think I was this gross, sweaty girl.

This was ridiculous. I was sixteen years old. I should be able to hold a guy's hand without analyzing it to death.

I released a big breath and decided the truth was probably the best in this situation. I forced myself to meet his gaze. His brown eyes were a lot less certain now than they had been a moment before. "I-I, um, think you should know that I've never actually held a guy's hand before and..." I let my voice drift off, not knowing what else to say. This was so humiliating.

"And you want it to be special? To mean something?"

Sure I'd go with that. That would be much less embarrassing than having him think that I just didn't know what I was doing.

He ran his hand through his shaggy hair. "I don't think I've ever been shut down like this before."

My throat constricted. I hurried to say, "I'm not shutting you down, Noah." *I'm such a loser.*

"But what about those guidelines we set yesterday? I thought hand-holding and cuddling were on the 'ok to do' list."

He was right. I'd been naive enough to think that I could handle doing those things with Noah. "Yeah, they're on the list." I looked down at my boots. "I guess I just want you to know how inexperienced I am, so you can help me not look so awkward in front of everyone."

Instead of laughing at me, he stepped closer and put his hands on my shoulders. "I promise to handle you with care and make sure you look good."

I slowly lifted my gaze to meet his again, and there was only understanding in his eyes. "Okay," I breathed.

He dropped his hands from my shoulders. "So, Lexi Stevens, will you do me the greatest honor of letting me walk you to my car?" He held his hand out to me once more.

My lips slowly turned up into a smile. "I would like that." And I did the bravest thing I'd done in a long time and slid my hand into his. His hand was warm and rough, but it also felt really nice. Like our hands were meant to be together always.

When Noah curled his fingers around mine, electricity traveled up my arm. I would have floated away if he hadn't been tethering me to the ground. And though part of me knew I should have wanted my first hand-holding experience to be real, and actually mean something, the other part of me was ecstatic that I was holding Noah Taylor's hand. His grip was steady and strong, and he knew what he was doing so I didn't have to worry as much as I thought I would.

As he led me through the crowd of students on the gym floor, a few eyes flicker to us. And then just before we made it to the back exit, I saw Raven and the sour expression on her face.

"Don't look now, but I'm pretty sure Raven wants to strangle me," I said.

Noah searched the crowd for a moment until his gaze landed on Raven. She immediately turned her scowl into a too-sweet smile and waved flirtatiously at him.

"She might," he said, shooting a smile in her direction. "And since that's what we're going for, I might have to hold your hand more often."

My heart really liked that idea. But instead of letting him know that my heart was being stupid, I said, "Why can't you just tell her you're not interested in her? Wouldn't that make more sense than getting a fake girlfriend?"

"Things are complicated with Raven right now. And I just want to take the easy way out."

I wanted to ask him why things were complicated but decided it wasn't really my place. Noah was the kind of guy who was an open book when he wanted to be, and a vault when he didn't.

We reached the back exit and Noah held the door open for me. I walked through and was surprised when he took my hand again. No one we knew was outside to watch us.

But I let the warmth of his hand envelop mine anyway, telling myself it was just so he could steady me if I happened to slip on the ice.

10

NOAH

I LOOKED at the current temperature on my weather app as I trudged back to my car after Mr. Stevens kicked me out for the night. It was ten degrees right now and it was going to get even colder. I really needed to figure something out. When I talked to my mom today, she told me that Paul was still uptight, worried about his job and still didn't want me there, but she assured me that I'd be free to come home this weekend. I just needed to make it through the next four nights. I hated how that man had the power to decide when I got to sleep in my bed and when I didn't. Hated that my mom lets him have that power. But I tried not to be too bitter about it. They did assume I was safe and warm at my dad's house.

It was already ten-thirty when I climbed into my car. I didn't have it in me to drive all the way out to the woods north of town, so I drove a couple of houses down and then pulled my sleeping bags and things from the trunk. I let the heater blast as much hot air into the car as I could while I did my nightly routine of brushing my teeth and spitting it out the door. Then I pulled a hoodie on and slipped my feet into the thick wool socks I'd bought myself when I got the extra sleeping bag.

I was going to have to wash my laundry somewhere soon. Maybe tomorrow I'd find a laundromat on the other end of town, so I could get my clothes unstinkified without anyone recognizing me. I climbed into my double sleeping bags, put on a beanie, and let the heater warm me until I was sweating. Then I turned it off and hoped I could just sleep through the night.

A TAP on my window woke me up. Then someone called my name from the other side, the sound muffled.

I sat up, wondering who was at my car door. The windows were frosted over and the light from the sun glared harshly, reflecting at just the right angle that I couldn't see anything outside.

"Are you in there, Noah?" I recognized Lexi's voice this time since I was more alert now. Adrenaline immediately shot into my veins.

What was I supposed to do?

No one was supposed to know I was sleeping in my car. Especially not her.

I whipped my arm out of my sleeping bag and pushed the lock button down, in case she tried to open the door. If I just stayed quiet, she might leave and assume it was someone else's car. She wouldn't know my license plate, would she? I didn't even know it. I always looked for the New York Jets magnet on my trunk.

It was then that I realized my mistake. That magnet would tell her it was definitely my car, and she was probably wondering what the heck I was doing parked on her street this early in the morning.

She knocked again.

"Noah. Are you in there?"

My heart thundered in my ears. She wasn't leaving. Was she going to stay out there until I came out?

If the windows weren't crystallized right now I would have just turned on my car, slid over the center console, and drove away. But I couldn't see a thing.

The handle on the passenger side creaked like she was lifting it, the frozen seal cracking.

Didn't I lock that?

But then the door opened the rest of the way, and I came face to face with a very worried-looking Lexi. She wore her gray thick coat with the furry hood pulled over her head, and her hazel eyes were wide behind her glasses.

"Noah!" She put her hand to her chest. "What are you doing in here?"

Her eyes traveled from my face to take in the rest of me.

"You're sleeping in your car?"

I pursed my lips and tried to decide what I was supposed to do. Should I just shut the door on her and actually lock it this time? Or tell her the truth?

Run, talk, run, talk?

I sighed and turned on the engine. It was freezing. Then I looked back to her and cleared my froggy throat. "I wanted to sleep near you after that awesome date we had last night."

She crossed her arms over her chest. "This is serious, Noah. Why are you sleeping in your car in the middle of winter?"

I adjusted my seat to sit up straighter. "Technically, it's not the middle of winter. It's only the first week of December."

"Noah."

I turned away, not wanting to meet her gaze. "Remember how I said my life is complicated right now?"

"Yes?"

I sighed. "Okay, I'll tell you what's going on, if you promise not to tell anyone."

"Not anyone?" she asked. "What about Easton?"

"Not even Easton." The fewer people who knew about my situation, the better.

She tucked some of her hair behind her ear, her face going through a range of emotions as if she was having an internal debate on whether she would keep my secret or not. But then she finally said, "I can keep a secret."

"Okay, climb in." I pointed to the driver's seat. While she made her way around my car, I shimmied out of my sleeping bags and stuffed them in the backseat.

She climbed inside. I angled the heater vents so they were now turned toward both of us instead of just at the passenger side like I did during the night. That was when I saw the time. It was already seven. I must have turned off my alarm and not even noticed. I wasn't going to get my sneaky shower in today.

"What are you even doing outside this early in the morning? Don't you have to get ready for school?" I asked, trying to distract her now that the moment of truth had actually arrived.

She shrugged. "Last night, I saw you drive the wrong way home and park down the road. I didn't think much of it, just figured you were pulling over to text someone or something, but then when I looked out my window and saw your car was still there, I got worried and had to check on you."

She was worried about me? No one else seemed to care when I came and went, but Lexi actually cared? I didn't know how I felt about that.

She became serious. "Are you going to tell me what's going on, or are you going to keep trying to distract me with questions?" she asked.

My shoulders sagged. I stared straight ahead. "My stepdad kind of kicked me out of the house last week."

"Your stepdad kicked you out?" Her voice came out loud and disbelieving.

I held a finger to my lips. "You don't need to announce it to the whole neighborhood." They didn't need to know that no one wanted me around.

"Why did he kick you out?" she looked worried—like she thought I might have done something unforgivable to get myself kicked out of my own home.

I sighed. If I *had* done something wrong, then I could at least understand what was going on and would have the power to fix things myself. But I wasn't the real problem. The real problem was Paul and my dad. "My mom told me to spend some time at my dad's place. But since I like him only a tiny bit more than the stepdad, I decided to give my good old car a try. It's actually not so bad."

"Do you hear how stupid that sounds?" She shook her head. "It's *freezing*, Noah."

Yeah, pretty sure I knew that better than anyone else in this car right now.

"I'm sleeping in two sleeping bags, and if it really gets that bad, I can just turn on my car and warm it up for a bit. It's not that big of a deal."

She didn't look like she accepted my reasoning, but she said, "What about your meals? Is this why you're always eating out?"

I shrugged. "Breakfast is overrated. You see me eat lunch at school. And your dad and those fast-food workers are pretty good cooks, so I'm good." At least I'd be good for a couple of days until my money ran out. I'd had to fill up my car with gas earlier than I'd expected, thanks to running the heater all night.

"Do you hear yourself? Why don't you just go home?"

I pinched my eyes shut. How could I explain without airing my family's dirty laundry to the world?

Nothing came to mind, so I went with lying. "I'm trying to prove a point to my mom."

"Freezing to death is not worth proving a point. What could be so important to risk that?"

I crossed my arms. "I don't really want to talk about it."

"Does anyone else know?"

"No, and if you're good at keeping secrets they won't know anytime soon."

She was quiet as if mulling something over. Was she trying to think of who to tell all my secrets to? Had she figured everything out and was going to report my mom to CPS or something?

Not that they would do anything since I was technically an adult now.

She finally turned back to look at me. "Just come home with me and you can at least eat some breakfast. My dad was making French toast when I came outside."

As if on cue, my stomach growled. "And how should I explain to your dad and Easton why I'm still wearing the clothes I wore yesterday? Or why I'm even at your house first thing in the morning?"

Her knee bounced. "My dad has to leave in a couple of minutes, so once he's out we only have to worry about Easton."

"Okay."

Her eyes brightened. "How about I just tell Easton that you thought picking me up would be a great addition to our fake dating plan? Then you can just come over early enough and still be hungry for a *second* breakfast."

My stomach rumbled again. It would be nice to eat something before lunch today.

"Okay, I guess I'll just change in my car and hope no one else comes peeking into my windows."

She narrowed her eyes at me. "How long does it take you to shower?"

"Five minutes. Why?"

"I just figured that if you're the 'jump in and get busy' kind of guy, you could probably fit a shower in after Easton leaves to school, and we could still make it to first period on time."

A shower would be nice. But that was also kind of weird. I'd never showered at a friend's house before.

She put her hand on the door handle, about to leave. "Just bring your backpack with some clothes. Once you see my dad drive away in his truck, come on over and we'll get you fed and showered. Okay?"

"Okay."

She still didn't climb out. "How have you been showering, anyway? Because there's no way that you're not. I would notice something like that."

"Locker room." I shrugged then let a smirk lift my lips. "Have you been sniffing me, Lexi?"

Her face turned red, which I was starting to think was one of my favorite looks on her. She was kind of cute when she was embarrassed.

She climbed out of my car. "I'll see you in a few minutes, Noah." Then she shut the door without answering my question.

Which had me thinking that maybe she had been sniffing me, and maybe she had liked my cologne.

I grabbed my backpack from the backseat, tossed some clothes and shower kit in it, and then also threw in my cologne, just so I could test my new theory out.

11

LEXI

I RUSHED BACK into my house, sneaking in through the back door so my dad or Easton wouldn't realize that I'd been gone. Dad was still in the kitchen puttering around like he wasn't in a hurry at all. I checked the clock on the wall. He was supposed to be gone by now. Had I heard him wrong? Was that tomorrow instead of today that he needed to go into the office early?

I took off my coat and stashed it in the corner before he saw me. Then I tried to walk into the kitchen with as serene an expression as I could muster at that moment.

My dad turned when he saw me. "I left breakfast in the oven. Just put the leftovers in the fridge, okay?"

Okay, good. It sounded like he was going to leave any minute. I inhaled deeply, trying to even my breathing out after my dash down the street.

"Thanks for breakfast, Dad." I grabbed a plate from the cupboard and pulled the scrambled eggs and French toast from the warm oven.

When I turned around, my dad was studying me. "Is something wrong? You seem more anxious than usual."

My dad didn't miss a thing.

I pasted on a smile and laughed lightly. "I-I'm fine. Maybe a little nervous for my history class today."

He put a couple of papers into his messenger bag and buckled it shut. "You have a test?"

"No, but I think we're about to start a group project and those always make me nervous."

He nodded like he understood. "I get that. Just don't let your partners make you do all the work. Stand up for yourself this time."

He knew me so well. I always ended up doing the majority of the work in group projects, because I was usually the person who cared most about my grades.

"Thanks for the advice."

He smiled like he'd just received a gold star for awesome parenting.

I checked the clock on the wall again. School would start in less than thirty minutes. My dad needed to go now, or Noah wouldn't have time to shower and eat, and I really wanted to be able to do this for him. He needed someone right now.

This must be part of why he said his life was complicated. He was practically homeless. How did he afford to eat out? I certainly didn't have that kind of money from what I made babysitting here and there. And Noah didn't have a job.

"I'll see you for dinner tonight," Dad said, interrupting my thoughts. "I'm thinking white bean chili might be good on this cold day."

Good, he was finally going to leave.

"Do you mind if Noah eats with us?" I asked, turning back to dishing up my food so he wouldn't see how anxious I was about his answer.

"You're helping him with his English homework again tonight?"

"Yeah." At least I would be, now that my dad mentioned it.

"Just tell him dinner will be at six." Dad put his bag over his shoulder and kissed me lightly on the head. "Have a good day at school, Lexi."

And then he finally left.

I watched out the window as my dad backed out of the driveway and onto the icy road. Once he was out of sight, I saw Noah's car turn around and then pull into our driveway. Nervous energy coursed through me, and I didn't know why. Noah had been to my house tons of times. He'd eaten hundreds of meals with us. Why did I suddenly have to be all anxious about him coming over for breakfast?

I busied myself, grabbing a second plate from the cupboard and loading it up with food for him. I could do this. I wasn't doing anything wrong. I was just helping out a friend who had no one else to turn to.

"Expecting someone?" Easton's voice came from behind me.

I jumped and almost dropped Noah's plate.

Easton strolled into the room and eyed the two plates I'd made up. "Or is this like one of those National-Bribe-Your-Brother-into-Doing-Something-for-You days?"

"You wish." I set Noah's plate down on the counter with a shaking hand then tucked some hair behind my ear. "Noah's picking me up today as part of our fake relationship thing. I figured I'd make him up a plate of food since he always seems to be hungry."

Easton pursed his lips. Would he be able to figure out what was going on?

"You sure you aren't hoping for this plan of yours to be legit?" He grabbed a glass from the cupboard and filled it with orange juice.

I wiped my hands on my pants. "Of course not. You know I like Harrison and not Noah."

He gave me a skeptical look. I didn't like that look. It made me remember all the reasons why I might have wanted this to be real in the past.

The doorbell rang, and I startled again. I really needed to get a grip on myself or my heart was going to be beating fast all day.

"I'll get that." My voice squeaked. Why was I acting like such a basket case?

I opened the door and found Noah standing there in his coat, with his backpack slung over one shoulder. His hair looked slightly less messy than it had been in his car a few minutes ago, like he had just run his fingers through it, pushing it to the side.

"Hi," I said.

He glanced around awkwardly. "Hey."

I stepped back to let him in. "You're still hungry, right?" I asked, hoping he'd play along and pretend like we hadn't just been talking ten minutes ago.

"Yep." He wiped his shoes on the rug before following me into the kitchen. "It smells good in here."

Easton was sitting at the bar with his plate piled high with food when we walked in.

"Hey, Noah," Easton said with his mouth full.

"Hey." Noah dropped his backpack on the floor by the pantry.

"So, sounds like you and my sister are getting serious if you're taking her to school." He elbowed Noah in the arm playfully when he took the stool next to him.

"Yeah." Noah eyed me anxiously before saying, "Raven's still not buying our fake relationship, so we thought it would be a good idea for me to give Lexi a ride to school today."

I brought our plates over then stood at the end of the counter. My hands were shaky as I tried to cut into my French toast. After attempting it twice, I set my fork down, hoping I'd be less shaky once I distracted Easton with some questions.

I urged my legs to stop feeling so wobbly. "H-how did things go with Mercedes?"

Easton swallowed his bite of eggs and took a sip from his glass. "Really good."

"So, are you official yet?" I asked to keep the small talk going since Noah was just shoveling his breakfast into his mouth, and was, therefore, no help during the conversation.

Easton stabbed a piece of toast onto his fork. "Not yet. But I think it might be headed there if I'm lucky."

I smiled. "Cool. She seems to like you. I noticed you two sitting pretty close at last night's game."

"Yeah, we weren't the only two people sitting close." He raised an eyebrow at us.

Was he talking about Noah and me? I hadn't even thought that my brother might be paying attention to us.

Noah pushed his plate away and set his arm around my shoulders to pull me in for a brief squeeze. "Yes, Lexi and I just can't keep our hands off each other."

My skin immediately flushed, and I remembered just how much I had liked holding his hand after the game. But I couldn't let either of them know that, so I pushed him away. "You know we don't need to pretend in front of Easton."

Easton's gaze narrowed at us, and I could just see the cogs spinning in his head. He was catching the vibes that something else was going on here.

He confirmed my suspicions when he asked, "This is still fake, right?"

Noah laughed. "Of course. I just like to give Lexi a hard time."

I laughed awkwardly. "Could you ever see Noah and I together in real life? That would be about as likely as having a unicorn sitting at our kitchen table."

Easton stood and walked around the island to put his plate in the sink. "Just making sure. Because I really don't want to have to make good on my threat to beat you up if you start to get confused on what's real and what isn't."

I swallowed and looked nervously at Noah.

But Noah seemed unfazed by the threat, which meant that in his mind, everything was really just for show.

"We're just doing this for the mutual benefits. No need to bruise your knuckles on my face." Noah stood then turned to me. "Are you about ready to go, Lexi?" he asked.

Did he not want to take a shower then? Or was he just saying it so Easton wouldn't suspect anything?

My food was still mostly untouched, but my stomach was such a ball of nerves that I didn't think I could eat much more, anyway.

I picked up my plate. "Um, yeah. I just need to grab a few things from my room."

Easton grabbed his backpack and then turned back to me. "Well, I'm gonna head out if you don't need a ride."

I nodded, trying not to let him see how relieved I was that he was leaving early. "See you at school."

Easton looked at Noah. "Try not to break Raven's heart too bad, okay? She was in a *bad* mood after the game last night."

Noah ran a hand through his hair. "Yeah, I feel kind of bad about that, but she'll realize soon enough that she's better off without me."

12

NOAH

LEXI and I both watched from the windows in the living room, waiting for Easton to pull away. Soon his beat-up Mustang was headed south on the road.

"You still want to get that shower in?" Lexi looked up at me.

"Yeah." I grabbed my backpack from the floor in the kitchen and then followed her down the hall to her room.

"You can just use my shower. There should be an extra towel in the cupboard above the toilet.

"Since when do you have a shower in your room and Easton doesn't?"

I'd never been in Lexi's room before, but it only seemed fair that the older sibling would have the nicer room.

She shrugged. "When Maddie and Grant moved out last summer, I got to move into their room. Easton likes it in the basement."

Now that she mentioned it, I remembered her and Juliette moving her stuff across the hall and complaining to Easton about him not helping them push her heavy dresser.

Lexi pointed to a door in her room. "That's the bathroom. You can use whatever you need in there. I'll just wait for you downstairs."

I swallowed, glad she wouldn't be waiting for me in her bedroom. This was already awkward enough as it was.

When I got in the shower, I realized too late that I'd somehow missed packing my bar of soap into my backpack. I must have left it at the school in my gym locker. I looked around the steam-filled shower, hoping against hope that she had something that didn't smell like a floral shop or bakery. But even nerdy Lexi's taste in scents wasn't on my side. I really should have insisted on using Easton's bathroom.

I found the least girly-sounding container along the tub wall —pomegranate and mango body wash—and lathered up. I'd just use an extra spray of cologne to cover it up.

Two minutes later I was out and toweling off. I skipped my morning shave, since we were running late on time, then went down to find Lexi.

"SO, since I know that you're not going home, what do you plan to do now?" Lexi asked me as we walked to my car after school.

"I don't know. I've been going to the library a lot lately."

Her eyebrows raised in shock. "You've been going to the library? That's surprising."

I laughed. Yeah, the library was probably the last place anyone would expect to find me. "People do crazy things when they have nowhere to go." Then I remembered that I was running low on clean clothes. "Actually, I'll probably head to the laundromat and wash my stinky clothes."

I'd never done laundry before, but it couldn't be that hard to figure out.

"How are you paying for all of this, anyway?" she asked. We

stopped at the edge of the sidewalk and waited for a guy—who looked too young to have a license—pull his giant brown truck out of its parking spot.

"My dad puts money into an account for me every month." I looked down at her. "I had to use a lot of my money on a second sleeping bag, but I think I should have enough to do laundry."

"You think?" She frowned. "Are you going to have enough for food still?"

The traffic stalled, so we continued toward where I'd parked my car in the back of the parking lot. "I should be able to go back this weekend. I think I'll have enough money until then." Not that I actually wanted to go home that badly. If it had been summer instead of winter, I'd probably never go home. Not after the way my parents had treated me. Why would I want to go live with a bunch of people who didn't want me around—who actually got mad at me for being part of their family?

I flexed my jaw, hating the way those thoughts made me feel. I needed to change the subject. My life was more depressing when I thought about it. It was much better to just live moment by moment and not worry about what I'd be doing tonight. Or tomorrow. Or the next day.

We made it to my car, and instead of focusing on things I couldn't change, I focused on something I could control. And that was being the best fake boyfriend that I could be and keeping girls like Raven from getting caught up in my messy life.

So I opened Lexi's door for her and pretended like I was a gentleman. And since no good deed should go unnoticed, I checked the area for any onlookers.

Was it such a bad thing to want people to know that I did have redeeming qualities some of the time?

Sadly for my ego, no one was paying attention to us. But that was okay. It would be good for me to do nice things like this, anyway.

I tossed my backpack in the backseat then climbed in my side of the car and buckled in.

Lexi's fingers fidgeted in her lap, as if she was trying to get the courage to say something.

She finally cleared her throat. "You could always just come over to my house right now. And, I don't know, I guess we could wash your laundry. I don't think anyone would notice since my dad will still be at work for the next couple of hours and Easton has work, too. It would save you money, at least."

She was looking at me carefully, like she was worried she might offend me with her offer. A big part of me wanted to tell her not to worry, that I was a big boy and could take care of myself. But then there was also a warmth growing in my chest, softening the hard shell I'd put up around my heart.

It would be nice to save more of my dwindling stash of money. So I nodded. "Okay, I'll take you up on that."

She smiled at me, a truly happy smile that made me feel like I'd just helped her instead of the opposite. "Great. And I already talked to my dad today, and he said that you can eat dinner with us if you wanted."

The warm feeling went away. "Did you tell him that I'm sleeping in my car?" If she had told her dad... I shook my head. I didn't even want to think about what would happen if she was telling people. I thought I could trust her!

"Of course not! I just said we were gonna be working on your school project for English today. He has no idea what's really going on."

I exhaled. "Okay, good."

We parked in front of the Stevens' house ten minutes later. I grabbed my duffel bag from where I stored it in the trunk with my other homeless-teenager stuff. Lexi led me inside. Our first stop was the laundry room which was just adjacent from their small kitchen.

"The detergent is in that cupboard." She pointed at the cupboard above the washing machine. "I usually have to use a stool to reach and fill the cup, but you should be fine."

Lexi discreetly ran her gaze up and down my body. And for the first time, I wondered what she thought of me. We'd known each other for years, but I'd never given much thought to how Lexi would see me. Did she like what she saw when she looked at me? Because I was starting to think that maybe glasses weren't nearly as nerdy-looking as I'd originally thought.

"I guess being a giant does have some perks." I shrugged, hoping she couldn't read my thoughts on my face.

"Yeah, don't rub it in."

"Being vertically challenged isn't the worst thing in the world," I said as I set my duffel bag on top of the washing machine.

She rolled her eyes. "It is, when your dad and brother are tall, and you have to take a stool everywhere just to reach the things they like to store up high."

"Better than hitting your head on ceiling fans everywhere you go."

She opened the door to the washing machine. "I guess we all have our problems."

I stared ahead at the duffel bag and the washer, wondering what I was supposed to do next. "Um, so I've actually never done laundry by myself before. Is there a certain way I should be doing this?"

Her mouth dropped. "You're eighteen years old and you've never washed a load of laundry?"

It wasn't that weird, was it? "I thought it magically appeared in my drawers every week." I grinned so she knew that I was joking. Of course, I knew that my mom washed my laundry. And I liked to think I was a good enough of a son to appreciate it.

She folded her arms across her chest. "Well, since not all of us have these magical laundry fairies at our house, I guess I can teach you. I've been doing my own since I was in elementary."

"Since elementary?" Really?

She shrugged. "Well, I kind of had to learn if I wanted to have clean clothes to wear every day, instead of just when my dad had time to get to it."

That made sense. I hadn't known her family then, but from what Easton had told me, it sounded like things were pretty crazy at their house when her mom first left them. Things had definitely been hard on my mom after she got divorced, but she'd only had one kid then. Mr. Stevens had three kids, and if I remembered right, I was pretty sure they'd all been under the age of eight at the time.

Being a single parent was hard. Which was probably one of the reasons why my mom wasn't willing to leave Paul. She'd been a single mom before. She didn't want to do it again.

"Let's teach you a new life skill, okay?" Lexi said. She taught me how much detergent to use, and then showed me the little compartment to put it in.

"It's probably a good thing I didn't try going to the laundromat today. I probably would've broken all the machines."

She smiled and pushed the detergent compartment shut, her shoulder brushing against my chest with the movement.

I stilled, not used to my body having a reaction to her. I wasn't supposed to feel *actual* sparks with Lexi. She seemed to notice something too, because when she moved back she was careful not to touch me again.

She laughed awkwardly. "I don't think even you could mess it up that bad."

I chuckled uncomfortably, suddenly aware of how small their laundry room was and how close we were standing to each other because of it. Was she wearing that pomegranate and mango bodywash I'd used earlier?

I shook my head—I couldn't be thinking about this right now. "You'd be surprised at how good I am at messing up things." I was about the last person who would ever have the Midas Touch. Pretty much everything I touched turned to mud instead of gold.

"Now you just separate your clothes into different loads and shut the door. It's not too difficult."

"Separate them?" How? Like all my pants in one pile and t-shirts in another? Or was it more like all the blue-colored shirts went with my green ones because they were kind of close to the same color? Did it matter if I put stripes in with the solids?

When I just stood there paralyzed by the task, she put her hands on her hips. "Just put all your colored clothes in one pile and any whites you have in another."

I dug through my duffel bag. Everything in there was pretty dang colorful, so I just shoved them into one load and wiped my hands together. "Well, that was easy."

Lexi chuckled and pushed a couple of buttons on the machine. Before I knew it, I had washed my first load of laundry.

I followed her back into the kitchen. "Is that really all there is to doing laundry? Am I, like, a pro now?" I sat on the barstool in the center of their kitchen. I loved the feel in their home. Even though it was run by a former drill sergeant, it was still a homey place. I felt welcomed there.

"Just wait till you have to fold the laundry and put it away. That's when the real work starts. Anyone can just drop a load in the washing machine."

I shrugged. "Lucky for me I'm living out of a duffel bag, so I can pretty much just shove it in there and call it good. Bet you wish you could do that."

She rolled her eyes and opened the fridge. "Maybe I should try out this whole sleeping-in-your-car thing. Just think of all the time I could save."

I laughed. "Yeah, wouldn't that be a great addition to our

scheme. Raven and Harrison would go crazy if they found out we were sleeping in my car together."

She turned back to me and gasped. "You know that's not what I meant."

I winked at her, unable to resist a chance to make her squirm. "Yeah, but just think how much warmer I'd be with you close by. I'd even be a thoughtful boyfriend and let you share my sleeping bags."

She shook her head and turned back to the fridge. "Only *you* would dare suggest a thing like that."

"Well, at least you know that if you were to ever get stranded with me in the middle of a blizzard, I've got you covered."

13

LEXI

EASTON, Noah, and I had all been sitting at the kitchen table for a couple of hours after dinner when my brother stretched and yawned. Easton said, "Well, I think I'm gonna head to bed."

Noah checked the clock on the wall behind him. "It's only eight-thirty. You're really going to bed this early?"

Easton shrugged and slapped his book shut. "I'm going to try to turn into an early bird. Mercedes was just talking to me about this book that she was reading about how much more productive you are when you wake up early. I figured I'd give it a shot."

"Like one of those self-help type of books?" Noah asked, disbelief written all over his face.

"Aren't those, like, old people books?" I asked.

Easton scooted his seat away from the table. "They're for people who care about their future. And I care about mine."

"You sure it's not to just impress your almost-girlfriend?" I asked skeptically. Easton was always doing things like that to impress the girl he liked.

Which I hated to admit seemed to be a family trait. I was fake-dating Noah after all just to get a guy's attention.

Man, I was an even bigger loser than I thought.

"I'm not doing it for Mercedes. I'm doing it for myself."

Noah laughed and stood. "Sure you can say that, but we all know what's true. And it's plain to see that you're whipped."

Easton scowled. "I'm not whipped."

"Whatever."

"Well, I'm gonna go to bed." He made ready to leave. "I'll see you tomorrow at school, Noah."

Once he had gone downstairs, I turned to Noah who was packing his things into his backpack.

"Are you leaving then?" I asked.

"Doesn't make much sense for me to stick around now. I've already been here all afternoon."

"But it's cold outside. Don't you want to stay indoors a little longer?"

He put a finger to his lips and quickly glanced around like he was worried someone might overhear us. But my dad was in the other room, probably watching some sporting event on TV. "I can finish reading this chapter in my car. It'll be okay."

But he'd already said he was running low on cash. And car gas wasn't cheap these days.

"I was gonna go read by the woodstove for a little while before I head to bed. Just come down and get warm before you leave."

He seemed to weigh the pros and cons of leaving now or staying like I suggested. And for some reason, my heart was pounding in my chest, not wanting him to reject me in this little thing.

He grabbed his copy of *Pride and Prejudice* off the table. "Okay, fine. I'll stay a little longer."

An hour later, when I looked up from my book, Noah was lying down on the reclined sectional with a blanket over his long body—he had fallen asleep.

His head was tilted to the side, his book falling out of his hand, about to drop onto the floor.

I knew my dad would be coming to the top of the stairs soon, to tell Noah it was time to go home like he did every night. But I didn't have the heart to wake him and tell him he had to leave. He didn't have anywhere safe and warm to go to. Just his car, which, yeah, at least it had a heater, but when I thought about how distraught he'd been last night at the game, talking about how cold it was going to get, my stomach felt hollow. He tried to make it seem like it was no big deal spending all night freezing outside, but it bothered him much more than he wanted me to know.

I studied his face. He looked so peaceful. Like all the worries he'd had etched on his face had disappeared. Would it be such a bad thing to leave him here, and hope my dad didn't notice? I could just go upstairs, turn off the lights, and tell my dad that I'd already taken care of the fire so he wouldn't have a reason to come down and find Noah.

But I knew Noah would be mad at me if I did that. He'd be worried that Easton and my dad would discover his secret.

So I slid out of my seat and knelt on the floor beside him, putting my hand on his arm to give him a gentle shake.

"Noah," I whispered.

He didn't budge.

My chest hurt. This was probably the warmest he'd slept all week.

My dad's footsteps sounded above me.

"Noah," I tried again. This time his eyes fluttered open. He looked disoriented for a moment before his eyes settled on mine.

The corner of his mouth lifted. "Hi."

"Hi." I couldn't keep a huge grin from returning his lazy smile. He was really cute when he was groggy, and his hair... I let my gaze flicker to the messy auburn tendrils falling over his forehead. I wanted to run my fingers through it and brush it to the side.

"Is Noah still here?" Dad's voice carried down the stairs.

That seemed to wake Noah the rest of the way up because he startled and immediately reached for the button to get the recliner back up to sitting position.

He cleared his throat. "Yeah, Mr. Stevens, I-I was just leaving."

He tossed the blanket he'd been using to the side and made ready to stand.

"Wait." I gripped his arm.

He looked at me with question in his eyes. "What is it?" He glanced around like he thought he must have forgotten something.

I drew in a deep breath, hoping it would make me braver. "What are you going to do tonight? Where are you planning to sleep?"

He grabbed his shoes and put them on. "I'll probably go to my usual spot in the forest. Can't risk having anyone else find me sleeping in my car."

"Do you really have to sleep in your car?"

He shrugged. "For the next few days, yeah. Unless I feel like going to my dad's house with my tail between my legs. But he's usually pretty annoyed with me anyway, so I can't imagine him welcoming me if I show up at ten o'clock on a weeknight."

My heart pounded in my chest. "H-how about you just stay here then?"

He paused and studied me with uncertainty in his eyes. "I don't think your dad would like that very much. He's a nice guy, but I know how he is about you and boys."

"We could tell Easton and have him ask."

Noah looked down the hall as if worried Easton would over-hear us from his room. He lowered his voice. "I love the guy, but I just want as few people to know about this as I can have."

"My dad will understand."

Dad's voice came from upstairs. "It's late, Noah. Your mom is probably worried about you."

"Just putting my shoes on, Mr. Stevens," Noah called. Then he turned to me and shrugged. "I'm not his problem."

Why was Noah so worried about being someone's problem?

"But I can't send you outside to sleep in your car. I checked the weather and it's going to be just as cold tonight as it was yesterday."

"And I survived last night just fine." He stood and wiggled his feet the rest of the way into his shoes. "I'll see you tomorrow, Lexi." And without another word, he grabbed his book and disappeared up the stairs.

I watched Noah trudge down the sidewalk from the darkness of my bedroom. The lights on his car flashed when he unlocked it. Then he opened the driver's side door and just stood there for a while, looking at my house. I couldn't see the expression on his face, but I imagined a look of longing for warmth and family.

It wasn't fair. He shouldn't be sleeping in his car. He shouldn't be worrying about where he was going to be staying the night, or how he was going to stay warm, or where he'd be getting his next meal.

How could his mom do that to him? How could neither of his parents know where he was staying?

But I knew from my own experience with my mother that not all parents were created equal. And just because you were related by blood didn't mean you necessarily loved your family.

Noah climbed into his car. I looked around my room, faintly lit by the moonlight streaming through the window. It was spacious enough. Maddie and Grant had both fit in here for years with the full-sized bed that was now mine, and the crib which later turned into a toddler bed for Grant.

My gaze traveled to my closet. It was pretty big. And I had

that air mattress in there that Juliette used when she had slept over this summer.

My mind made up, I did what was possibly the stupidest thing that I've ever done in my life: I texted Noah.

Me: **Just come sleep in my room so I'm not worried about you all night.**

My heart banged against my rib cage as I waited for him to respond. The read receipt changed from sent to read, then the conversation dots appeared on the screen.

I ran to the window to see if his car was still there. It was, and I could see a small blue light coming from his phone in the front seat. But when a message didn't immediately come through, I started to doubt myself.

He had to know that I was just being a good friend and not offering something more, right?

I read over the message I sent him again and realized that it could be taken either way. So I hurried and sent another text.

Me: **On the air mattress in my closet. Not my bed.**

His message came an instant later.

Noah: **Ok**

I sighed, relieved that he was at least letting me help him a little.

Me: **Just park your car down the street so my dad doesn't know. Text me when you're back and I'll open my window.**

I tried not to panic too much when I heard the swoosh telling me that my message had gone through.

I was just about to make my dad's worst nightmare come true and have a boy spend the night in my room.

I PACED my room for the next couple of minutes as I waited for Noah to text me back. If anyone knew what we were about to do, I'd be so dead. So, so dead.

But I just couldn't think about that too much right now. I really didn't need anything else to stress me out.

My phone vibrated in my hand, and I almost jumped out of my skin.

Noah: **I'm here.**

My heart pounded in my ears as I unlocked my window and pushed against it to open it up.

The glass was so cold. But when I tried to slide it open, it didn't budge.

I tried again. It still wouldn't move.

This wasn't good. I couldn't help Noah stay warm tonight if I couldn't even get him into my room.

I pulled out my phone, my fingers shaking as I typed my message out.

Me: **I can't open my window. I think it's frozen shut.**

Through the frosty glass, I saw him hovering outside. He checked his phone.

Noah: **What if I helped slide it?**

It was worth a shot, so I stepped closer to the window and nodded.

His hands moved to the glass. I positioned mine with one hand on the frame and the other on the glass, and then pushed.

But it still didn't budge. Why did my dad have to be so cheap that he couldn't update the windows in our home?

My phone vibrated again.

Noah: **What do you want me to do? Should I just go back to my car?**

I looked at him again. He was just looking back at me through the window. I couldn't read the expression on his face since it was so dark outside, but his silhouette showed a sagging posture that told me how badly he wanted me to figure out something else.

Me: **Let me see if my dad is in his room. Maybe I can figure something else out.**

I pushed my phone into my back pocket and creaked my door open slowly. The hall was dark.

This was looking promising.

I peeked my head through the crack and swiveled my head to get a view of my dad's room.

His door was shut, but light was coming from the gap underneath. Did I dare sneak out of my room? My dad was a really light sleeper, but I thought he used a sound machine at night to add white noise, so he could sleep better.

But did he turn that on before or after he got in his bed for the night?

I didn't know.

I shut the door to my room again and texted Noah.

Me: **How good are you at slipping through dark houses unnoticed?**

Noah: **I only got caught 1 of the 4 times I robbed a house. So pretty good.**

I laughed and it came out all shaky with my nerves. This was about the wrongest time to be joking.

Me: **Meet me at the back door.**

I checked outside my room again, slowly opening my door and bracing myself in case it decided to creak. It squeaked when I got it five-sixths of the way open. I froze and listened for movement in my dad's room. When I didn't hear a sound, I tiptoed down the hall.

By the time I made it to the back door I was sweating. I slowly undid the deadbolt. The chain on the door would be a little trickier.

My dad had placed it clear at the top when we were little since Easton had been an escape artist back in the day. I stood on my very tippy toes, pretending like I hadn't quit ballet after only a few weeks when I was five, and eventually got the chain to slip out. I gripped the handle with my clammy hand and opened the door as quietly as I could.

Noah filled the threshold two seconds later, startling me with his huge form.

I threw my hand to my chest and gasped. "Just jump right out at me, why don't ya?" I whispered, stepping back to let him in.

"Just trying to be fast." He removed his shoes from his feet before stepping the rest of the way inside.

I wouldn't have even thought to remove my shoes, which had me wondering if maybe he hadn't been joking earlier about robbing houses. He had said something to Ashlyn about no one pressing charges a couple of months ago. Was that because he'd actually stolen things?

I shook those thoughts away. No. This was Noah. He didn't do things like that. He may have a chip on his shoulder, but he wasn't a criminal.

At least I was ninety-five percent sure he wasn't in trouble with the law.

I shut the door after him and did up the deadbolt. I was standing on my toes to lock the chain when Noah stepped right behind me, his torso brushing against my back as his fingers took the chain from mine and easily slipped it into the lock.

I almost had a heart attack at his unexpected closeness and had to work hard to hold in my shriek.

Once the door was secured, we slipped down the hall and past my dad's room. I wanted to cheer when I saw no light coming from under his door.

His sound machine was on.

I'm not doing anything bad. I'm not doing anything bad. I told myself as I shut my bedroom door behind us. *I'm just helping Noah out.*

I ran my thumb along my promise ring. It was still there. And there was no way it was going anywhere. I had nothing to worry about.

And if Noah even tried to lay a hand on me while we were in here, I would kick him.

I made quick work of showing Noah to my closet.

"Just grab as many blankets as you think you'll need to be comfortable." I pointed to the stack of quilts my grandma had made me through the years. They were on the top shelf, so I'd usually have to use one of my step-stools to get to them, but Noah easily pulled three of them down.

He turned to look at me expectantly. "You said something about an air mattress."

Right. Air mattress.

I looked around my large walk-in closet. I frowned when I didn't see it in the corner. Had my dad or Easton taken it out of here?

I rummaged through the pile of dirty laundry on the floor, wishing I'd cleaned my room instead of pacing anxiously after texting Noah, but the air mattress was nowhere to be found.

I whipped myself up and turned to face Noah, the blood rushing out of my face because I'd stood too quickly. I stumbled backward, feeling lightheaded.

Noah quickly gripped my arm to steady me, and my skin burned where he touched me.

"You okay?" he asked, concern etched in his eyes.

I nodded, unable to speak. This was not the right time for my body to have a reaction like that to him. Me helping Noah out as a friend was one thing. But me having romantic notions for the boy staying in my room was another.

I brushed the hair out of my eyes. "I'm fine. But no air mattress."

He nodded, seeming to take in my closet. It was probably barely just long enough for him to sleep in.

"You sure there's not enough room on that full-sized bed of yours?" He raised an eyebrow.

I shook my head. "Oh no. Definitely not."

He nodded. "Okay, I'll take what I can get."

He spread out a few blankets on the floor to give himself some padding.

I just stood there dumbly as he did it. I didn't realize I'd been standing so closely until he stood again. I tripped on his backpack and lost my balance—I was turning into that freaking Bella Swan girl!

I tried to right my balance, hoping he wouldn't notice how clumsy I was becoming around him, but he grabbed my arm again.

"Sorry my backpack was in the way," he said.

Noah stepped closer but didn't let go of his hold on me. He ducked his head down until he was looking directly into my eyes. I swallowed. Wow, his eyes were kind of mesmerizing.

"Thank you for letting me stay here tonight." He spoke in a low voice that was way too intimate for this confined space.

I nodded and tried to find my tongue. "I-I'm glad I could help. I didn't want you to freeze."

His hand went from holding me upright to gently rubbing my arm. I wondered if he knew he was even doing it. Electricity raced all over my skin, like his touch was lightning and my body wanted to absorb the full charge. Did he have any idea what his soft touch and alluring eyes were doing to me?

He looked at his hand, and then finally seemed to realize what he was doing and removed it.

But then his gaze flickered to my lips. My heart, which was

already beating faster than I ever thought it could go, started thrumming like a hummingbird's wings.

His lips parted.

He was going to kiss me.

But then he spoke instead.

"You have something on your glasses."

"My glasses?" My voice squeaked, and I didn't know if I was relieved or disappointed that he had not been looking at my lips.

I pulled my glasses off and wiped them with the corner of my shirt before replacing them.

"Did I get it?"

He nodded. "Yes." He looked thoughtful for a moment before he said, "I can see your eyes much better now."

I drew in another breath, trying to fill my lungs with the oxygen I would need to get my brain working right again.

"Thanks." I adjusted my glasses again. I really needed to stop this nervous tic of mine. It was making it totally obvious how much he was affecting me. "Well, uh, I'm going to bed now."

"Me too." He stepped to the side, so I could escape from the too-small closet.

A few long, heart-pounding minutes later, I was in my bed and he was five feet away in my closet.

He'll be sleeping less than five feet away from me.

I would not think about that.

I plugged my phone into my charging cord on my nightstand, made sure my alarm was set for six-thirty, and then fluffed my pillow. Once I'd finished my nightly routine, I glanced over at Noah one more time before turning off my lamp. He looked comfortable enough. "Remember, no sneaking out and climbing in my bed."

He laughed. "I was only joking about sharing your bed. You really don't need to worry about me. That's, like, the last thing I'd do tonight."

I bristled at his response, my muscles going taut. "Why? Is it because I'm not mainstream?"

"No. I— Well, first of all, you've said it yourself, we're only fake dating. And second of all, I still want Easton to be my friend. And third, I've seen your dad's gun cabinet and would rather not be on the other side of the barrel of his shotgun."

My muscles relaxed. "Okay, those are good reasons."

He yawned. "I know you have this whole Noah-only-likes-mainstream-girls notion in your head, but don't lock me into that category. I might surprise you."

My heart raced when I thought about what his words could mean. Should I be reading into them? Should I be reading into everything that had happened tonight?

He put his hands behind his head, and I couldn't help but think that his arms looked really nice that way.

Yeah, I definitely shouldn't be reading into what he'd said.

I quickly took off my glasses then flipped off my lamp before I could find anything else to admire about him. I couldn't admire him if I couldn't see him.

"Good night, Noah," I said.

"Good night, Lexi. Thanks again for letting me in tonight. I really appreciate it."

14

NOAH

MY ALARM WENT OFF and I immediately silenced it. Just five more minutes.

I turned on my side and fluffed up my pillow, releasing a long, contented sigh. Then I opened my eyes, realizing where I was. I hadn't woken up this warm all week. I took in my surroundings as the memory of last night came to mind. I was sleeping in Lexi's closet.

Fully alert now, I rolled over to my other side, so I could see out her closet door. Had my alarm awakened Lexi? Did I alert her dad to my presence?

Lexi was still asleep on her bed, one arm hanging off the side, her hair a huge mess over her eyes.

I stifled a laugh. She was dead to the world. And if she hadn't woken with my alarm when she was only a few feet away, then hopefully, her dad hadn't heard it either.

I turned the alarm and ringer sound down on my phone just in case it decided to try and alert everyone to my presence again.

I still had over an hour and a half until school started, but what was I supposed to do now? Should I risk sneaking out of

Lexi's house and possibly getting caught by her dad and the now early-bird Easton? Or should I stay hidden until they all left, and then bum another shower in her bathroom?

I tried to relax my breathing and perked up my ears for any sounds in the house. I was pretty sure the Army had turned Lexi's dad into an early riser. Which meant he was probably already up and at 'em.

Sure enough, a moment later, I was able to pick out the sound of pots and pans clanking in the kitchen.

I glanced at Lexi again. She was still sleeping.

I looked over to her window, wondering if I could get it open now that I was inside and had better leverage. If I were to leave now, I could still get to school in time and just shower in the locker room. I didn't want to risk getting caught in Lexi's room and have her get into trouble because of me. She'd already done so much to help me out.

I pushed the warm blankets off me then stood.

My head immediately crashed against the rod in her closet. I swore and rubbed at the sore spot. *Stupid giant-people problems.*

"Who's there?" Lexi said, her voice full of alarm. Panicked, she scrambled and reached for something on her nightstand.

"It's just me," I said through gritted teeth, the throbbing pain in my head making it hard not to release a string of curse words that would probably make angelic Lexi blush.

But telling her it was just me in her room and not a serial killer didn't seem to calm her down at all. Instead, it had the opposite effect. Her hand groped around for another few seconds —touching her phone, a book, and then her lamp before it stopped on her glasses. She pushed her hair out of her eyes and slid her glasses on.

Her eyes focused on me a second later. "Why are you making so many loud noises?" she whispered. "Are you trying to get us caught and me grounded for the rest of my life?"

I continued to rub the spot on my head that was already turning into a big bump.

"You think I purposely banged my head on your closet?"

That seemed to bring her back to reality, and she took a deep breath before relaxing against her headboard. "Sorry, I just heard this loud sound and woke up."

I leaned against the closet door frame. "Sorry to scare you."

"Is your head okay? That sounded pretty painful from how loud it was."

It *was* pretty tender. "A bag of ice might be nice."

She pushed her blankets away and kicked them the rest of the way down. "Okay, I'll see if I can sneak some up here. Just stay in there, okay? I'm going to leave my bedroom door open, so my dad won't think I'm hiding something in here."

"Okay." And I stepped back into the closet, shut the door, and waited in the dark for her to return.

I listened to the muffled sounds of her family going through their morning routine. It sounded like her dad was talking to her about something. It took a while for her to come back, but eventually, her bedroom door clicked shut, and then she was opening the closet door for me to come out.

"Here, sit on my bed and let me look at it," she instructed.

I did as I was told. She stood in front of me, handed me the ice pack, and then was looking intently at my hair. "Which side hurts?"

"Right on top." I pointed to the spot about halfway down the center of my head.

She gently touched a couple of places on my scalp.

"Ouch," I said, once she'd found the spot.

"Sorry." She leaned closer to get a better view. And I couldn't help but notice how good she smelled. Pretty sure I stank first thing in the morning, but she smelled amazing.

Which reminded me to shut my mouth, so she wouldn't be as

likely to catch a whiff of my nasty morning breath. I may be a homeless guy at the moment, but that didn't mean she needed to smell it on me.

I closed my eyes as she pushed my hair aside to get a better look. Chills ran down my neck from the way it felt to have her hands in my hair, nerve endings sparking to life. I wondered what it would feel like to have her run her hands through my hair as I kissed her...

"Looks like you hit your head pretty good there. But there isn't a cut or anything, so I think you'll be okay."

I opened my eyes, coming back to reality and stopping myself from daydreaming about pulling her onto my lap and keeping her there.

She'd probably scream if I did that anyway, and then our secret would definitely be out. So I kept my hands obediently in my lap even though they were itching to touch her.

She took the ice pack from my hands and gently set it on top of my head. "How about you just lie down on my bed and keep this on your bump for the next twenty minutes?"

"You don't think your dad or Easton will find me? I can try to get the window open and sneak out to my car."

She stepped back and seemed to study me. "My dad has to go into the office early again today, so I can just tell Easton that you're coming to pick me up again and you can come out once he's gone."

"Okay." I lay down on her bed, trying not to think about how she'd just been asleep here moments before.

What was happening to me? Why was I suddenly having these kinds of thoughts about Lexi? This was not part of our plan.

She wrung her hands in front of her. "I, um, have to take a shower, though. Just, uh, stay over there, okay?"

She was cute when she was nervous. And for the first time, I was thinking that maybe she did have a reason to be nervous, because I was starting to have physical reactions that I shouldn't be having to her presence.

I cleared my throat. "You don't have to worry about me sneaking in there."

She laughed awkwardly. "Of course I know that." But her face turned bright red, and I was pretty sure mine was already that shade as well.

She grabbed some clothes out of her dresser, making sure to block my view, hugging them to her chest before she disappeared into the bathroom.

I lay back on her pillows and sighed. I was in trouble. And if Easton could read the thoughts running through my mind, he would kill me.

"THANKS FOR LETTING me stay in your closet last night," I said as I stuffed my dirty clothes into my backpack after my quick shower.

"No problem," she said. Then, with a pause, seemed to think better of it. "Well, thankfully my dad or Easton didn't notice, so it didn't become a problem." She laughed.

"Yeah, that would definitely be bad." I zipped my backpack shut and threw it over my shoulder, ready to leave her room for the first time that morning.

"I'm sorry I wasn't able to sneak you breakfast up here."

"It's okay." And thankfully, my stomach behaved and didn't grumble at me.

"I'll figure out something better tomorrow."

"Tomorrow?"

Her face flushed. "Well, didn't you say something about going back home on Saturday? I'm feeling brave enough that I'm stupid enough to think that we can pull this off again. I know my closet isn't the most comfortable place in the world, but it was better than sleeping in your car, right?"

"Definitely better."

She turned off her bedroom light, and I followed her down the hall, trying not to notice how good she looked in her dark jeans today.

Eyes up, Noah, I chided myself.

She stopped in the kitchen before heading out and rummaged through the pantry for a moment.

She came out holding two energy bars. "Will these tide you over until lunch?" she asked.

A warm feeling spread through my chest at her thoughtfulness. I took the bars from her hand. "These will be perfect. Thank you." I gave her a meaningful smile, hoping she'd understand how grateful I was. "You're kind of the most thoughtful fake girlfriend I've ever had before."

"You say that like you get fake girlfriends on a regular basis." She raised an eyebrow.

I laughed. "Nope. You would be the first."

"And hopefully the last. I don't think faking relationships should be a regular thing for either of us."

I nodded. "Yeah, they tend to make things confusing." Like how I was starting to get confused into thinking I wanted this to turn real.

She nodded and held her hand out to me. "Well, are you ready to go, fake boyfriend?" she asked.

I looked at her outstretched hand for a moment before taking it in my own. "Yeah, let's go." I gave her hand a squeeze and forced myself not to think about how good it felt in mine and how happy I was that she'd offered it to me even when no one from school was around to see it. I would just let this be whatever it was right now and try not to mess Lexi's life up too badly.

15

LEXI

I BREATHED a sigh of relief once Noah and I were on our way to school. We had done it. We'd successfully made it through the night without Easton or my dad suspecting anything was going on.

Maybe, just maybe, trying it again tonight wasn't such a terrible idea.

"How did you sleep, anyway?" I asked as he turned down the road just off my street.

He shrugged. "Surprisingly really good. I thought I'd be awake all night since that has become kind of my thing this week, but I slept like a baby."

"You do realize that phrase 'sleeping like a baby' is a total lie, right?"

He glanced away from the road briefly to give me a confused expression. "What do you mean? Don't babies sleep through everything?"

"Grant didn't." No, my little nephew was a downright terrible sleeper from the time my sister brought him home from the hospital. "Now every time I hear someone say that phrase, I take it to mean that they're saying they woke up every two hours to eat, and then cried the other half of the night. Babies are not a good example of someone who sleeps soundly at all."

He laughed. "Duly noted." He looked at me and winked. "I promise to never use that phrase so carelessly in the future."

I couldn't help but smile back. Noah didn't always smile, but when he did it was contagious.

"So how is it having Maddie and Grant out of the house now?"

"It's a lot quieter for sure. Grant had so much energy. I miss them a lot, but I'm really happy that she and Jaxon finally worked things out. It's good for Grant to have both parents." My sister and her high school boyfriend had a rocky relationship for years, being too young to be thrust into parenthood and an adult relationship. My dad's attitude toward Jaxon, the guy who had impregnated his teenage daughter, hadn't helped either. But Maddie had been able to stay at home her first year of college and our family had been able to help her out a lot with Grant. She'd gotten her feet under her and now things were really looking good for them.

"I hope things are better for them now that they're on their own. I know from experience that your homelife can affect you in more ways than you like."

I couldn't help but wonder what exactly was going on with him and his family. You didn't just sleep in your car instead of your bedroom for nothing.

But I didn't ask him. If he was willing to talk about it, it seemed like it would be a pretty long conversation and we were almost to the school.

We pulled into the parking lot a minute later. Noah parked and then hurried over to my side of the car to open the door. As I got out, he took my hand and we walked into the school together. I had been scared to death to hold his hand after the game on

Tuesday, just two days ago, but now it seemed like the most natural thing in the world. And I kind of wanted it to never stop.

I WAS in a happy daze the rest of the morning. Everything seemed to be going so well in my life now. Things at home were good and calm. My grades were pretty good. And for once, I didn't feel like an outcast at school. I had spent the first few months of the year just trying to get Harrison to notice me, but now that I was fake-dating Noah, I kind of didn't really care if he ever did.

I knew in the back of my mind that this was probably not the smartest way to feel right now since it was fake after all, but I would just let myself live in the contented bliss of not having to work so hard to fit in for a while.

"You and Noah seem to be enjoying having your relationship out in the open now." Raven sidled up to me on my way to the cafeteria for lunch.

I forced a smile and tried to ignore her jealous tone. "Yeah, it's been really nice not having to sneak around anymore."

I almost laughed when I realized exactly how big of a lie those words were. After last night, we'd been sneaking around more than ever.

"I've noticed you've been coming to school with him. And his car always seems to be parked on your street."

I nodded. "Yeah." But he'd been coming to my house a lot before anyway, because of Easton.

"I couldn't help but notice he was at your house really late when I drove by last night." She looked down at my left hand—not so discreetly—and eyed my promise ring. "He's a pretty good kisser, isn't he?"

Why was she looking at me like that? And was she trying to

hint that I shouldn't be wearing my ring anymore? My face paled. Did Raven know that he'd slept at my house last night?

I laughed, hoping to dispel my anxiety. "Yeah, he's a good kisser."

She raised her eyebrows. "Those big pouty lips of his aren't just for talking."

I furrowed my brow, wondering if she was trying to say something else. Girls like Raven always had some sort of secret agenda when they talked. Was this a test to find out if I had really kissed Noah? Had she somehow found out that I wasn't really Noah's girlfriend?

"It is interesting though..." she said when I didn't say anything.

"What's interesting?" I knew it was stupid for me to jump on the bait she was giving me, but I couldn't help it.

She lifted her shoulder in the way all the mean girls do in movies—when they're trying to look like they aren't being conniving little witches when that's exactly what they were doing. "I guess I'm used to seeing Noah constantly kissing his girlfriends, and it's hard not to wonder why he's not doing that with you."

I knew I shouldn't have taken her bait.

I looked around anxiously, wishing someone would jump in and save me from this conversation. But of course, everyone was minding their business for the first time as they walked down the hall.

So I did something that I could only blame on desperation.

I looked at Raven with as much confidence as I could muster. "We haven't been kissing in public because Noah kind of thought you might have a crush on him, and he didn't want to make you feel bad when you saw it."

"He what?" Finally, it was her turn to be the most uncomfortable person in this conversation.

I nodded, not having to fake my confidence quite as much now. "I think he felt sorry for you." I shrugged and broadened my smile. "But I'm actually really happy that you brought it up. Because you have no idea how hard it has been to see those soft lips of his at school and not just kiss him in front of everyone."

She didn't say anything, just pressed her lips together and stared straight ahead.

We were almost to the cafeteria now, and I needed to make sure I came out of this conversation swinging.

"So can I tell Noah that you don't mind?" I waited for her reaction.

The corners of her mouth slowly turned up into what I could only describe as a smile-grimace. "Of course you can tell him. Don't let me stop you."

In the cafeteria, my gaze immediately zeroed in on Noah who was already sitting at our table. It was amazing how instantly my senses were able to find him now. Like I had some sort of Noah tracker in my brain.

Before we could reach him, I turned to Raven. "Thank you so much for chatting with me. I can't wait to tell Noah."

I scooted my seat closer to Noah, my palms getting all sweaty. I wiped them on my pants, trying to get them less clammy in case Noah decided to hold hands again.

"I need to talk to you," I whispered. "Something came up with Raven."

Noah glanced at Raven who was setting her purse down and taking her seat.

"Private conversation or public?"

"Private."

"Okay, come with me." Noah tugged on my hand and pulled me out of the room. I only caught a slight glimpse of Raven's reaction, but I hoped she assumed we were sneaking away to make-out.

Noah pulled me through the cafeteria's back exit, down the hall, and then to the stairs that led to the gym.

"Is this private enough?" He stopped us about halfway down the stairs.

"Yeah."

"So what did you need to talk about? Does Raven know that I slept at your house last night?"

I covered his mouth with my hand and quickly looked around. "Shh. Don't say that here."

"I thought this was private enough."

I shook my head. I didn't think there was a place secluded enough for us to start talking about *that*. I could still barely believe it was real. An image of us standing in my closet, so close with his hand caressing my arm, came to mind.

I blinked my eyes to get the memory out of my head, telling myself that it hadn't been a romantic moment. He'd just seen something in my glasses after he'd kept me from falling over like a klutzy fool.

I drew in a deep breath and stared into his dark eyes. "Do you still want to continue this fake-relationship thing?"

A worried crease formed on his brow. "Why do you ask?"

"Raven was asking me questions today, and I'm thinking she might be onto us."

He leaned in closer. "What kind of questions?"

"Um..." I tried to remember, but the way he was looking at me made it hard for my brain to form coherent thoughts. I had to look at my hands, unable to return his intense gaze. "She asked me why we never kiss in public." I blew out a long breath and adjusted my glasses. "She said you've never had a problem with PDA before, and so something must be off with the way you feel about me."

He scrubbed a hand over his face. "She really is paying attention, isn't she?"

I nodded. "So what are we going to do about it?" I dared to look at him, anxious for his answer.

"Do you think we need to do something about it?" His voice was more gravelly than usual, and my mind had a really, really hard time not thinking about how it sounded super sexy.

I was not supposed to think that way about Noah anymore. I had gotten over my crush a long time ago. Noah was out of my league. A non-option, unless we were just pretending.

But I couldn't bring myself to say no. Because deep down, I still wanted Noah Taylor. "I don't know. Maybe?"

"Maybe?"

Couldn't he just make the decision for us, so I didn't have to give away that I might still have feelings for him?

But him letting me have a say was kind of sweet in its own way. Could it be possible that he might want something to happen, too?

I cleared my throat and tried to appear much more level-headed than I felt. "I guess we have two options. If we want to keep this going, we'll have to ramp everything up. But if not, we'll need to stage a break-up soon."

Please don't pick the second option.

There was a gentleness in his eyes that I wasn't used to seeing. He seemed to be forming his thoughts carefully. "I'm not ready to break up with you. I don't want to stop this yet."

He didn't? Hope blossomed in my chest and I sagged with relief. I shouldn't want to keep dating him like this, because it wasn't real. But spending so much time with him was becoming addicting.

"I don't want to stop it either," I admitted.

"Which leaves us only one other option," he said.

"And what's that?"

"We might have to break those rules we set in the beginning.

If we want this to be believable, I'm probably going to have to start kissing you."

My heart jolted to a stop. "Kissing?" I couldn't keep my voice from raising an octave. I knew that was why I'd started this conversation in the first place, but having him actually say it caused butterflies to flap uncontrollably in my stomach

"I think that's what we'll need to convince Raven." He reached over and took my hand in his.

"There's just one problem with that." I had never kissed a guy. And if I was going to kiss Noah, something I had daydreamed about a thousand times, I didn't want to mess it up. Especially not with an audience.

He squeezed my hand and studied my expression. "What is it?" he asked, like he was worried I wouldn't want to kiss him.

"Remember how I've never been on a real date before?"

He nodded slowly. "Yeah."

My stomach turned with nerves. This was so humiliating. Why did I have to keep having these kinds of vulnerable moments with Noah?

His fingers were drawing circles on the back of my hand. I wished I could just focus on how incredible that felt instead of what I had to say to him. "I-it's probably really obvious, but I've never kissed a guy before, and I don't want to look stupid doing it in front of other people. We've been letting them think that we're constantly making out. It can't look like I've never kissed you before." I said the words as fast as I could, hoping that the quicker I got them out, the less stupid they'd sound.

He didn't say anything immediately. Maybe I'd stunned him into silence with a new level of social-ineptness that had never been before reached by humankind.

My heart pounded wildly in my chest.

But then he finally spoke. "I guess we could practice first." He peeked at me through his lashes. "If you wanted."

"Practice?" I searched his face for a hint that he was kidding. But he looked totally serious.

He shrugged. "Sure. You said you don't want it to look like we've never kissed before, so we can just practice first, and the problem will be solved."

Well, when he said it like that...it still sounded crazy.

Then he stood and helped me up beside him.

"Oh, are you thinking we should practice right now?" I asked.

"Yeah."

"Right here?" I squeaked.

"Follow me." He took my hand and led me down the stairs to the gym. The bleachers were already rolled out for the assembly that we'd be having later this afternoon.

He pulled me under the bleachers.

"Just watch your step," he said, as we went farther under. I watched his shoulders as I followed behind him. And then he suddenly stopped, and I bumped right into his back.

"Sorry!" I jumped back.

"Don't be." He turned and leaned one shoulder against the brick wall. I decided to follow suit and pressed my back against the wall. I needed it for stability anyway, since my legs were so wobbly.

We just stood there staring at each other, his towering frame hovering inches from mine.

When he didn't do anything, I spoke with a shaky voice, "We should probably hurry so we still have time for lunch."

He nodded. "Okay."

"Okay." I sighed, hoping he'd just go for it.

He stepped in front of me, placing one hand on the wall near my head to brace himself as he leaned closer. I suddenly had an understanding of how powerful "leaning" really was. Maddie's favorite movie, *While You Were Sleeping*, totally nailed it. Noah was a giant compared to me, but I loved how it felt to feel so petite next to him. He was powerful and strong. He'd make an awesome protector if I ever needed one.

He ducked his head closer. "You sure you want to do this?" He was giving me one last chance to back out.

My heart was beating out of control, and I was pretty sure I was on the verge of melting as I returned his hot stare.

"Yes," I whispered. I wanted this. I wanted him to kiss me. And it definitely wasn't because I cared about keeping up a fake relationship anymore.

He ran a thumb over my cheek. "You know Easton will kill me if he finds out about this."

I swallowed. He probably would. "We can break up if you don't want to do this."

"Do you think that's best?"

"Do you?"

He shook his head and spoke in a husky voice, "I don't want to think right now." And then Noah closed the distance between our lips.

I gasped, caught off guard. But his hand cupped my neck, steadying me and pulling me closer as he coaxed my lips to move slowly with his. I had no idea what I was doing. I'd never done this before. But for some reason, my inexperience didn't seem to be an issue as Noah gently brushed his lips across mine once... twice. Then again and again.

He kissed me gently, like he actually cared and wanted to make my first kiss a good experience. I'd always assumed he was more of the go-for-the-gold, kiss-without-abandon kind of guy. But instead of attacking me with his lips and making me feel way out of my element, just trying to catch up, he kissed me as if I was fragile and he didn't want to break me. It made me feel unbelievably special. Noah knew what he was doing, and the slowness of the kiss made my stomach twist and shake with pleasure I'd never felt before.

I could barely draw in a decent breath as his warm lips caused crackles of electricity that sparked mine to life in a brand-new way. I'd had my lips for sixteen years, but until this moment I had no idea how many nerve endings they had or how sensitive to his touch they could be. And I never wanted this practice kiss to stop. It felt much too good to be so close to Noah with his lips capturing mine between his.

Feeling a little braver, I let my hands trace their way up his arms to rest behind his neck. He was so tall that he was almost bent in half to kiss me. I raised myself up on my toes to help him out, and he reacted by pulling me closer and wrapping his arms around me.

"You sure you've never kissed before?" he asked, breaking the lock his soft lips had on mine.

"Pretty sure this is my first time." I sighed, trying to catch my breath, but it was coming in short little bursts. "Do you think everyone will buy this then?" I asked. I really hoped so, though I wouldn't mind practicing for a few minutes more.

"Pretty sure you're a natural." His breathing was more uneven than usual. Could he possibly have enjoyed that kiss as much as I did?

"T-that's a relief."

He rubbed his hands along my back, making it really hard for me to think. "So do you feel that was enough practice before we make our kissing debut?"

The thought of kissing in public scared the crap out of me. But maybe with Noah taking the lead, it wouldn't be so bad.

His eyes dipped down to where I was nervously biting my bottom lip. Then his gaze met mine. "Maybe just a few more minutes?"

I nodded. "Just to make sure."

But before he could close the distance between us again,

Ashlyn Brooks and Luke Davenport—of all people—appeared at the opening under the bleachers.

Just let me die, please.

Noah immediately straightened, standing to his full height. I pushed myself away from him at the same time, feeling my cheeks burn with embarrassment over getting caught by Noah's ex and her new boyfriend.

It took them a few seconds, but they soon noticed us, too.

"Sorry, we didn't realize this was your spot," Luke said. "Mr. Sawyer locked the Chem lab today."

Okay, I did not need to know where those two usually made out. It was so weird.

"It's okay. We were just leaving." Noah's jaw flexed as he took my hand and led me out from under the bleachers. I kept my eyes trained on my feet, partly so I wouldn't trip on anything and partly because I was too embarrassed to meet Ashlyn and Luke's gazes. What would Ashlyn think of her ex-boyfriend kissing a lowly sophomore under the bleachers?

I hoped she was too infatuated with her new boyfriend to really care much about it.

And I hoped Noah was over Ashlyn enough not to care about being caught, either. I didn't want him to be embarrassed by me.

Ashlyn and Luke moved aside so we could get past them. "It's all yours." Noah's voice was more gruff than usual.

"Thanks," Ashlyn said, without any hint of awkwardness in her voice. "And I've been meaning to tell you all week, but I think it's so cute that you two got together."

16

NOAH

WALKING BACK to the cafeteria with Lexi and our trays of food felt different this time. I was even more aware of my surroundings than usual, hyper-aware of her. While I hated that Ashlyn and Luke had interrupted us, I knew it was probably a good thing, too. Kissing Lexi once under the bleachers for practice was one thing. Kissing a second time—when it was clear she didn't need any practice at all since her trumpet-playing skills really must have translated into kissing skills—now that was crossing the line.

But that didn't keep me from thinking about the kiss. It had been amazing. Better than amazing. Usually, when I kissed a girl, all I wanted to do was slip my tongue down her throat and satisfy some sort of hormonal hunger that was out of control. I never cared about the feelings of the girl I was with. It had always been about me, and what I wanted to feel. But it was different with Lexi. Maybe it was because she'd never been kissed before, or maybe it was because I knew her dad would kill me if he found out. But I wasn't so sure it was either of those things. Maybe, just maybe it was different with Lexi because I was starting to like her as more than just my fake girlfriend.

This was so bad. So messed up. I shouldn't want to kiss Easton's little sister—the girl I'd always thought was too nerdy to check out when she walked by. But spending so much time with her these past few days was making me notice things I'd never taken a second glance at before. Like how Lexi's eyes were more than just the typical hazel. She had lots of green flecks in them, and that had caught me off guard. And I loved that because her glasses were so thick, it made her eyes even more magnified and easier to get lost in.

It was so weird that I liked that about her.

The smattering of freckles across her nose were kind of adorable. I'd probably never used that word before in my life, but Lexi Stevens was freaking adorable and it was making me lose my mind.

"You want to hang out again after school?" I asked Lexi as I walked her to her next class after lunch. She was hugging her books to her chest, and I was worried that kiss might have weirded her out too much to hold my hand at school anymore.

She looked up. "Got more laundry to do?"

I shrugged. "No. I was thinking of actually just hanging out."

"Because Easton has work and you have nothing better to do?" she asked.

Man, I really had ignored her pretty badly over the past few years, hadn't I? If I wanted her to see me differently than she always had, I needed to step up my game. Maybe I should suggest a movie? I did have that *Pride and Prejudice* test coming up, and while I had understood some of the book, I could definitely use a refresher.

"Would you mind watching *Pride and Prejudice* with me?"

She gave me a wary glance. "You know I don't like movies like that, right?"

Was she trying to turn me down? Was I annoying her with how much time I was spending with her?

"Um, okay... Yeah, I'll, uh, find somewhere else to watch it. That's okay."

Wow, I had definitely interpreted everything wrong between us. Here I'd thought that maybe she enjoyed spending time with me, but clearly, she saw the time spent together as more like a job.

I looked around for a reason to just leave this conversation right now, since walking her to class was probably not the gentlemanly gesture I thought it was.

I bit my lip. "Well, I'll just go—"

"Hey, Noah." She touched my arm and I froze.

"What?" I held my breath because I had literally no idea what she was going to say next.

"I wasn't trying to turn you down. I just don't want you to get offended if I fall asleep during the boring parts. I used to do that all the time with Juliette and her chick flicks."

I narrowed my eyes. "So you don't absolutely hate the idea of spending more time with me?"

The smile she gave me calmed my nerves enough to let me take a small breath. "Of course not."

She removed her hand from my arm, and I was able to convince my feet to walk down the hall again.

"Okay, so I'll come find you after school?" I asked when we stopped in front of her classroom.

She nodded. "Yeah."

I watched her walk in, and even though a movie with Lexi should seem like a small thing, I kind of felt like I'd just won something.

JAKE HALEY, one of my football buddies, stopped me in the hall after English.

"I couldn't help but overhear you talking to Easton's sister in the hall. But is it true that you're watching *Pride and Prejudice* after school?"

"Yeah." Hopefully, he hadn't noticed the way she'd almost rejected me too. That wouldn't be good for my plan to make everyone think we were dating.

"Mind if I join you? I could use a refresher, but my mom is weird and thinks that's cheating."

"It's only cheating if you don't read the book."

"I've read most of it." He bounced his backpack higher on his shoulder. "Are you the English test police or something?"

"Of course not." I was the one who was watching the movie as a refresher, wasn't I?

"So can I come?"

"I'll have to ask Lexi first. I'll text you when I find out."

Jake clapped me on the shoulder. "Thanks, man."

Then he disappeared down the hall.

I rounded the corner to the sophomore hall a minute later. Lexi smiled tentatively when she noticed me.

"Hi," I said breathily when I reached her. She looked so vibrant right then. Had something changed since lunch? Or was she just happy to be done with school for the day?

"Hey," she said.

Her books were in her backpack this time, so her hands were free. Free for me to just take in my own.

"Ready to go?" I asked, chickening out from touching her.

"Sure."

I turned back the way I'd come from, and we started walking toward the school's exit. I asked her, "Is it okay if Jake Haley comes over to watch the movie with us?"

"Jake Haley? Why?"

"I guess he heard us talking about it."

She bit her lip. "Sure. Yeah, he can come."

It didn't sound like she liked the idea.

"I can tell him no if you want. It's really no big deal."

She shook her head. "No that's fine. I mean, we have plenty of room downstairs."

"Great." I hurried and shot Jake a text, telling him to come around three-thirty. That should hopefully give us enough time to scrounge up a copy of the movie from somewhere.

"YOU KNOW you're going to owe me big time for watching this movie with you, right?" Lexi asked as she took the DVD out of the case. We'd been fortunate enough to find a copy of *Pride and Prejudice* at the library, so I didn't have to borrow from Ashlyn, the only other person who I knew for sure would have one of them on hand.

"It can't be that bad." I shrugged. "I mean, I read the book and didn't hate it too much, and I'm a guy."

"Yeah, but two hours and nine minutes without even a single action scene is a really long time."

"You don't have to watch it if you don't want to." I didn't want this to be some sort of chore for her.

"No," she hurried to say. "I'm going to watch it..." She looked around uncomfortably. "I mean, what would Jake think if I didn't watch it with you?"

"He'd probably wonder if something was up between us."

"Exactly."

"So what do I owe you, then?" I asked, feeling guilty about having her watch a movie she clearly hated.

She slid the disc into the movie player then looked at me over her shoulder. "Information."

Information? Really? That was a weird request.

"What do you want to know?" I wasn't going to give her my social security number if that's what she was hoping for.

She stood up and walked toward me. "Why did your stepdad kick you out of your house?"

Oh, that kind of information.

I ran a hand through my hair, and then dropped myself onto the sectional.

"It's stupid."

That was kind of the truth. The whole situation with Paul and my mom was stupid because she should have left him a long time ago.

Lexi sat on the cushion next to me, tucking one leg under her. "Just tell me. Ever since I found you in your car I've been going through all sorts of reasons in my mind for why you got kicked out. You're not in some kind of legal trouble, are you?"

"Legal trouble?" I laughed. She really did think I was some delinquent, didn't she?

She looked at her hands in her lap. "I-I overheard you talking to Ashlyn a couple of months ago about someone not pressing charges. And I just thought that with your reputation..."

"My reputation?" I blinked my eyes shut as my temper flared. "I'm so sick and tired of people thinking I'm a bad guy."

Lexi touched my arm briefly. "Hey, you don't need to get mad. I'm sorry if I offended you. I'm really just trying to figure this out with the few facts that I do have."

I sucked in a breath, trying to calm down my boiling blood. She just wanted to know why I was sleeping in my car. And she deserved to know after everything she'd done for me.

"You don't have to tell me if you don't want to." She trained her gaze down. "I'm just worried about you, Noah."

I wanted to tip her chin up so she would look me in the eyes, but I settled for sitting up straighter.

"I'm sorry I got mad. My dad is always talking about me being into trouble, since every time he sees me it looks like I've been in a fight." A fight with Paul. "I'm just tired of being the bad, messed-up kid, I guess. And I'm trying to be better."

She nodded and slowly met my gaze. "I know. I've noticed how much you've mellowed out since last year, even more so the last couple of months."

"You have?" She had watched me that closely?

She seemed to grow uncomfortable and adjusted her glasses. "I notice a lot of things about you, Noah."

She did? My throat grew thick, and I suddenly found myself wanting to tell her more. "M-my stepdad is the real reason I got kicked out. I got in his way when I thought he was about to hurt my mom, and he punched me."

She gasped. "He punched you?"

I nodded. "And it wasn't the first time, either."

Fear and shock filled her eyes. "You can't go back there, Noah."

My heart squeezed in my chest. "I don't want to." I flexed my jaw. "But I have to watch out for my mom and my sister. My mom thinks Paul will calm down, but I'm not so sure. He goes through phases."

"Why doesn't your mom leave him?"

I leaned my head back against the high headrest, letting my eyes fall closed for a moment before meeting her worried gaze. "She tried, once."

Lexi waited for me to say more, so I continued, "Last fall, he was on one. My mom got beat up pretty bad. I was just coming in from a party when it was going on. They were in the kitchen, dishes were smashed all over the floor. And then when I tried to stop him, he went nuts. My mom and Brielle were able to get out of the house, and then I followed them. We went to the women's shelter, but I wasn't allowed to stay since

I'm too old and other women see me as a threat because I'm a guy."

"Is that why you said this wasn't your first time sleeping in your car?" she asked, probably putting all the puzzle pieces together.

I nodded. And just because I didn't want her to find out from someone else, I said, "Your family was out of town that weekend, so I went to Ashlyn's house that first night. But then, yeah, I stayed in my car for the next few days."

She rubbed her arm and raised her eyebrows as if trying to get up some courage to say something about that. Was she going to kick me out for being in the habit of sneaking into girls' rooms?

I was about to tell her that I'd only done it out of desperation when she finally spoke up and said, "So I'm not the first girl whose room you've snuck into?"

Was I a terrible person because I liked the hint of jealousy in her voice?

"Ashlyn even let me sleep in her bed." Yeah, I couldn't help myself with that one.

Lexi gasped and scooted back, like my words had burned her. "I thought you said you didn't do that with her..."

She *was* jealous. And maybe I'd pushed a little too hard with my last comment.

"Ashlyn slept in her chair that night. I literally fell asleep as she was bandaging me up."

"Don't tell me she gave you ice, too? I thought that was *our thing.*" She smiled, and I was happy she wasn't too put off by me spending one night at my ex-girlfriend's house.

"I tend to need ice a lot in my life." I shrugged. "Hazard of being Noah Taylor, I guess."

"So why did your mom go back if he treats her that badly? Why doesn't she press charges?" Then realization dawned on her face. "'That's what you meant by 'not pressing charges' when I overheard you, huh?"

"Yeah." I looked at her solemnly. "I don't get it. He treats her terribly, but she's scared to leave him." I drew in a shaky breath. "I'm worried that one of these days, I'll come home and find she stayed one fight too long." I turned my head to the side, trying to ward off the tears that pricked behind my eyes. I would not lose it in front of Lexi. I would not be a wimp.

But I couldn't help but be scared for my mom. She was a good mom: loving, caring, smart, and fun. She was just brainwashed into thinking she needed Paul for some reason. And I blamed that on my dad. If my dad hadn't betrayed her— If he hadn't left us for a younger woman, my mom wouldn't have gotten it in her head that she was lucky to have any man at all. She would know that she was worth so much more than what the men in her life had been giving her.

My lip trembled, and I wiped at the tear threatening to leak out my eye. My voice wobbled when I spoke, "I just wish she knew what she was worth."

Lexi's eyes filled with compassion, and before I knew what was happening, she moved closer to me and tentatively touched my shoulder. "I'm so sorry you have to deal with this Noah. It isn't fair."

She looked at her hand and seemed to get embarrassed for touching me, so she removed it. I felt cold when she did that. Like she was rejecting me.

Awkwardness permeated the room as we had a hard time meeting each other's gazes. What was going on between us? We'd been fine holding hands this morning as we walked into school. Why could we only touch when other people were around? Had that practice kiss really scared her off from me?

She tucked some hair behind her ears. "I want to tell you to go home and watch out for your mom and sister, but I also don't want you to be in danger."

"I know what you mean. But I'm going back this weekend. I can't overstay your much-too-generous hospitality for long. I don't want to risk your dad taking away your college tuition if he finds out that you're letting me sleep in your closet."

"Does Easton know about any of this with your mom?" she asked.

I shook my head. "No. I, um, like to keep some things just in the family."

She nodded and gave me a small smile. "I appreciate you telling me. I know it wasn't easy."

"That's the understatement of the year." I blew out a low breath. "Just try to forget the whole part where I teared up. I kind of have a reputation for being a tough guy."

She laughed lightly. "That secret is safe with me, too."

17

LEXI

THE DOORBELL RANG a few minutes after Noah and I had finished our conversation.

"I'll get it." Noah stood from the couch.

I watched him as he walked up the stairs. His broad shoulders carried much more of a load than I'd ever imagined. I still couldn't believe what he'd told me about his stepdad. I'd always wondered who Noah was getting into fights with, but I'd never imagined it was happening in his own home. It hurt my heart to think about what was happening to his mom and how because she was too scared to leave, she was putting Noah and his little sister in danger.

Noah was even stronger than I'd known. I definitely couldn't deal with all the stuff he had to. He should be having a fun, carefree senior year. Not sleeping in his car or sneaking into my bedroom because he had nowhere else to rest his head for the night.

"The movie is all set up downstairs," I heard Noah say to Jake as they walked closer to the top of the staircase.

"Hi, Lexi." Jake waved when he made it to the family room. "Thanks for letting me join you guys."

I nodded and adjusted my position on the couch. "No problem."

"I don't think we've officially met, but I've definitely been hearing a lot about you this week." Jake sat on the opposite end of the sectional, tossing the throw pillows to the cushion next to him.

"Hopefully good things," I said. Though I knew the reason why everyone was talking about me was because of my new 'relationship' with Noah.

Jake laughed. "Yeah, mostly good." He turned to Noah. "How was it to have Ashlyn and Luke find you two making out under the bleachers today?"

"What?" I asked, feeling my neck grow hot. I knew Jake and Luke were good friends, but why were they talking about that?

"Who told you they saw us?" Noah asked.

"Luke overheard Raven talking in P.E. about how she thought you guys were only pretending to date. So when he heard what she was saying, he told everyone what he saw."

I looked at Noah, anxious to see what he felt about this. His jaw flexed. He wasn't happy about Ashlyn and Luke catching us after all. I should have known. I knew he wasn't over Ashlyn yet. It was obvious with how he hadn't touched me again after they'd found us.

But he pushed the annoyed look off his face and took his seat on the cushion next to me, putting his arm around my shoulders and squeezing me against his side. "Oh, it's real, right babe?"

"Yeah, definitely real." I managed to croak out.

But I wondered if Jake bought it, since Noah removed his arm from my shoulders the next moment to grab the controller and get the movie started.

He really didn't want to touch me anymore, did he? He'd

been so touchy-feely in front of people at school the past couple of days that his complete lack of physical contact after our kiss was messing with my mind.

What *did* he think about me after that kiss, anyway? Had I really been that bad of a kisser? I'd thought it had gone well enough. It had definitely been good on my end, at least.

And he wouldn't have told me those things about his family if he'd felt nothing for me, right?

But then again, he *had* invited Jake to watch the movie with us. Was that so he wouldn't have to be alone with me again?

Noah started the movie and reclined his seat, so I found the lever between the cushions to recline mine as well, hoping the show would take away my worries for the moment.

"You two aren't going to start making out, are you?" Jake narrowed his eyes at us. "I really don't need a second showing to prove Raven's accusations wrong."

Noah and I looked awkwardly at each other for a moment before Noah pasted on his signature bad-boy smirk and said, "You're the one who wanted to watch the movie with us. Beggars can't be choosers."

Jake threw a pillow at Noah, but it fell on Noah's lap instead of hitting his face. "Thanks for the pillow." Noah smiled. "We'll use it as a shield if we do decide to make-out."

Jake just rolled his eyes and shook his head. "Maybe I really should read the book instead."

"Now that would be the day." Noah laughed before focusing back on the TV screen.

About a minute later, just as I was finally beginning to relax, Noah leaned closer with his mouth next to my ear and whispered, "You should probably sit closer than that." His eyes darted over to Jake briefly, indicating that we had an audience and therefore a show to put on.

I scooted an inch closer, so now there were only five inches between us instead of six.

"So much better," he said sarcastically. I'd hoped that he'd do the typical Noah thing of pulling me closer, forcing me to cuddle with him, but he didn't.

I sighed. Trying to dissect every little movement Noah made would only make me crazy. I needed to stop trying to figure him out. So I tried to shut my brain off. I was doing a pretty good job of focusing on the movie, and to its credit, I did find myself actually enjoying it a little, but about halfway through, Noah stretched and adjusted his position to get more comfortable. His arm bumped against mine. My skin warmed on contact, and I wanted him to bump into me again.

Why didn't I scoot closer when I had the chance?

Maybe I could accidentally move closer to him? Or was that stupid? Would it be totally obvious that I wanted to touch him?

I glanced over at Jake to see if he was watching us. If he was, that would give me a good enough reason to move closer, right? But he was super focused on what was happening on the screen, he had even pulled a notebook out and was taking notes on the movie.

I chuckled to myself. He wouldn't read the book, but he was diligent enough to take notes.

I gestured at Noah to check out what Jake was doing. He grinned at me, and it kind of felt like we had a moment. But then he went back to watching the movie.

I sighed and pulled out my phone to give my mind something else to focus on. Juliette had posted a bunch of photos of her and some guy at the Eiffel Tower. He was cute and had his arm around her. I would need to ask her about him the next time we talked.

"What are you looking at?" Noah leaned closer, his cheek almost touching mine as he peeked at my phone's screen.

I cleared my throat, surprised at how close he was. "J-just some photos of Juliette. Apparently, she doesn't have a problem finding guys in foreign countries, either."

He glanced down at her photo briefly before shrugging. "Eh, she's not my type."

What? "She's always been the type of every guy I've ever known."

Noah shook his head. "I don't see it."

I rolled my eyes. He had to be totally lying, but it was nice of him to try to not make me feel as self-conscious.

"I'll make sure to tell her she's not your type when she gets back next week."

He smiled back. "Make sure that you do."

"Hey, shhh." Jake waved a hand to quiet us. "Mr. Darcy is proposing to her like a boss."

Noah and I just looked at each other and laughed.

"You're really getting into this, aren't you?" Noah asked after his laughter died down.

Jake held a finger to his lips. "Seriously guys, he's asking her to marry him and insulting her at the same time. This guy is my hero."

Noah shook his head, as if realizing he wasn't going to get Jake to take his eyes away from the *riveting* movie.

I shoved my phone in my pocket and settled back in my seat. But as I resumed watching, I couldn't help but notice that Noah kept glancing at me out of the corner of his eye.

18

NOAH

LEXI FELL ASLEEP SHORTLY after Mr. Darcy's failed proposal. She hadn't been lying when she told me about falling asleep during chick flicks. I didn't think I knew of a single girl like her—she was so different from what I was used to. But I kind of loved that about her.

The movie ended, and I successfully got up from the couch without waking Lexi and walked Jake out.

"Thanks for letting me chill with you and your girlfriend." Jake shrugged into his coat at the top of the stairs. "I think I might actually crack my book open now."

"You could probably ace the test without reading it. The movie was actually pretty true to the book." From what I'd understood of the book, that is.

Jake shrugged. "I know. I kind of liked how much Mr. Darcy and Elizabeth were always fighting. If I'd known about that when Mrs. Phillips assigned the book, I might have actually read more than the first two pages."

"Well, the test isn't until Monday, so there's still time."

He nodded. "See you at school tomorrow. Tell Lexi I said bye."

I smiled and opened the door for him to leave. "Yeah, I'll tell her when she wakes up."

Who would have thought that when two jocks sat down to watch a romance movie with a sixteen-year-old girl, it would be the *girl* who fell asleep?

I shut the door behind Jake and checked the time on my phone. It was close to six. Easton and Mr. Stevens should be home soon. But instead of heading out, I found myself wandering back downstairs to sit next to Lexi.

I browsed through the channels on their TV and ended up stopping when I saw the weather forecast on the news station. Apparently, a huge snowstorm was supposed to roll in tonight. They were telling everyone to bring their animals in if possible, so they could stay warm. I really hoped Lexi was still okay with me sleeping in her closet again. The floor wasn't the most comfortable thing in the world, and it was a really tight fit, but it was warm.

The commercial break came on next, and for some reason, the commercials were louder than the news report had been. Lexi startled in her seat, and for a second, I thought she might wake up. But instead of opening her eyes she just turned on her side, and somehow, her head ended up resting on my shoulder.

I went still at her unexpected closeness, my heart coming to a stop before taking off like it was in a race. She nuzzled against me as if to get more comfortable, and soon the side of her head was resting on my chest.

Was she really that deep of a sleeper that she wasn't aware of cuddling up to a human instead of the throw pillows that were usually in the corner?

I held completely still for about half a minute, worried she'd wake up and jump away from me. She hadn't seemed to want to get very close to me during the movie when I'd asked her to sit closer. But she didn't stir, and after another ten seconds, I released the breath I'd been holding.

The news ended so I started flipping through the channels again until I found a hockey game to watch. I let my muscles relax. My gaze landed on Lexi's hair, which was long and would probably feel silky in my hand. I'd threaded my fingers in it as we'd kissed earlier, but I hadn't really been concentrating on the softness of her hair so much as I'd been lost in the way her lips felt pressed against mine. But now her strands looked soft and inviting. I felt the urge to reach out and touch them.

She did seem like the deepest sleeper in the world, so maybe I could just... I slipped the tips of my fingers into her hair, letting them slowly trail down her back. She twitched, and I went still. Did I wake her up?

But then she resumed her regular breathing again, so I traced a line along her side and then down her arm, watching the goose-bumps rise on her skin where I touched her. I smiled, liking that I could have this effect on her as she slept.

What was happening to me? I shouldn't be growing more and more attracted to Easton's little sister. I was eighteen. She was only sixteen. But the more I got to know her and the more time I spent with her, I found her stealing small pieces of my heart. Pieces I didn't know were even there anymore. I had the feeling that if I wasn't careful, she might just go and steal the whole thing.

Footsteps sounded on the stairs, and before I could even register what those footsteps signaled, Mr. Stevens stared down at me. And he did not look happy.

Oh crap! This couldn't be good.

I glanced down at Lexi, wondering what I should do with her. She was practically cuddling up to me. Should I just shove her off and jump to the other side of the couch, hoping that Mr. Stevens somehow wouldn't notice?

I pushed the thought away almost as soon as I had it, because I knew from the angry glint in his eyes that he had most definitely noticed how Lexi and I were sitting, and he'd probably also seen the way I'd been looking at his daughter while running my fingertips along her arm.

"H-hi, Mr. Stevens." I sat up straighter. Lexi startled a little but didn't wake up.

Mr. Stevens gritted his teeth. "Hi, Noah." Then his gaze went down to his sleeping daughter, his expression darkening further. "Sit up, Lexi." His voice was gruff, and he just glared at Lexi, not even looking at me.

Lexi, who had been dead to the world for the past hour, sat up faster than lightning.

"I'm awake. I'm awake." She pushed her hair out of her face and looked around, clearly disoriented.

"What's going on here?" Her dad crossed his thick muscled arms.

I swallowed the lump in my throat, knowing I was in huge trouble.

Lexi seemed to finally break out of the daze from her nap—her eyes went wide and she jumped off the couch. "We were just working on Noah's school project and I fell asleep."

Her dad narrowed his gaze, clearly not believing her. "I think it's time for you to go home, Noah."

I launched myself out of that couch, faster than I'd ever moved before. "Uh, yeah. Of course, Mr. Stevens. I was just leaving anyway."

I slipped past him, feeling his glare burn a hole in the back of my head as I walked up the stairs. I could just imagine him debating whether to grab his shotgun.

My hands were shaking as I pulled on my letterman jacket. I

was about to walk outside when I heard Mr. Stevens' voice again, speaking to Lexi. "You can stay sitting, Lexi. We need to have a talk."

19

LEXI

MY DAD SAT down on the other side of the couch. I wasn't usually afraid of him since he was my dad, but he didn't look happy at all. And I had a feeling it had everything to do with him finding me at home alone with Noah Taylor. I'd fallen asleep while watching a movie, but that wasn't a crime, was it?

My dad looked at me with his stern expression. "Is there something going on between you and Noah?"

What exactly had he seen? Did he somehow find out that Noah had slept in my closet last night? Or had someone said something to him about Noah and I pretending to date?

"What do you mean?" I asked, hoping my non-committal answer wouldn't make him even more upset.

"I saw the way you were laying on him. We have rules, Lexi." Okay, so he didn't know about everything else. But this still wasn't good.

"Laying on him?" My voice squeaked. I'd been sleeping, but I hadn't been sprawled on Noah, had I?

"Don't play stupid with me. Why were you two sitting alone in the dark basement?"

My stomach shrunk in on itself. When he put it like that, it sounded *really* bad.

"I wasn't l-laying on Noah." I stuttered. "We were watching a movie for his class, and I fell asleep. And we weren't even alone—Jake Haley was here, too."

Where had Jake gone, anyway? How long had I been asleep?

"You were alone with that boy when I got home. I wouldn't put it past Noah to pull some kind of stunt with you. Just yesterday, his dad was telling me about how Noah's always getting into trouble. I don't want you spending time with him anymore. In fact, I'm going to talk to Easton about it when he gets home."

Frustration bubbled up inside me, my muscles tensed into knots. He couldn't do that.

"His dad doesn't have any idea what's going on with Noah."

"His dad thinks he's getting into drugs."

"His dad is a jerk who doesn't even take five minutes to listen to his son," I said before I could think better of it. At my father's glare, I shut my mouth.

"Then why else would Noah be getting into fights all the time? Mr. Taylor says he's pretty much emptied his bank account in the past week."

Because he's homeless! I wanted to shout. And I wanted to march up to Mr. Taylor and tell him what was really going on with his son. But I bit down the words. That was Noah's secret to tell. I made him a promise and I wanted him to trust me.

So I said the only thing I could. "He's not getting into drugs. I would know if he was."

"And why would you know, Lexi? Are you sure there isn't anything going on between you two?" Dad narrowed his eyes at me, and I couldn't get over the feeling that he might see right through me.

"I just know, Dad. Nothing's going on."

"Didn't look like nothing from the look on that boy's face when he saw me. That was the look of trouble."

What had Noah been doing while I was sleeping? My dad made it sound like I was on top of Noah. Had I really fallen asleep on him...and he didn't shove me away? Was it possible that he was okay with me being so close to him? I really hoped I didn't snore.

I shook my head. "We're barely friends. He just needed a place to watch a movie for class."

"And he couldn't do that at his own house?"

I looked down. "No."

My dad pursed his lips. "I don't want you spending any more time alone with that boy in this house. It's against our rules, and you know that."

"But we weren't alone. Jake was here until a few minutes ago."

"Those are the exact same things your sister said to me. And I love Grant, he's my little buddy, but your sister had a hard time of it. She was lucky to have you to help out so much with Grant. But I won't let that happen to one of my girls again. You need to be smart."

Why did he always have to think I was up to something bad? I hated how just because Maddie had gotten into lots of trouble when she was my age that he assumed I was going to follow in her footsteps. I hadn't done a single thing wrong.

I laid my head back and blew out a frustrated breath. "We're just friends. He wouldn't dare do anything with me, anyway, even if we did want to...which we don't. Guys know all about my purity ring and my drill sergeant dad. Pretty sure I won't get asked out on a date until I'm hundreds of miles away at Yale. If then."

Which reminded me of exactly why Noah, or Harrison, or any guy for that matter would never dare touch me.

My paranoid dad was ruining my life. It wasn't fair that I was being punished for my sister's actions. When was I going to get to stop proving myself to him?

My dad stood then touched my shoulder. "I just want you to have more options in your life. Getting mixed up with the wrong crowd has more of an impact than you know."

I crossed my arms and glowered at him. "All I did was fall asleep. I'm not going to end up like Maddie."

"That's all I want to hear. Just make good choices and your life will be easier."

Except for the fact that I had always made good choices, yet my sister's choices were the ones making my life hard at the moment.

But instead of saying anything about that, I just sighed and said, "You don't have to worry about anything. I'm still planning to go to Yale. Nothing will get in the way of that."

My dad gave me a small smile, though his eyes told me he was still worried about me. But I tried not to look too hard or it would just make me feel guilty. I wasn't going to do what my sister did. But I wasn't going to just cut Noah out of my life. He needed someone right now, and at the moment, that someone was me. I wouldn't let him down.

20

NOAH

"I'M SORRY, but your card was declined." The girl at the first drive-thru window at McDonald's gave me an uncomfortable look. It was the kind of uncomfortable that made me think she knew who I was. Which meant we probably went to the same school.

I cleared my throat, feeling awkward myself. "Are you sure?" I had checked the balance on my account yesterday. There should be at least thirty dollars left.

"I can try another card," the girl offered.

I tightened my grip on the steering wheel. "I don't have another card. Could you just try once more?"

The girl nodded before ducking back in to swipe my card again. How could my money have just disappeared from my account? I needed that money to get me through until at least Saturday. I had to eat somewhere, and from the way Mr. Stevens had reacted to finding me at his house, I doubted I'd be bumming food off them much more.

The girl came back, holding my card out to me. "It still wouldn't go through."

"Okay, thanks." Without meeting the girl's gaze, I took the card back and tossed the useless thing onto the passenger seat. Then I rolled up my window and stared ahead at the car in front of me, wishing I could just drive straight through and hide my shame.

Had someone hacked into my account somehow and stolen my money?

The brake lights went off on the car ahead of me, having successfully gotten their food into their vehicle. I followed it out of the drive-thru, not bothering to stop at the second window since they wouldn't be giving me my order after all.

I drove down the next block and pulled along the curb to call my dad. Maybe he would know what had happened to my money.

He picked up after the third ring. "Hi, Noah." His deep voice came through my earpiece.

"Hey, Dad," I said, trying to figure out how to proceed. Our last conversation had ended with him accusing me of getting into drugs. "Um, do you know what happened to the money in my checking account? I had thirty dollars yesterday, but my card just got declined."

"Yes," he said. I could hear the chattering of my step-siblings in the background.

I waited for him to say more, but when he didn't, I asked, "Yes as in yes you know where my money is?"

I heard his chair scrape across the floor in the background, like he was standing from his nice warm dinner with his perfect little family. "I put a hold on your account and transferred the rest of your money out this morning."

"You *what?*" I raised my voice.

"I noticed that your account went from about two-hundred fifty dollars to only thirty in less than a week. And the only reason I can think of for a high school student to blow that much money that fast is if they're up to something illegal."

"Are you serious right now?" I blinked my eyes in frustration.

"I told you to stay out of trouble, Noah. To not get into drugs. But since you can't seem to take responsibility for yourself, I had to take matters into my own hands."

Hot anger burst through me. "For the last time, Dad, I'm not doing drugs! I'm not getting into trouble anymore." I stopped getting into fights—aside from the ones Paul picked with my mom. I stopped making out with random girls. I had practically lived like a saint for the past two months.

He sighed loudly like he didn't believe me. "Then what is it, Noah? Why did you withdraw so much money this week?"

"Like I told you, I got kicked out for the week. Paul went on a stupid rampage and I'm the one being punished for it." My throat constricted with the emotions threatening to bubble over. "I had to go buy myself a freaking sleeping bag, so I could sleep in my car since I'm not good enough to stay with either of my parents. I withdrew the cash for my expenses, so you wouldn't know I was homeless!"

Tears sprang to my eyes, and I hated that I was getting emotional over this. I would not let my dad hear me cry like a baby. I'd cried the day he moved out and I had watched him drive off to his new life with his mistress. After that day, I promised I wouldn't show emotion in front of him ever again.

The line was silent for a moment. Then after about ten seconds, my dad's voice came through again, "Y-you're sleeping in your car?"

I bit down, already regretting telling him that much.

When I didn't respond, he said, "Noah?"

"Yes," I grunted.

"How can you be sleeping in your car?"

"Well, I park in the woods and just don't get out of it. Eventually, I fall asleep."

"This is not something to joke about."

Oh, believe me, I knew that.

When I didn't say anything, he said, "You know what? Let me give your mom a call. Let me see if I can arrange for you to go home again tonight."

I rolled my eyes. Of course, when faced with the option of inviting me to stay in one of the spare bedrooms at his house, or push me onto someone else, he still chose to keep me away from his precious perfect children.

"Don't bother, Dad. I'm fine, really."

"Don't be like that, Noah. I'm trying to help."

"Dad, we have to go now, or I'll be late for my recital." I heard my step-sister, Paige, say in the background.

"Noah," my dad spoke again. "I need to go. But I'll call your mom and get you back home."

I leaned my head back against the headrest, fighting the wave of emotion threatening to topple over. Once again, my step-siblings came first. I was never going to be as important to my dad as they were. "Don't worry about me, Dad. I don't want you to be late for your recital."

And then I hung up and tossed my phone onto the seat beside me before he could say anything more.

I pulled onto the road again, driving back to the north woods. If I wasn't going to be getting any dinner tonight, I might as well go to sleep now. Then I'd swallow my pride in the morning and use some of the money in my school lunch account to buy myself breakfast. I could ignore the gnawing, empty feeling in my stomach until then.

THE ROAD to the campground hadn't been plowed since the recent snowstorm, so I ended up driving toward the school. Maybe I could park in the back lot and go unnoticed for the night.

I passed my house on the way and couldn't help but look in the windows as I drove by. The warm, yellow glow coming from inside would have me tricked into thinking it was a nice cozy environment if I didn't know any better. But I did know better. I just hoped my mom and Brielle were okay. Paul should have heard about his promotion by today.

I pulled my car into a corner spot at the back of the parking lot, popped my trunk, and grabbed my camping stuff. After shoving them in the backseat, I slammed the door shut, but it popped back open—I hadn't put my sleeping bags in far enough.

Stupid sleeping bags. I shoved them into the middle of the seat, my temper flaring as I did so. Then I slammed the door shut with much more power than it needed. *Stupid car. Stupid everything.*

I gripped the handle on the passenger side and swung the door wide open before stomping my feet on the ground to get the snow off. Then as I lowered myself into my seat—my bed for the night—I bumped my head, hitting the same spot I'd banged this morning in Lexi's closet. *Stupid small car.*

I'd been on the verge of tears since my conversation with my dad, but I couldn't fight them back any longer as the reality of another long, freezing night loomed ahead.

Tears clouded my vision as I pulled my wet shoes off and dropped them into the back.

My phone buzzed under my butt. I reached my hand around until I found it. I wiped the moisture out of my eyes, so I could see the screen. If it was my dad again...

But it wasn't. It was Lexi.

Lexi: **Are you coming back tonight? I had my dad**

**work on my window after dinner, using the excuse
of it being dangerous in case of a fire.**

I drew in one of those shuddering breaths that told me I'd
been crying too hard as I punched in my response.

Noah: **Your dad doesn't want me there. I don't
want to get you in any more trouble than I already
have.**

Lexi: **Don't worry about me.**

My windshield was already covered in a thin sheet of snow.

Noah: **I'll be fine.**

I could survive this. Lots of people went to bed cold and
hungry each night.

My phone started ringing, and Lexi's name popped up on the
screen. I sighed then swiped my thumb across the screen to
answer.

"I'll be fine, Lexi. I have two sleeping bags."

"Stop trying to be a tough guy, Noah." She apparently wasn't
one to give up easily. "I already checked the weather and it's going
to be really bad, worse than yesterday. Just come over. Please. I
won't be able to relax tonight if you don't."

I looked out the window again, watching the big snowflakes
come down fast and hard.

"Okay," I finally said.

"Okay?" The relief in her voice made me feel a little warmer
inside.

"Yes, I'll come. Just don't blame me if your dad finds out and
grounds you for the rest of eternity."

"He won't find out."

I PARKED at the end of her street ten minutes later and filled my backpack with a change of clothes and everything I'd need to keep me until the next morning.

Then I headed down the sidewalk to her house, sneaking down her side-yard like I had last night.

I texted Lexi to tell her that I was there, and she appeared at her bedroom window a moment later. Her hair was pulled back in a ponytail and it looked like she was already wearing her pajamas—a gray tank top and sweatpants. Had she pretended to go to bed already just for me? It was just barely after eight o'clock.

I grabbed the old bucket that I'd seen sitting against the tree last night, turned it on its lip and used it to help myself through Lexi's window.

It was a tight fit, so I had to fall forward to get myself the rest of the way in, but once I was inside her warm bedroom, Lexi shut the window.

"My dad is still in the living room watching TV," she whispered.

I nodded, brushing the snow off myself as I stood. "Thank you for sneaking me in again."

She shrugged. "It's no problem." Then she turned to walk away.

I gripped her arm and dipped my head down to really look her in the eyes. "I know what you're risking, so don't say it's no problem. I was there to see your dad's reaction this afternoon."

She looked to the side, clearly uncomfortable on the subject of her dad. How bad had that conversation been, anyway?

"My dad is overprotective. We aren't doing anything wrong." She met my gaze again. "If I get grounded for keeping you out of the cold, it's worth it."

She sat on her bed and watched me as I took off my backpack and then my letterman jacket. I felt uncomfortable under her scrutiny, but I tried to ignore it. What did she see in me? In her mind, was I still just her brother's annoying best friend, or could she possibly see me as something more?

When I met her eyes, she looked away before I could figure her out.

She cleared her throat. "So what restaurant did you hit up tonight?"

"McDonald's." I sat in the chair at her desk.

She squinted. "I never would have pegged you for a McDonald's kind of guy."

I shifted in my chair. "When you eat out as often as I do, you gotta try everything."

"So what did you get tonight?"

"I ordered chicken nuggets. And to try and be a little healthier, I added a side salad in there, too."

She pulled one leg on the bed and set it under herself. "Their chicken nuggets are the best. My dad made this weird Asian dish that one of his coworkers told him about."

"And I'm guessing it wasn't a new family favorite?" I asked.

She shook her head. "Definitely not. I could really go for some chicken nuggets, though. Maybe I should take this whole rebellious daughter thing to an extreme and sneak out to get some."

I laughed. "Yeah, I'm sure the ones I ordered would have tasted good."

"Wait, *would* have tasted good? Didn't you get some?" She gave me a confused look.

I realized my mistake and looked around awkwardly. "I didn't actually get to try them. My card was declined."

Her eyebrows raised. "It was declined? So you didn't eat any dinner?"

I shrugged. "No. But I had a pretty good lunch, so I should be okay."

She stood right up from her bed. "I'm not about to let you starve, Noah. Just tell me when you don't get food. I can get you some."

"But you said yourself that your dinner was gross. I figured I wasn't missing out on much."

"I can find something else. It's not like that's the only thing we have to eat in the house." She gave me a scolding look and headed for the door. "You should've said something, Noah. I'll be right back."

I stood and grabbed her hand to stop her. "You really don't have to. I'm fine."

She looked back at me meaningfully. "It's really no problem, Noah. It's not like my dad guards the fridge or takes a count of exactly how much leftover food there is. I mean, we usually have you and Easton eating us out of house and home, so it really isn't going to be that big of a deal."

I nodded and released her hand, feeling a wave of emotion coming over me. I didn't deserve this. She was being too good to me. "Thank you."

She opened the door slowly, peeked her head out to make sure no one was watching, and then left. She was back five minutes later with a sandwich.

She shut the door behind her before handing me the plate. "I wasn't sure which kind of sandwich you liked, so I just made ham and cheese. I hope that's okay."

"This is great. Thank you again, Lexi, you're kind of like my guardian angel right now."

She shook her head and waved me away. "I'm just being a good fake girlfriend."

I smiled. "Pretty much the best fake girlfriend ever."

She looked down, and there was something in her expression that made me wonder if I'd said something wrong. I'd only repeated what she'd said about the fake boyfriend/girlfriend thing.

But after today and everything that had happened—the kiss, me telling her about my family, getting caught by her dad, her taking care of me again—it really didn't seem like it was fake anymore. If it was, I should be going to Easton for all of this stuff. He was the one I was really supposed to be friends with.

But maybe that was just it. Maybe Lexi had moved up higher in level of importance in my life.

And if that was true, I needed to find a way to let her know that this wasn't pretend to me anymore. This was real. And I wanted it to be real for her, too.

I just hoped I wouldn't scare her off while I tried to figure this out.

21

LEXI

WHILE NOAH ATE HIS SANDWICH, I went to hide in my bathroom with the excuse of brushing my teeth, uncomfortable with how he had looked at me after I'd made the comment about us being fake. Today had been crazy. My dad didn't want me anywhere near Noah. But I just couldn't do what my dad wanted me to do anymore. I was sixteen years old. I had things that I wanted in my life. And right now...I wanted Noah. Deep down I had always wanted Noah.

Even though it was impossible to think he might want me back.

But that kiss... Oh. That kiss and the way he'd confided in me and no one else was making me think that crazy things like that might be possible.

The memory of our kiss under the bleachers swirled over me as I gripped the sink, trying to calm down my racing heart. We kept saying this thing between us was just for Raven, or Harrison's benefit, but I barely even cared what Harrison thought of me anymore.

I brushed my teeth in fast circles as I tried to figure this whole thing out. If by some miracle Noah did like me, was it even possible for us to have a future? Easton had been okay with us pretending to be together, but I doubted he'd be okay with it being real. He'd said so himself that he knew what Noah was like with girls, and that he'd beat him up if he touched me for real.

And I already knew for sure that my dad wouldn't be okay with it.

But was it so crazy to think that none of that mattered? That if Noah did share my feelings, we could beat the odds stacked against us?

There was a quiet knock on the bathroom door. I stilled my toothbrushing. "Yes?" It came out sounding all garbled.

"Is it okay if I brush my teeth?" Noah asked from the other side of the door.

I quickly rinsed my mouth and said, "Yeah, sure." Then I let him in.

He stepped inside, shutting the door behind him. He must have noticed the alarm on my face because he said, "I'm just shutting it in case your dad or Easton come into your room while we're in here."

My eyes went wide, but I nodded. "That's a good idea." I was tempted to lock it too but didn't, since that was probably taking things too far.

He squeezed past me, his frame towering over mine, and went to the sink. He turned on the water.

I leaned against the wall behind him, looking at his reflection in the mirror. I hadn't noticed when he'd first gotten here since my room was only lit by the lamp in the corner, but his eyes were tinged with red around the rims.

Had Noah been crying?

On the phone, he had sounded like he might be trying to cover up a wobbling voice. It hurt my heart to think about it.

His hair was messier than usual. He sported a few-days-old

scruff on his face. I touched my chin, vaguely remembering how it had chaffed against my skin earlier as we'd kissed. I'd been so caught up in the sensations of everything else that the roughness of it hadn't bothered me. In fact, I wouldn't mind feeling it again.

Would it be wrong to tell him I needed more practice?

I forced my gaze away from his face, not wanting him to think I was staring. I took in his broad shoulders instead. He was so much taller than me, I was practically a dwarf next to him. But that was part of the pull I had for him. It made me feel petite, like a girl instead of the tomboy I felt like most of the time—though it was also probably part of the reason why he'd always treated me like I was such a kid.

His arms were really nice, too. Toned, and still tanned from football season. And I found myself wanting to find a reason to be wrapped up in them again.

I shook my head. What was coming over me? Daydreaming about Noah when he wasn't around was one thing, but daydreaming about him when he was looking right back at me through the mirror was another thing entirely.

So I decided to talk about something that would make my ogling less obvious. "Do you know why your card was declined?"

He spit in the sink and shrugged. "I called my dad, and turns out, he transferred all my money out."

"What? Why would he do that?" Because there was about no chance he was having money problems. Noah's dad was loaded.

Noah set his toothbrush down on the counter, not really looking at me. "He thought I was using the money for drugs."

"Drugs? Really?" My dad had said as much, but it was still weird to hear it from Noah.

"Apparently, your dad isn't the only one who thinks that I'm bad." He turned and leaned against the sink, so he was facing me instead of my reflection. "Anyway, when I told him that I was sleeping in my car, he kind of changed his tune."

"If he knows you're sleeping in your car, why didn't he invite you to his house?"

"He said he was gonna talk to my mom or something, but it wouldn't surprise me if he got too distracted by Paige's dance recital tonight. He was in a hurry again to get off the phone with me."

"That's so messed up. I'm so sorry, Noah."

He shrugged like it was no problem. "It's what I'm used to. Whatever." He picked up his things. "Anyway, I think I'm ready to turn in for the night."

I pushed myself away from the wall. "Right. Me too."

We both tried to go out the door at the same time and ended up bumping shoulders. My skin sparked to life where our arms touched. And I wanted to touch him again.

But he stepped back, creating some distance between us. "You first." He gestured for me to walk ahead of him.

"Thanks."

I led the way back into my bedroom. He turned off the light in my bathroom before coming out.

I went into the closet and turned on the light. "I, um, put away the blankets you used last night since I didn't want my dad to see them."

He stepped up closer and easily pulled them off the top shelf, his bicep flexing with the movement.

"Do you know how unfair that is?" I asked.

"What?"

"That you never have to use a step stool."

He smiled. "Do you really want to be six-three like me?" he asked.

"No."

"Good. Because I bumped my head in the same place twice today."

"Ouch."

He chuckled. "Yeah, ouch." He dropped the blanket to the floor before turning back to me, looking like he wanted to say something.

"What is it?" I asked.

He shrugged, and when he looked at me, his dark eyes made me feel warm all over. He tucked a stray hair behind my ear. "I like how short you are."

"Y-you do?" I asked, my pulse starting to thrum to life again.

"Yeah." He let his hand drop to his side. We just stood there staring awkwardly for a moment as I tried to figure him out.

Did he like me?

I really, really wanted him to.

But instead of asking and possibly making things really awkward between us, I turned to walk back out of my closet. "Well, I'm going to bed now."

"Lexi?" he said.

I turned back, my heart in my throat. "Yeah?"

He took my hand in his, stepping closer. After just a moment's hesitation, he leaned closer and pulled me against his body in an embrace. "Thank you for being there for me," he whispered in my ear, sending warm, blissful chills down my spine.

I hugged him tighter, taking advantage of this rare moment to breathe Noah in. He smelled amazing. He felt amazing. I didn't ever want to let go. "I'm here for you anytime you need me. Always have been."

I expected him to step away, but he didn't. Instead, he just kept holding me. We were so close. I could hear his heart beating against my ear. I wasn't a doctor or anything, but it seemed like it was beating a little fast. Possibly as fast as mine.

He *was* affected by our closeness.

I could actually make his heart race. All these years of thinking the feelings between us were one-sided, and I finally had evidence that Noah Taylor might feel something for me.

He slowly pulled back, and when our eyes met, I burned. Because the way he was looking at me was like nothing I'd seen before. His eyes were full of desire, and when his gaze flicked down to my lips, my stomach muscles tightened. He was going to kiss me.

But he didn't. He just kept looking at me in a way that made my stomach twist up in so many knots I didn't think it would ever come untangled.

"What do you think is the most appropriate way for me to show you my thanks?" he whispered as he ran his thumb across my lips. My nerve endings went nuts, and I had to bite my lip to keep from going crazy.

I swallowed. "Um..." But I couldn't say anything more because Noah Taylor was touching me and making it impossible to think. Impossible to talk.

He smiled in a detached sort of way at my reaction, and then his hand traveled down my neck and along my shoulder, a path of fire following everywhere he touched.

Maybe it wasn't such a smart idea to wear a tank top to bed after all, because the way his electric touch was making me feel made it hard to remember why I shouldn't just throw myself at him right now.

I blinked my eyes shut.

This is Noah Taylor. He's a player. My dad would kill me if I got involved with him.

But when I looked back at him, all I saw was the guy I'd wanted for years. And he was looking at me the way I'd wanted him to for as long as I could remember.

"Lexi, I..." he started.

"Yes?" I asked, my heart swelling with anticipation. This seemed like it might just be the most important moment of my entire life.

"I—" He blinked his eyes shut and shook his head. When he

opened them, the look in his eyes had changed. "I-it's getting late. We should probably go to bed."

I swallowed, feeling my hopes drop into a tailspin of broken dreams. "Yes. W-we should."

It took all my strength to make myself step back from him and break the magnetic hold he had on me. I slowly turned, trying not to let him see the disappointment crashing over me like waves on a sailboat in the middle of a storm.

I moved one foot out of the closet. Then the next. Forcing myself to leave when all I wanted to do was stay.

"Lexi, wait." He gripped my arm and my pulse turned frantic. *Knock. Knock.*

"Can I come in?" Easton's voice sounded from the hall.

I jumped away from Noah like he was on fire and pushed him back in the closet, shutting the door on him. Then I quickly turned around to make sure Easton hadn't opened the door already. Thankfully, he hadn't, so I launched myself onto my bed.

Just as I was about to tell him to come in, I saw Noah's backpack in the middle of my floor.

"Just a minute," I called, my heart beating wildly in my chest. "I'm just putting on my pajamas."

He hadn't seen me already wearing them when I was in the kitchen making a sandwich, right?

I jumped off my bed and swooped Noah's backpack up, and quickly shoved it at him in the closet. I didn't get a chance to actually see him since he'd thankfully thought to shut off the light, but I heard him groan like I'd just hurt him with his backpack.

I'd probably thrown it at his head, like everything else he'd bumped into today.

Once I'd shut the door, I jumped on my bed again and pulled my phone off my nightstand, hoping I'd look like I was calm and relaxed. "You can come in now."

Easton stepped inside and shut the door behind him. "Hey, I just got done talking to Dad."

"Yeah?" I asked.

Act cool. Don't look at the closet.

"What exactly were you and Noah doing when he got home? I thought you two were just pretending to date. This didn't somehow suddenly turn real, did it?"

My stomach went into my throat, but I tried to make a face that didn't show him anything weird was going on.

"Of course it's not real. I just fell asleep, and I guess Dad thought I was cuddling with Noah or something."

Easton leaned against the wall. "I knew it was probably something like that."

"Could you imagine me and Noah together for real?" I laughed awkwardly. "That's nuts. I'm sure he can barely stand to be around me most of the time."

"That's true. You guys do fight a lot."

"Yeah," I agreed, though we hadn't really been fighting very much lately. Sure he teased me here and there, but it was starting to be more like flirting than anything else. Was that stupid of me to think he was flirting with me? Because it sure seemed like he was about to kiss me a few seconds ago. And I wanted to believe that I didn't have a reason to think it was just another practice.

"Good. That's what I told Dad. So your secret fake relationship is still safe with me."

Fake relationship. I was really starting to hate those two words. I wanted it to be real.

"Thanks."

"Speaking of you and Noah spending more time together, have you noticed anything off with him this week?"

"What do you mean?" My voice came out higher pitched than usual. I sat up a little straighter, feeling uncomfortable talking about Noah when I knew he could hear everything from his hiding place in my closet.

Easton slid down the wall until he was seated on the floor. "I don't know. It feels like he's been avoiding me. I know I've been working a lot this week, and you two have your thing going on. But it just seems like something is off. And after what his dad told Dad today..." he trailed off.

"He's not into drugs, if that's what you're wondering."

Easton looked up at me. "Okay, that's good. I didn't think so, but I just wanted to see if you knew anything."

I did know something. But I couldn't betray Noah's trust. If he wanted my brother to know, he'd tell him.

"So, are you grounded from Noah, too?" I asked.

He laughed. "He tried, but I learned through the years that sometimes you just have to stand up to Dad."

"Wish I was better at that. According to him, I'm going to end up just like Maddie if I spend any more time alone with Noah."

Which was so stupid. I knew how babies were made. And Noah and I were most definitely not going to do those things together.

I still didn't even know if he even liked me in *that way*.

I glanced at my closet and my cheeks heated when I realized Noah had probably just heard what I'd said. *Stupid, stupid, stupid.*

Easton looked away and coughed. "Anyway," he said awkwardly, clearly not liking the thought of me and Noah being together. "Maybe I'll see if Noah wants to do a hot tub night tomorrow after the game. We haven't done one of those in a while."

"I'm sure he'd like that." Then an image of Noah without a shirt popped into my head. He really looked good without his shirt on. It probably would be a good idea for me to find something to do tomorrow night, so I wouldn't be tempted to watch them.

I shook my head. *Way to be creepy, Lexi.*

"Yeah, I'll shoot him a text."

Just don't text him right now. Because a ringing sound coming from my closet would not be good.

I expected Easton to get up to go now that we'd covered the topics at hand. But he just stayed there with his back against the wall.

Why wasn't he leaving?

"So random question," he said, "but doesn't Juliette get back soon?" He stared at his hand which he was rubbing along the gray carpet absentmindedly.

I frowned. "Yeah, she gets back next week. Why do you ask?"

"No reason, really. She just popped into my head today while I was working." He shrugged, but still wouldn't meet my eyes. Weird.

"Is everything okay between you and Mercedes?"

"Sure. Things are fine. We're gonna go to the game together tomorrow. She's nice."

Nice? Hmm. Something was off with my brother. He'd just called her "the hottest girl in school" last week. But now she was simply *nice*?

Did any of this have to do with Juliette coming back? They had acted really weird around each other before she went to Paris.

"Well, I better get to bed. Thanks for the chat." He stood and made ready to leave. *Finally.*

But just before he opened the door, he turned back and asked, "Hey, do you still have your skateboard repair kit?"

The repair kit that was currently in my closet?

"Why?" I asked, since opening my closet to look for something was about the last thing I wanted to do right now. "Are you going skateboarding? It's the middle of winter."

He scratched the back of his neck. "I was thinking about going to the indoor skatepark in Syracuse soon. I just wanted to get my skateboard ready."

"Um, well, it's probably buried in there. I'm kind of tired and don't really want to dig through my whole closet if you don't really need it."

"That's okay, I can look for it."

I jumped from my bed and blocked him from opening my closet door. "No. That's okay. I'll..."

He narrowed his gaze. "Why are you acting so weird?"

I laughed awkwardly. "No reason. It's just...um...I hung my bras up in there to dry and I don't want you to see them."

He stepped back, clearly not wanting to see my underwear, either. "Okay, yeah. I'll, um, just get it from you later."

I nodded, and my erratic heartbeat slowed a little. "I'll get it to you tomorrow."

He put his hand on the doorknob. "Thanks. Goodnight."

"Night."

I collapsed against my closet door as soon as he was gone. *Whew. That was close!*

The closet door behind me opened a crack, making me jump.

"Is it okay to come out for air now?" Noah asked through the crack.

I swung the door wide open, feeling bad for trapping him in there for so long. "Yes." I looked around quickly just to make sure Easton really was gone and not coming back in. "You can come out."

He crawled out and stood, giving me a lopsided grin. "Now wasn't that exciting?"

I shook my head but smiled despite myself. "I don't know if exciting is the right word for it."

22

NOAH

THIS WAS GETTING DANGEROUS. Not only did Lexi's dad not want her to spend any more time with me, but now Easton had almost caught us.

But it was probably a good thing that Easton had come in when he had. I'd been about to kiss Lexi, and that would have been really bad. We were just fake dating, and I couldn't have any feelings getting involved. I wasn't supposed to be with a girl right now. I was supposed to stay single and not let anyone else get mixed up in my messy life. I needed to figure things out myself.

But something Lexi had said bothered me. I needed to ask her about it.

So after we were in our respective sleeping areas—her in her bed, me scrunched up in her closet—I asked. Hoping the darkness, and the inability for her to see my face, would make this less uncomfortable.

"Is it true what you said to Easton?"

"What do you mean?" she asked. "I kind of told a lot of lies just barely."

"I'm talking about what you said about me. Do you really think I don't want to be around you?"

She was quiet for a moment too long, and I worried I may have messed something up. "Well, kind of. I mean, ever since I've known you, it seems like I've just been this proverbial annoying little sister of your best friend."

That may have been true in the past. But it wasn't true anymore. "That couldn't be further from the truth, Lexi." My heart raced, feeling like I'd practically admitted that I liked her. What would she say? Would it scare her to death? I was two years older than her.

"What do you mean?" she asked in a quiet voice.

I turned on my side so that I could see her silhouette better in the darkness. "Well, in the very least, I'd like to think that we became friends this past week."

She turned to face me, too, her head resting on her arm as she laid on her pillow. "Yeah, I guess we're friends."

That was good. At least she saw me as a friend.

"But how long do you want to keep this fake relationship going? I mean, for me and my purposes, I think that it has fulfilled its need. I thought I liked Harrison and all, but I don't really care anymore."

She didn't care about the trumpet player anymore? "I guess if you don't want to keep this up we can stop," I offered. It probably wasn't fair for me to keep this going with Lexi anymore. Things were already confusing as they were. "Do you want to break up tomorrow?"

"Um, sure. That would probably be good. I think Easton is missing you, anyway."

"Yeah, probably time to get things back to normal around here." The thought made me sad. Really sad. I didn't want to lose what Lexi and I had together.

"So you want to do it tomorrow at school? Make it a big public thing? Or just tell everyone?"

"I think I've had enough of public spectacles to be good for a long time," I admitted. I was tired of always putting on a show.

"Okay, yeah. We can just tell people if they ask. I don't want to make it a big production, either." She rolled onto her back.

I wanted to say something more but didn't know if I had the guts to say it.

But it was time for me to start acting like a man. So I said, "It's going to be kind of weird not hanging out with you as much after this week." Which was strange. We'd known each other since I was in middle school, yet in just one week I'd gotten to know her better than I had in the last six years.

"It was fun while it lasted." She sighed. "But Juliette will be home next weekend anyway, so I guess the timing is probably about as perfect as it could be. Things will go back to normal and it will be as if this week never even happened."

She said it like it was a good thing. But I couldn't help feel the complete opposite.

"WELL, I guess this is probably the last time you'll have to hold my hand," I told Lexi as we walked into school the next morning. My heart squeezed in my chest just a little bit as I thought about how our week of pretending was coming to an end. If I'd known how things were going to go from the beginning, I probably would've done things a lot differently. Found more reasons to cuddle with her. Hold her hand. Kiss her. Just be with her more. But we were ending. And I needed to be okay with that. It had been fake from the start. We'd only kissed that one time because the situation had demanded it.

And if I'd known that one kiss was all I was going to get, I would've made it last longer. Savored it. And probably have tried to steal another.

But we had accomplished what we set forth to accomplish when we started this. Kind of.

Except for the fact that she didn't really care what Harrison thought of her anymore. And I didn't care what Raven thought, either. All I cared about was if Lexi wanted to date me. All I cared about was what Lexi thought of me now.

"Yeah, you can go back to hanging out with all your girl-friends after tonight." There was a sadness in her eyes that I couldn't miss.

I squeezed her hand. "We'll still see each other all the time. I mean, it's not like I'm going anywhere. I'll still be Easton's friend unless your dad really does stay true to what he said yesterday."

We made it to her locker, but I didn't want to let go of her hand. I wanted to hold onto it forever. She didn't seem in a hurry to let go either. Which made me wonder if we were really doing the best thing. Would it be so bad if what started out as fake turn out to be real?

She cleared her throat and let go of my hand to open her locker. I watched as she set her books inside, just soaking in everything that was Lexi. Her long brown hair that she liked to keep in a ponytail most of the time. Her thick-rimmed glasses that I'd always thought made her look geeky, but now I found them adorable. Her tomboyish clothes and Chuck Taylors. Everything I had never thought I would like about a girl was suddenly all my favorite things.

She finished putting her books away then turned to me, catching me staring at her. She bit her lip. "So do we start telling people this morning? Or just save it all for after lunch?" she asked.

If we waited until after lunch, I'd still have another chance to hold her close. More possibilities to enjoy being with Lexi without worrying about it being wrong. But also, more opportunities that I knew wouldn't be real.

Which was better? To cut it off now? Stop myself from pretending that there was a future between us? That she might possibly someday see me as something more than this homeless guy she pretended to date once?

Or was it better to get my head out of the clouds and face reality now?

"Let's wait until after lunch."

I tried to get a read on what she was thinking, but I couldn't tell. She just appeared neutral about the whole thing.

Maybe this wasn't affecting her as much as I'd hoped.

But then she said, "Yeah, I think that's best. I don't usually like answering questions this early in the day, anyway."

"Me neither." I smiled, happy that she was at least going along with this with me. "Want me to walk you to class for old time's sake?" I offered my hand to her again, my heart pounding as I prayed she wouldn't turn me down.

She only hesitated for a second, and the feel of her hand in mine made my heart calm down. It just felt right. Like I was meant to hold her hand forever.

"I'd like that," she said.

23

LEXI

IN JUST UNDER AN HOUR, my long-time dream of dating Noah Taylor would be over. I knew this day would come eventually, but now that it was here, I wanted to tell it to go away. I'd never dated anyone before—this fake-dating experience was all that I had, but I wouldn't trade it for anything in the world. In fact, if I had the option to fake-date Noah or date Harrison for real, I'd pick the fake. It had been one of the craziest, but also one of the best weeks of my life.

When I entered the lunchroom, Noah was already sitting at our table. He must have been watching for me because as soon as I looked at him, he smiled and waved. My heart squeezed in my chest. He was smiling at *me*.

I forced myself to walk at a regular pace, though all I wanted to do was run to him so that I could have just a few more seconds to bask in what it was like to be Noah's girlfriend.

He pulled the chair next to him out for me.

"Hey," he said, smiling as I took my seat.

"Hi," I said, scooting closer. We still had a few more minutes. It would be okay for me to glue myself to his side, right?

"Do you want to eat lunch before we go somewhere and pretend to break up?" he asked.

My stomach was all tied up in knots. I didn't think I would be able to eat even if I tried. "I'm not really that hungry today," I said.

"Okay, let's just go now then. I have something I wanted to talk to you about, anyway."

Noah took my hand and led me from the cafeteria. He intertwined his fingers with mine, squeezing my hand. I was going to miss this so much.

We bumped into Easton on our way.

"Hey, where are you two going?" he asked, his expression darkening when his gaze flicked down to our entwined hands.

Noah stepped closer to Easton and bent his head down to speak in a lowered voice. "We're going to the auditorium to 'break up.'" He held one hand up to make air quotes.

"Ah, gotcha." Easton gave us a knowing look. "Well, make sure you don't take too long because I want to talk to you about your plans for tonight."

"Will do." Noah nodded.

Soon he was pulling me away with him to the auditorium's back entrance that led to the stage. "They sometimes leave this unlocked." He gripped the handle and pulled. And just like he had suggested, the door opened right up. It was pretty dark when we stepped inside, just a couple of emergency lights on in the back.

"Should we just sit right here?" Noah pointed to the stairs that led down from the stage.

"Sure." I sat down on the first step.

I looked at the rows of red cushioned seats as Noah lowered himself next to me, and I couldn't help but have a sense of déjà vu.

"This kind of reminds me of our first date," I said.

Noah glanced around as he tugged on his pant legs to get better situated on the step. "Yeah, it kind of does."

It was crazy how much had happened since he'd saved me at the movie theater.

I put my hands in my lap, wondering what he needed to talk to me about.

After a brief pause, he said, "So, my mom called me this morning during second period."

"She did?" I asked.

He nodded. "Yeah, she left me a message since I couldn't answer it during class, but it turns out my dad did call her last night. She just didn't get his message until this morning. I snuck out of class early to listen to what she had to say, since I was worried something might have happened with her and Paul."

"Nothing happened, right?" I couldn't imagine always worrying the way Noah had to.

He shook his head. "No, she actually told me to come home. So, looks like I won't need to sleep in your closet again tonight."

While I was happy that he was able to go home and not live like a homeless teenager anymore, I couldn't help but feel disappointed over not having him to myself for a few more hours. Once we left this auditorium it would really be all over.

"I'm glad you get to go home."

There was a question in his eyes. "You don't sound happy."

I shrugged and looked at my hands. "No, I'm happy you can go home." I peeked up at him. "Really." I sighed. "I just— Would it be so bad if I admitted that I've kind of liked hanging out with you this week? Once we go back to the lunchroom, everything will go back to the way it was before. You'll go back to just being Easton's friend. And I'll go back to being Easton's little sister."

"And you don't like that idea?" He studied me carefully.

Just tell him you don't want to break up. Don't let him get away like you do with everything else in your life.

Tell him you want him for real.

I swallowed, trying to get up the nerve. But when I looked at him I knew it was pointless. He was Noah and I was Lexi. He was everything I wanted in a guy while I couldn't even hope to be on his radar. The only reason why he was talking to me right now was because I was his best friend's sister. If we hadn't had a mutual connection to Easton, there was no way he would've ever noticed me. He went for the gorgeous girls: the Ashlyns and Ravens of the world. He didn't go for the band geeks.

"It's probably for the best. I mean, it was already absurd tricking people into thinking we would actually work out for a whole week. I'm sure everyone will be relieved to see that the world has finally righted itself. Popular people hanging out with popular people. Nerds with nerds."

"Do you really think I'm that shallow?" he asked.

I shrugged. "Since when have you ever dated a girl like me before?"

He opened his mouth but nothing came out. And I knew it was because he couldn't think of one single time.

"It's okay, Noah. We all have our types." I always went for the unattainable guys. He always got the girl.

"Do you remember what I told you a couple of nights ago?" he finally asked.

I tried to remember a specific thing that stood out. "Can you give me a hint? We've had so many conversations this week that it's hard to know which one you're referring to."

"It was when you were accusing me of only liking mainstream girls. It seems to be a revolving theme when it comes to how you see me."

Because he'd never given me a reason to think otherwise. Yes, we'd had that moment in my bedroom last night. But now that I'd had more time to think about it, I realized that it was only because he'd been so overcome with emotion because of everything with his dad and the cold outside—he'd momentarily confused his feelings of gratefulness for actual desire for me.

We wouldn't even be having this conversation in the auditorium right now if he ever had actual feelings for me. He wouldn't have suggested we break up right after the almost-kiss. He must have realized that he was leading me on, so breaking up was the best way to put a stop to it.

I should probably be thanking him right now for saving me from my crazy notions of us actually working out in real life.

I decided to let the subject drop. This way, neither of us would be tempted to say something we'd regret later.

I sighed. "Well, do you think we should get back to the cafeteria?" Easton was ready to get his friend back.

"If you think that's best," he said.

If I thought that was best? What did he mean by that? This was our plan, wasn't it?

"Would it be so bad if I tell you that I'm having second thoughts about this whole thing?" he asked.

I looked into his eyes, not sure I'd heard him right. In them, I found a vulnerability I hadn't seen before.

"You are?" I asked, my voice coming out in a whisper.

He shook his head slightly and bit his lip. "I don't know, Lexi. This week..." He trailed off, not finishing his sentence.

I really wanted him to finish that sentence.

This week what? What was he going to say?

I waited. I *would* hear him out. I would make him say what he was going to say. I needed to know.

But Noah just stared at me. He reached over and pushed some hair behind my ear, his warm touch causing a rush of heat to flush on my face and neck. Then his hand ran along my shoulder again, just like it had last night. And I was instantly transported back to my room. The look in his eyes. The unfiltered desire. I'd been sure he was going to kiss me, until he turned around and suggested we break up today.

But could it have actually been real?

He swallowed, his Adam's apple shifting. He was nervous...

He sighed, looked down, and then looked back at me, his eyes seeming to search my soul. "There's this one last thing I want to do."

But before I could find out what that one last thing was, the door creaked open behind us and Easton poked his head inside.

Of course. My brother or my dad were always there to make sure I never even had a chance at romance.

"Hey, are you two done breaking up yet? I wanted to talk to you before Raven did."

Irritation flashed on Noah's face before he blinked it away and turned to my brother.

"Yeah, we were just finishing up," Noah called. Then he stood and offered his hand to help me up as well. It was probably the last time I'd ever be this close to Noah Taylor. "Are you ready to face everyone then?" Noah asked.

"You guys go ahead first. It'll probably be more believable if we don't walk in together."

He rubbed his thumb across the back of my knuckles. "You're probably right." Then he let go and stuffed his fingers in his pockets. "Well, it's been a fun week. I'm sure we'll still see each other around."

Why did he have to make it sound like we were saying goodbye?

Probably because it really did feel like a goodbye. Goodbye to all my hopes and dreams ever coming true where we were concerned. After today, he'd probably forget all about this week.

"I'll see you around. Good luck with your Mom today. I really am happy you get to go home."

He nodded. "Thanks, Lexi. I couldn't have made it through this week without you."

Right as he was about to leave me, he hesitated and leaned closer, pulling me in for one last hug. And I couldn't help but melt against him. I really liked Noah. I knew he wasn't perfect. I knew he had his own faults. But for the past week, he had been mine, and he'd made me feel special. I'd never had a guy pay attention to me before, and I didn't know if I'd ever have something like that again.

He spoke in a low voice beside my ear. "I hope you find what you're looking for, Lexi. You're an amazing girl and any guy would be lucky to have you." Then he kissed me gently on the cheek. Before I could respond, he disappeared out the door to join Easton in the hall, and I just stood there frozen in shock with my fingers touching the place he'd kissed me.

24

NOAH

I WALKED BACK to the lunchroom with Easton, cursing myself the whole time for being such a chicken. I should have told Lexi that I didn't want to break up. But of course, like every other good thing in my life, I was practically pushing her away.

I needed to stop sabotaging myself.

But what was done was done. And my week with Lexi was over. Now it was back to reality.

Along our way, Mercedes stopped Easton, so I went ahead to grab my lunch, and then I took a seat at my regular table, hating the fact that the chair next to me was empty and would remain empty.

"Where's Lexi?" Raven asked after looking around for her.

I ripped a piece off my roll. "We broke up."

"You broke up?" Raven's jaw dropped, and she actually did look surprised. Maybe we really had been convincing to people.

"Yep." I stuffed a piece of roll in my mouth, so I wouldn't have to say anything more. I really didn't feel like talking about it right now. It was crazy that even though our entire relationship had been fake, I felt even worse than I had when Luke and Ashlyn had started dating.

It would seem that I'd finally found a way to move on.

Raven pushed her tray closer to mine, and then moved her chair closer as well. "Why did you break up? When she first walked in here today, I was watching you. I've never seen you look at a girl like that before. It was like you were in love or something."

She'd seen that in my face?

That couldn't be good. I couldn't be in love with Lexi. She was my best friend's sister. There wasn't a chance at a future with her.

"Was she the one to break up with you?" Raven pressed when I didn't say anything.

Just then, Lexi walked into the room with her tray. I watched her as she walked past my table, and my heart blipped in my chest at the sight of her. She was scanning the room for a place to sit, and I remembered that earlier this week, she'd said something about not having a regular lunch table ever since her friend went away.

Maybe I should leave, so she could at least sit with her brother?

But then she moved in the opposite direction, toward a table full of kids that I recognized from the band and they made room for her. I sighed, relieved she wouldn't have to eat alone.

"Earth to Noah." Raven's voice interrupted my thoughts.

I shook my head. "Sorry, what did you ask again?"

She rolled her eyes. "I asked who did the breaking? You or her?"

"It was mutual."

"Certainly doesn't look that way."

And boy was she right. I could barely keep my eyes off Lexi.

My heart pounded in my ears when Lexi glanced at me over her shoulder. Was she telling everyone at her table then?

I blinked my eyes shut. *Get yourself together, Noah. This is going just the way you planned it.*

Except for the fact that I thought it was about the stupidest plan I'd ever come up with.

Easton, who had been talking to Mercedes, finally made it back to our table.

"What did I miss?" He scooted his chair up and opened a carton of milk.

"Noah and your sister broke up," Raven said.

Easton raised his eyebrows, playing his part of being surprised surprisingly well. "Oh, that's too bad."

I shook my head and laughed despite how sad I was feeling. "You know you're happy about that. You never were excited about me and your sister dating in the first place."

Easton smiled. "Yeah, it was weird. Just imagine how happy my dad will be when he finds out." He winked.

"Well, considering he already threatened to ground both of you from seeing me this week, I'd say he'll be happy to know that your sister won't be spending much time alone with me anymore." Yet another reason why it could never work out between Lexi and me. Mr. Stevens would probably lock her up if he had any idea of half the things I'd done with his daughter this week.

I stabbed a meatball with my fork. I needed to talk about something else. Anything that would keep my mind off the fact that I could never have a future with Lexi.

"So you wanted to talk to me about something?" I asked Easton.

He wiped his mouth with his arm after downing his whole carton of milk. "Yeah, I was hoping that since you won't be sitting with Lexi at the game tonight that you might want to sit with me. And then afterwards, I was thinking it might be fun to hang out in my hot tub and catch up. It seems like I've barely spent any time with you lately"

"Sure. That sounds fun."

"Great."

THE REST of the school day, people bombarded me with questions about why Lexi and I broke up. I mumbled vague responses such as how we just weren't meant to be. Or how it was too weird with Easton. But I could tell people thought my answers were weird. I'd probably have been able to think of much better reasons for our "break-up" if there had actually been problems between us. As it was, all I could think of were all the reasons why we should still be together.

I drove home, to my actual home, after school. I parked out front and just sat in my car for a while, trying to figure out how I should act. My mom had let Paul kick me out—that wasn't something I could just forgive and forget about, was it?

But she also hadn't known about where I would be staying. So I grabbed my duffel bag before I could overthink things too much and went inside.

"Noah." My mom stood from where she'd been working on her computer when she saw me come in.

"Hi, Mom."

When she held her arms out to me, I gave her a quick hug.

"It's so good to see you." Her smile was more forced than usual, and I knew she was trying to make up for the past week.

I decided not to make things too hard for her, so instead of throwing in a snide remark like I would have a year ago, I said, "It's good to see you, too. Is Brielle home?"

I looked around, anxious for my little sister to be here—she could help bounce some of this awkwardness away.

"She doesn't get off the bus for another thirty minutes. But she'll be so excited to see you. She's been asking when you're coming home all week."

I had missed my sister. She was probably the main reason why I felt comfortable coming back here. If not for her, I'd probably find a job and get a place of my own.

"Did Paul hear back about his job yesterday?" I asked, watching my mom closely for any signs of distress.

Her expression fell. "Not yet. We thought he'd know by now, but his boss wanted another day to consider the candidates. We should know by five, though."

I nodded. "That's good. I hope for everyone's sake that it's good news."

I didn't miss the flash of anxiety in my mom's eyes. "I hope so, too."

Would she leave him if he acted out again? Was she worried that if he did get the job, it wouldn't be the magical fix his temper needed to keep from hurting her?

She went into the kitchen to fill a glass with water. "Anyway, we're planning to go out to dinner tonight once we find out the news. Would you like to join us?"

I set my duffel bag on a stool at the bar and grabbed a bottle of Coke from the cupboard. I twisted the cap off. "Easton and I are going to the game tonight and then hot tubbing. But you have fun without me."

I knew it was probably bad of me to turn down her offer, especially after the past week, but I really didn't want to sit down at a table across from Paul after he'd kicked me out. We didn't need a waitress picking up on the vibes I'd be sending. I wasn't nearly as good at hiding my frustration with my stepdad as my mom was.

"Well, we'll miss you. Brielle especially." My mom's shoulders slumped, and I felt a stab of guilt pass through me.

I turned the cap back on my soda after taking a long pull on it. "How about I take Brielle sledding tomorrow?"

Mom's face brightened. "She'd love that, Noah. That's a great idea!"

I lifted my bag back onto my shoulder, ready to head up to my room and get everything put away. But just before I turned the corner, my mom stopped me.

"And Noah," she said. I turned to her, my heart splitting at the look of pain on her face. "I really am sorry that you had to sleep in your car this week. I had no idea. If I'd known, I would have brought you back home myself."

I nodded, feeling a wave of emotion about to come over me. I cleared my throat, hoping my voice wouldn't come out sounding too wobbly. "It's okay, Mom. I survived."

"I know. I just feel bad that it happened in the first place."

I adjusted the shoulder strap on my bag. "It's okay. Just promise me there won't be a reason for it to happen again, okay?"

She looked down at her hands. "Okay."

25

LEXI

"NOAH AND I BROKE UP TODAY," I spoke into the computer screen as I video-called Juliette after school.

"Already? That was only, like, five days," she said.

The best five days of my life. But it was all over now. Whatever Noah and I had had together ended the moment Easton came to take him away from me. It was fate making the world balanced again—in a way. Easton had always been there. Always the one Noah had chosen.

"At least I got to kiss him once."

"You kissed Noah? How did I not know about this?" Juliette pretty much shouted at me through the screen.

I'd been so busy with Noah the past twenty-four hours that I hadn't even thought to tell my best friend about it. "Sorry, it all happened so fast."

She scowled, like she wasn't going to accept my apology, but then she grinned. "I guess I can forgive you, but only if you tell me every little detail."

"*Every* detail?" My cheeks heated further as memories of

Noah pressing himself against me under the bleachers came to my mind.

"Yes, Lexi. It isn't fair that I'm the one who goes to Paris, and you're the one who gets this big adventure."

I rolled my eyes. "You are so overdramatic sometimes. I saw those photos you posted on Instagram this week. You can't tell me that you're not having fun when I can see the hot guy you've been hanging out with."

She laughed. "Um, don't believe everything you see on the Internet these days." When she saw my confused look, she continued, "That was just Evan. He was helping me make someone jealous."

"Who are you trying to make jealous?" I asked. Juliette was always up to something, it seemed.

She waved her hand. "No one important. Anyway, you still need to give me details of your epic kiss with Mr. Hottie McHot Hot, Noah Taylor."

I laughed at her use of our old nickname for Noah. "It was good."

"Good?" She shook her blondish-gray hair on the screen. "You cannot just tell me that you kissed Noah and say it was good. This was your first kiss. Were you nervous?"

Nervous would be an understatement. "Yeah, I was pretty nervous. But, I don't know, Noah somehow made it okay. At least it was way less awkward than I imagined it would be." Yes, even in my past daydreams of kissing Noah, I still failed at the kissing thing. Apparently, my subconscious really didn't think much about our chances, either.

"So, was it just like a peck or a full-on make-out?"

I laughed. Juliette was going to get all the details out of me that she could. "Probably somewhere in the middle."

Her eyes went wide, and her jaw dropped. "You practically made out with him! This is huge, Lexi!"

I smiled, unable to keep the goofy grin off my face. It *was* kind of surreal. "And you want to know one of the best parts?"

"Of course."

"He didn't seem like he wanted to end it. He actually told me that I'm a natural." I bit my lip to keep the excitement from bursting out of me.

"Of course you are, Lexi. You're pretty much good at everything you try. School, band, skateboarding...dating your brother's best friend."

That sobered me right up. "Well, we both know that last one can't be true. Because if I was an expert at that, he wouldn't have broken up with me so soon."

"Or maybe he just didn't want to risk the wrath of protective Mr. Stevens."

"Maybe." Or maybe it was just that our relationship had served its purpose and it was time for me to come back to reality and move on.

"So what are you guys doing from now on? Are you going to try to talk to Harrison again?"

I gave her a small shake of my head. "I don't think so."

"I'm sure you could get any guy you want now after dating Noah. If nothing else, guys can't be as scared of your dad after seeing that bad-boy Noah Taylor was able to date you."

I sighed. "I doubt that. My dad freaked out when he saw Noah and me alone in the basement last night."

I told her all about that conversation.

"So maybe it really is your dad's fault that Noah got scared off."

I thought about it. It was possible. I wouldn't put it past him.

"Did he say anything about his future dating plans?" Juliette asked.

I shook my head. "No. It seemed like he was going to say

something to me before we had to finish our break-up, but Easton came in and ended that."

"Easton is interesting." She said it like she was talking about something else. I wanted to ask her what it was, because after my conversation with Easton last night about Juliette coming back, I couldn't help but wonder if something had happened between them that I didn't know about.

But before I could ask, she said, "So since we know you're not going to try to go after Harrison, and it doesn't look like Noah had another conquest in mind, how are you going to get him back?"

"Get him back? I don't think I ever really had him."

"From what you've told me, it kind of sounds like you did."

I let that thought sink in. Did I have Noah? Was that even possible? The memory of the way he looked at me before we departed. That hug. The gentle kiss on the cheek. Maybe I had him more than I thought.

"I can tell from the look on your face that it might be a possibility," Juliette interrupted my musings. "So, I'm going to share my expertise on the subject. You said when you started this thing that Noah told you guys wanted what they can't have. I think you should put that to the test. Make it so Noah can't help but notice you. Make him step up and be a man."

The thought of doing that gave me hives. "I'm not like you, Juliette. I don't do the whole make-him-jealous kind of thing. I could never pull off something like that."

"We may be different, but you have your own set of qualities that I could never even dream of having. Just use those. There's a basketball game tonight, right?"

"Yes..." I said slowly, clueless to what she might be getting at.

"Okay, so watch for Noah while you're there. I know you can't help the band shirt, but you can wear your favorite jeans. Maybe even put on some mascara. I don't know, just make sure he can't help but notice you." She got a devilish grin on her face. "And, you might think this is totally evil of me to suggest, but just talk to other guys. If I know Noah like I think I do, that one thing alone will make him want to mark his territory."

"Eww, not the image I need in my mind right now."

"I don't mean get him to pee on the fire hydrant." Juliette laughed. "You just watch, Lexi. Do those things that I've said, and you will have Noah Taylor not only begging you to be his girl-friend, but to be his everything. I think you have set this up perfectly for you that you may possibly get your second kiss this week."

Butterflies erupted in my stomach at her last words. "Okay, I'll do my best."

She beamed at me all the way from Paris. "Make sure to keep me updated on what happens tonight."

"I will."

"Great. I'll see you in a week!"

I nodded. "*Au revoir.*"

She blew me a kiss through the phone. "*A bientôt.*"

I WENT through every combination of jeans and boots I had after getting off the phone with Juliette. I still wasn't convinced that her plan would even work, but I figured it was worth a shot. It wasn't like I had anything to lose.

After pulling on a pair of black skinny jeans and my cute boots with the fringe, I went into my bathroom to see what I had to work with as far as cosmetics. I found an old tube of mascara in the back of my drawer, ran it through my lashes a few times—only having to clean up with makeup remover once—and then I added some brown eyeshadow and lip gloss, and called it good. I was wearing more makeup than I had worn in months. I hoped it wouldn't look like I was trying too hard.

I pulled my hair down from the ponytail it had been in all day and blow-dried it to get the kinks out. I didn't own a curling iron, so the straight look would just have to do.

Once I was sufficiently dolled up, to my low expectations anyway, I grabbed my trumpet and met Easton downstairs to head to the game.

He stared at me for a minute. "You look different."

I looked around awkwardly. "Yep."

And that was all we said on the subject of my altered appearance. I hoped Easton wouldn't realize that I was trying to get his best friend back.

When I got to the gym, the pep band was already mostly set up. I took my seat on the end—the place I had sat earlier this week next to Harrison—and got myself ready to play the part of a super confident girl who had just broken up with her hot boyfriend.

"Will Noah be joining us again?" Harrison asked as I opened my trumpet case.

He apparently hadn't noticed our quiet breaking apart during lunch time. There had been quite a few questions for me about it through the rest of the day, but mostly from sophomores and people I'd usually talked to at school.

I swallowed. "No, he won't be. We broke up."

Harrison's blonde eyebrows arched. "Really? That's surprising."

I nodded. "Yeah, it just wasn't meant to be, I guess."

"Sorry to hear that. It looks like you two got along really great," Harrison said.

And we had. Things had been amazing. And before I could prepare myself for it, a wave of emotion chose right then to hit me. I hadn't cried in years, but now, sitting in the crowded gym, my eyes suddenly decided it was time to finally let out the emotions I'd always liked to keep bottled up.

I shook my head to try to push the urge away.

But then I saw him. Noah.

He was standing at the bottom of the stairs, just like he had been at the last game, searching the crowd. But he wasn't looking for me like he had been last time. He did a little head nod after a second, and then walked over to where Easton was waving at him —right on the row in front of the cheerleaders.

His usual spot. It was the final sign that the world had officially gone back to normal.

"That's got to be rough, seeing him right after your break-up," Harrison said quietly.

I nodded and wiped at my eyes. "Yeah."

"I'm lucky my ex goes to another school," Harrison said.

I turned my gaze away from Noah to peer at Harrison. "Your *ex*-girlfriend? Did you just break up, too?"

He let out a long breath. "We broke up Wednesday night."

My lips pulled down into a frown. "I'm sorry to hear that. She seemed like she was a really nice girl."

Okay, so it was kind of a lie. I had hated her when I'd seen her on Friday. But I was over him now, so I didn't really need to let him know that I'd been jealous.

"I should've known it was gonna happen. Turns out her ex-boyfriend found out that she had moved on and he didn't like it. So he asked her to take him back, and she did."

"Let me guess, he was popular and hot."

Harrison nodded. "Yup. Student Body President."

In this, Harrison and I were very similar. We were the band geeks who would always be tossed aside when something better came along.

I gave him a sympathetic look. "For what it's worth, it's her loss, really."

He gave me a sad smile. "I could say the same for you." He put his arm around me and gave me a brief squeeze before letting his arm drop. And I couldn't help but think about how ironic everything was. I had done so many crazy things this week that could qualify me as a good candidate for a mental institution—and I did them all just so that Harrison would talk to me like this and put his arm around me. But now that he had done it, I didn't even care. Because I only cared about Noah.

I was so pathetic.

I looked down at where Noah was sitting and noticed him watching me. But instead of the almost-sad gaze that he'd given me during lunch when I sat at the other table, his face contorted into a grimace. I looked away.

So maybe he hated me now.

Perfect.

26

NOAH

IT TOOK ALL my willpower not to go up to that Harrison kid and tell him to get his hands off my girlfriend. I was just about to stand up and go give him a piece of my mind when reality brought me back: she wasn't my girlfriend, she never really had been. So I needed to be okay with her talking to other guys. That was our plan after all. And, at least where she was concerned, it had worked. So, it was time for me to move on as well.

I swiveled forward to watch what was happening on the floor. The cheerleaders were doing one of their routines. Raven was straight in front of me, smiling as she waved her pompoms and chanted with the rest of the cheer squad in their short skirts that I used to drool over.

And Easton was sitting next to me with his new girl Mercedes by his side. Everything was back to normal. It was almost as if this last week hadn't even happened.

The announcer's voice came through the loudspeakers, introducing tonight's game and the players. Raven took a few steps closer to me as the guy read through the visiting team's roster.

"So now that you're broken up with Lexi, do you want to

come to my house tonight? I was thinking about getting the old gang together and watching a movie or something." I couldn't miss the way her dark eyes ran along my body before lingering on my mouth. She was hoping for a rebound make-out.

And that was exactly what the old Noah would've wanted in a situation like this. Break up with a girl or get into a fight with his stepdad, and then go numb himself with another girl's lips.

But I didn't want to fall back into my old habits. So I said, "Thanks for the offer, Raven. But I'm actually going to Easton's house tonight. Maybe some other time."

Her expression fell, but she soon replaced it with a smile. "Okay, maybe next time."

I nodded. "Sure."

———

"HAVE YOU SEEN EASTON?" a familiar voice asked after the game was over.

I turned to find Lexi standing right behind me with her trumpet case.

"No, I think he already left to take Mercedes home."

"Oh, that's weird." Her expression fell. "I thought he was going to give me a ride home after the game." She adjusted her glasses on her face, a habit I had noticed her doing a lot when she was nervous about something.

"I can give you a ride home if you want."

She looked around as if to check the perimeter for anyone who might be watching or listening to us. I understood her agitation, since we probably did have a lot of people watching us today.

"Don't you think that's against the rules?" she whispered.

I shrugged. "I don't think there's a manual for this kind of thing. I think it's fine—just adds more interest to the Noah and Lexi show," I said, hoping it came across lightly.

She nodded. "Okay yeah, that would be great. I think my dad is out on a date or something."

I raised my eyebrows. "Your dad went on a date?" I'd never heard of him going on a date since I'd known him.

Lexi shrugged. "Yeah, I know. It was weird when I got his text a few minutes ago, telling me not to wait up for him."

Interesting. Maybe if her dad was busy dating someone else, he wouldn't have time to be so paranoid about his own children. That could be a good thing.

I shook the thought out of my head, though. Lexi and I were done. Over with. I was just giving her a ride home.

I pulled my keys out of my jacket pocket. "Ready to head out?"

"Yeah." She nodded.

I almost held my hand out to her, the habit that I'd formed over the last week, but I shoved it back in my pocket before she could notice—hopefully, she hadn't noticed the impulse, anyway.

I was going to have to get used to that.

I led her out of the gym, and I couldn't help but notice that we did have quite a few people looking at us as we walked past. I was tempted to tell them to mind their own business and that I was just giving her a ride home. But I didn't. I would let them think whatever they wanted. Whatever happened between me and Lexi was now just between me and Lexi. The public didn't need to be a part of this anymore.

"I noticed you and Harrison getting close during the game. Does that mean that our plan ended up working out after all?"

I couldn't get that image of his arm around her shoulder out of my head, no matter how hard I had tried throughout the game. And each time I had looked over my shoulder to check on them, an image of my fist connecting with Harrison's pretty-boy face came to mind.

I needed to stop thinking these violent thoughts.

Lexi buckled her seatbelt and looked at me with a smile that I didn't understand. "Yeah, actually, Harrison was asking me out."

"You're going on a date?" My voice came out too loud for my small car, and it felt like she had just kicked me in the stomach. Lexi wasn't supposed to go on dates with other guys.

Her smile broadened. "I'm kidding, Noah. He was just comforting me over our break-up."

I released my grip on the steering wheel, feeling more relief than I should have. "Oh, that's good."

I turned on my car and pulled out of the parking lot a moment later.

"What about you and Raven?" Lexi glanced at me with an expression that I didn't understand. Was it a curious one? Or jealousy?

"What *about* Raven?" I said it like I didn't understand what she was getting at. Lexi had teased me, I might as well do the same.

"She just seemed like her old self again. I'm guessing she isn't handing out too many 'I'm sorry you broke up' condolences."

I shrugged as I turned the corner onto the street that led to her house. "She invited me to watch a movie at her house tonight."

"Oh." That was all she said.

I smiled. She *was* jealous.

When I didn't say anything, she asked, "And are you going?"

She was really cute when she was jealous.

But I had had my fun. We were even now. "Easton invited me over to hot tub tonight."

Her shoulders sagged like she was relieved. "That's good."

"Yep. So, me giving you a ride home actually isn't that far out of my way."

We pulled up to her house a few minutes later, and I followed her inside.

"Well," she said, turning to me, and I could tell she felt awkward about being alone with me in the house. "I guess I'll see you later. I'm sure Easton will be back in a few minutes."

"You could join us in the hot tub if you wanted?" I offered before I could think better of it.

She scratched the back of her neck like she was actually considering it, making my heart pound in my chest. But then she said, "No, that's okay. I think Easton wanted some guy time tonight. I would just be in the way."

My heart, which had swelled in my chest, shrunk again. "Well, you have a good night. I'll just wait for Easton then."

She nodded. "Yep." And she went down the hall to her room.

27

LEXI

I SHUT the door to my bedroom and walked straight into the bathroom to look at myself in the mirror. What was I doing? Noah had just invited me to go in the hot tub with him and Easton. Why was I turning him down?

I stared at my reflection in the mirror. I was so stupid. Why couldn't I just follow through with Juliette's plan? Make him want what he couldn't have.

I shook my head. He wouldn't want this. I looked ridiculous. I already had smudges of mascara under my eyes, probably from those stupid tears that had wanted to escape when I'd seen Noah at the game. I probably looked like a mess the entire time.

I wiped angrily at the smudges then went back into my bedroom. I opened my dresser drawers and tore through them until I found the one swimsuit I owned—a plain blue one-piece. Definitely not eye-catching at all.

I sighed and dropped it back into the drawer.

Who was I kidding? I was not the kind of girl that could get a guy with her looks. That wasn't something that had ever even remotely worked for me in the past.

Plus, going into the hot tub with Noah and Easton would be totally obvious—even if Noah had invited me. I could just imagine how awkward it would be. Me sitting there, trying to look cool like I belonged in their world while surreptitiously taking sneak peeks at Noah and his perfectly sculpted chest.

No, I would not follow them into the hot tub. I refused to look desperate. Plus, it was freezing outside. Sure the hot tub was hot, but I had to actually make it there first. And it was, like, five degrees outside.

I would just hang out inside where it was warm. Maybe I could bake something in the kitchen. There was the perfect window that could give me a view of Noah from here.

Not that I was going to be creepy—that was so me three years ago. I did have some pride.

Noah did like to eat... Hmm. Maybe I could find my way into his heart through his stomach. That usually worked in the girly movies, right?

But first I needed to get out of this ridiculous band polo. I went to my closet next. When I opened the door, I was greeted with Noah's gray shirt on my closet floor. He must have left it there this morning. Would it be so bad if I kept it as a souvenir if this plan of mine didn't work out?

I shook that thought away. This would work. It had to.

But first, I needed something to wear.

I fingered my way through the clothes hanging inside. I had to have at least one thing that said, *hey, remember me?* I pulled outfit after outfit off the rack, holding them against myself and looking in the mirror before ultimately tossing them to the floor. I stopped when I found something that might work. It was a white and teal striped knee-length dress that I had worn to one of the few parties I'd let Juliette drag me to last summer. Noah had been there, and I had noticed him take a second glance when he'd seen me. I hadn't really thought anything of it at the time since he had just broken up with Ashlyn. But maybe he had liked the dress. It was worth a shot, anyway.

Once I was ready and I had touched up my makeup once again, I went downstairs, feeling a fluttering of nervousness in my chest.

When I walked into the kitchen it was empty. But a quick peek out the window above the sink showed me that Easton and Noah were already in the hot tub. And my memory did not do his physique the justice that it deserved. He was a *very* nice specimen of a man, if I didn't say so myself. Now if only I had a reason to just stand here and stare without looking too obvious.

That's right, baking. I pulled out a cake mix from the cupboard, deciding I would make some chocolate cupcakes with the peanut butter frosting that I loved.

I grabbed what I needed from the cupboard and then got to work mixing the batter together.

As I stood at the counter stirring, my gaze wandered out the window again. What were they talking about? Could they possibly be talking about me?

I shook my head. Of course not. Noah wouldn't talk to Easton about me.

But when I checked again, I was surprised to find Noah looking at the window. Heat prickled across my skin as I held his stare. He was just talking to Easton and staring at me. Had the dress actually worked?

I was pouring batter into the cupcake liners when the sliding door opened and Noah walked in.

"It's cold out there," he said, shivering as he grabbed a towel off the chair and started drying off his arms and chest, and then his hair. I just stood there in a daze, with my mouth hanging open until he looked back at me, snapping me back to reality.

"A-are you done already?" I asked.

"Yeah, Easton's just covering it up. We were thinking about making ourselves a snack."

"I'll have cupcakes ready in about twenty minutes if you want one," I offered, concentrating hard to keep my tone from sounding too eager. I realized too late that I had been pouring the batter into the cupcake paper for too long and it had spilled over the side.

Noah stepped closer, his chest rubbing across my shoulder. "A little distracted?" He winked.

My whole body flushed with heat. Noah had just winked at me. And his bare chest had just brushed against my shoulder. I tried to even my breathing. "Um...just a little."

He leaned over and whispered in my ear. "I'll try not to be so distracting."

Chills ran down my spine. He was definitely flirting with me.

With shaky hands, I grabbed a spoon from the drawer and tried to scoop the excess batter off the side of the pan and into a new cupcake paper. Noah just watched me. I tried to come up with some sort of witty response to his flirtatious whisperings, but my brain apparently had stopped working with the overload.

He took a seat on the stool next to me. "So, what kind of cupcakes are you making?"

I focused on what I was doing, not allowing myself to take a look at him even though I really wanted to. "Chocolate cupcakes with peanut butter frosting."

"My favorite?" he asked.

I tucked a lock of hair behind my ear. "Yeah." I guess they were his favorite, too.

The sliding door opened again, and Easton stepped inside with his towel wrapped around his shoulders.

"Remind me not to try that until it's at least twenty degrees outside."

Noah laughed. "Will do."

"Do you want a sandwich or something?" Easton asked, going to the fridge.

"Sure, I could eat." Noah stood and grabbed the sandwich makings that Easton handed to him.

I tried not to watch Noah too much as he made his food. But I caught myself sneaking glances at him.

And when he talked about how he wished he knew how to make a sandwich the same as the one he'd had earlier this week, I couldn't help but remember last night.

They finished their food quicker than I'd wanted, and Easton took their plates to the sink. "I think I'll go take a shower real quick before we start our gaming again," he said to Noah.

Noah leaned over the counter next to me, his shoulder blade standing out. He really needed to go and put a shirt on. He was making me so uncomfortable...in a good way. Making me want to see if his muscles felt as good as they looked.

"Yeah, go ahead. Mind if I wash the chlorine off in the shower up here?" he asked.

His gaze slid to mine, and it was like he was trying to tell me about how this wouldn't be the first shower he'd taken at our house this week.

"Go ahead," Easton said as he walked out of the room. "There should be clean towels in the closet. I'm sure Lexi could help you."

"I'm sure she could," Noah said under his breath. Then he looked back to me. "Or I could just take one in your bathroom, right?" He wiggled his eyebrows at me suggestively.

I shook my head and couldn't keep the blush from rising on my cheeks. "You are going to get us caught if you keep that up," I whispered in a hushed tone.

He laughed. "You know what? After this afternoon, I kind of don't care."

What did he mean by that?

As if he could read my thoughts, he leaned closer, his hot breath on my cheek. "I think we broke up too soon."

And then before I could say anything, he grabbed his towel off the back of the chair he'd set it on earlier, threw it over his shoulder, and walked out of the room.

I was in so much trouble.

But I was really hoping it would be good trouble this time.

28

NOAH

I LOCKED MYSELF IN THE STEVENS' bathroom before I could do anything more. I didn't know what was coming over me. Maybe it was the fact that I had already gone through the last few hours without Lexi by my side and knew what it was like and didn't want that anymore. But if I wasn't careful, Easton was going to find out that I wanted his sister.

Wanted.

I showered off the chlorine and changed as quickly as I could. If I hurried, I might be able to get back to Lexi before Easton was ready to play games.

"Done already?" Lexi asked. "I'm pretty sure that's the fastest shower I've ever seen you take."

I raised my eyebrows.

"Not *watched* you take, but *noticed* you take." she waved her hand. "You know what I mean."

I did know what she meant, but it was fun seeing her get so flustered. She went back to mixing her frosting with the beaters. It was too loud to talk, so I took the opportunity to just stare unabashedly at her. She was gorgeous. I wanted to run my fingers through her hair again—it looked so long and soft and silky.

And she looked great in that dress she was wearing. She had always looked good in teal; it made her skin glow.

She glanced at me as she finished beating the frosting, and it seemed like we were having some kind of unspoken conversation. Had she missed me as much as I had missed her over the last ten hours?

"You want to test it? Make sure it's sweet enough?" Lexi gestured to the bowl of creamy brown frosting.

"Sure." I dipped my finger in and sucked the frosting off. It was delicious.

"Was it good?"

I nodded. "Very good."

She dipped her finger in the bowl as well and licked off the frosting, the gesture more seductive than it probably should have been.

"It *is* good," she said. "I could probably eat an entire bowl of this."

I noticed she had a little smidge of frosting on the corner of her lips.

"You got a little something right there." I pointed to the spot.

She looked down for a second before looking back at me through her long lashes. "Maybe you should get it for me."

My heart jolted to a stop. Was she flirting with me? Who was this girl?

But I was not about to pass up the opportunity. So I rubbed my thumb across her lip and slowly licked the excess frosting off it.

She watched me in a dazed sort of way, and I couldn't help but wonder if she was feeling the same desire I felt crashing over me.

We may have broken up today, but I had a feeling this wasn't over.

29

LEXI

EASTON WALKED BACK into the room just after Noah had finished removing the frosting from my lips. What was coming over us? We were *not* being careful. Was the fact that we were no longer fake-dating somehow making it possible for us to finally be more open with our feelings?

Whatever it was, I didn't know if I could handle being alone with Noah anymore. He was *so* good-looking. *So* amazing. And I kind of wanted to throw myself at his feet like all the other girls I'd made fun of in the past. This was ridiculous.

"You ready?" Easton asked from where he was standing about three steps down.

"Sure," Noah said. "I'll be right down."

When Noah left and I was alone in the kitchen, I somehow pulled myself together again. I put the last batch of cupcakes in the oven and let the others cool on the counter. Then I stored the frosting in the fridge.

I looked around at the messy kitchen. I could clean it all up right now...or I could go downstairs. The cupcakes still had twenty-two minutes left. I tapped my fingers on the counter, internally debating with myself. I wanted to be with Noah. But would it look too obvious if I went downstairs?

But there was an even better question than that. *Should* I care if it looked obvious anymore? I had liked Noah for six stinking years, and in those years, I'd never really done anything about it. And where had that gotten me? Nowhere. I had simply wanted something and always wondered if I was going to ever have a chance at it.

I shook my head. This had to stop. I needed to listen to Juliette for once. Seize the day. And if I came out of this looking like a huge fool, at least I'd know that I tried instead of always wondering *what if*.

I'd always put Noah on a pedestal because he was older than me and more popular. But I needed to stop that too. I was a great catch. I might not be the same as all the girls he'd dated in the past, but I had my own set of qualities going for me. I was smart and spunky. And I may not look exactly like a supermodel, but I wasn't ugly either. I had caught Noah checking me out enough times this week to know that he was attracted to me.

I needed to stop making excuses to push my feelings for him away.

So I folded up my apron, stuck it in the drawer, and went downstairs. Easton was sitting in a gaming chair in the middle of the floor while Noah was sprawled out on the couch, watching him play.

When Noah saw me, he quickly sat up. "You joining us?" he asked. And I couldn't help but detect a slight hint of hopefulness in his tone.

I shrugged, hoping to come off as nonchalant. "I'm just waiting for the cupcakes. Figured I'd come and see what all the hullabaloo is about this game of yours."

Noah moved to the end of the sectional and patted the spot beside him quietly.

I hesitated for just a moment before taking the seat beside him.

We sat in silence as Easton played the video game. And I was all too aware of Noah. He was only inches away. I watched his chest rise and fall with his steady breathing. He seemed as calm as could be while I felt like I had hundreds of bouncy balls flying around in my chest.

He sighed loudly, and I peeked at him through the corner of my eye. And it was then that I noticed his hand resting on his knee. It was just sitting there, like he was waiting for me to grab it.

I'd held his hand so many times this week, but if it happened again, it would be different. This time it would actually mean something.

So I set my hand on my leg, hoping he'd see the signal and take it easy on my heart. My pulse started racing when his hand slowly slid off his leg and onto the space between us. I held my breath. If he held my hand now, it was over. I'd be his.

It took all my courage to let my hand slide off my leg to the space next to his. And in just a couple of seconds, my whole world tilted on its side because Noah Taylor ran his pinky slowly along mine. It felt amazing. Then, he gently took my hand in his.

I couldn't keep the huge smile from creeping up my lips. Noah Taylor was holding my hand. And for the first time, it was real.

He shifted in his seat until our arms were pressed against each other. Warmth radiated from everywhere we touched, and that blissful feeling that I was having more frequently around Noah swept over me.

"Regis is supposed to be hidden in that cavern," Easton said, breaking me out of my foggy daze. "Do you want a turn?" His thumbs were still going crazy all over the buttons, so he didn't take the time to look back at us—which I was thankful for.

Noah cleared his throat. "No, I'm good."

Then in a quieter voice that only I could hear, he said, "Real good."

We watched Easton play for a little longer, and I let myself settle more firmly against his side, loving being so close to him—and actually being awake this time. Before long, Noah placed my hand onto his leg so he could draw slow circles along the back. My nerve endings shot to life. I just loved the way he was touching me. It was so gentle, and slow, and it made me feel cherished.

"I like that," I whispered, daring to look at him again.

His big brown eyes were soft when I met his gaze, and he lifted my hand slowly to his lips, gently kissing the back of my hand. "I like this too." His voice was even more gravelly than usual.

I almost swooned—finally understood why all those girls in the old-fashioned movies fainted around men. It was a real possibility for me if Noah kept treating me like I was some sort of treasure.

Then, as if that wasn't enough, he leaned closer and kissed me on the forehead and then on the cheek. My heart beat like crazy when he let his head rest against mine. We were being so dangerous right now. My brother was just sitting right there in front of us. But for the life of me, I couldn't pull myself away. I was officially addicted to Noah.

We just sat there for the next few minutes—so close, but ready to pull apart the instant Easton looked back. Too soon the timer went off on my phone, signaling that I needed to take the cupcakes out of the oven.

I groaned, and the sound seemed to bring Easton out of his gaming trance.

"What's that for?" he asked.

I sat up straighter, pulling myself away from Noah just before he could see us. It took a moment for me to find my voice. "It's the timer for the cupcakes. They're done."

I didn't want to get up. Not when the last twenty minutes had been so perfect. But I forced myself to stand, and when I did, I immediately felt cold without Noah right beside me.

"Do you want any help?" Noah asked when I was at the base of the staircase.

I darted my gaze to Easton. He was back in his game, so I said, "That would be nice." And then I turned around and headed up the stairs, listening to the sound of Noah coming up right behind me.

I pulled the cupcakes out of the oven and set them on the stove to cool.

"Did you want to help me frost these ones?" I gestured to the cupcakes that had already cooled.

He leaned against the counter with a half-smile on his lips. "I think I'll just watch."

I shook my head and smiled. "You didn't really want to help, did you?"

He chuckled. "No, I just wanted to be with you."

My smile grew bigger at his words. *He just wanted to be with me.* I pinched myself to make sure I wasn't just dreaming.

Nope, this was really happening right now.

I pulled the frosting out of the fridge and grabbed a small spatula. As I worked at the counter, Noah stepped behind me— the warmth of his body against my back made it really hard to concentrate on my work. I slowly spread the frosting on the cupcake with a shaky hand. Noah pressed his lips to the top of my head, taking my shoulders in his hands and massaging them.

"I really like you, Lexi," he whispered. "Even though I shouldn't."

He brushed the hair off my neck and kissed me there, too. Chills raced down my spine. I tried to draw in a decent breath, but his closeness and the way I was feeling was making it impossible.

"Tell me you want me, too?" His voice was low and husky. He kissed the skin near the neckline of my dress.

I released a shaky breath. "I do," I whispered as his hands ran down my shoulders, along my arms, and up again, and it felt so amazing.

I couldn't concentrate on frosting the cupcakes anymore. I set the spatula back in the frosting bowl and the half-frosted cupcake on the counter. "You're making it really hard to work, you know." I peeked over my shoulder at him.

"And you're making it really hard for me to get you out of my head," he whispered in my ear before spinning me around to face him. He stepped closer, trapping me between the counter and his strong body. My heart, which was already racing, catapulted to new speeds that I was sure would put me at risk for a heart attack.

And before I could register what was happening, he tilted his face down and pressed his lips to mine. His warm lips moved slowly as he kissed me tentatively—giving me a chance to move away. But I didn't. I leaned closer, sliding my hands up his neck until they could tangle in his hair—the hair I'd been dying to touch all week. It was even softer than I'd imagined.

"I think I need to warn you now about how much I love to have my hair played with," he whispered against my lips, his hot breath making me tingle all over.

"Y-you do?" I couldn't breathe. Couldn't concentrate on anything but how much I wanted his lips back on mine.

"Yeah," he said before closing the distance between our mouths once again. Electricity sparked in my veins as he coaxed my lips to move with his. He kissed me slowly, passionately, and all I could think about was how he'd said that he liked me. I'd waited years for him to notice me the way a guy notices a girl, but I never thought it was really possible. So I moved on. Then I found someone else to crush on...but I should have known my feelings for Noah would never really go away.

I had liked Noah from almost the moment we'd met.

"If someone told you a week ago that we'd be doing this, would you have believed them?" he asked, briefly breaking the lock he had on my lips.

"Definitely not." I sighed. Wished for, yes. But actually happen? Never in a million years.

And then he was kissing me again. His soft lips sent shivers through my nerves, shivers that made my whole body tremble in a way it never had before. When he'd kissed me yesterday, it had been because of our arrangement. But this wasn't an agreed-upon kiss. He was kissing me because he wanted to.

And the thought that Noah Taylor wanted to kiss me, when he could be kissing any other girl at school, made my muscles go weak. He really did like me, right? It couldn't just be a physical thing, could it? He would have taken Raven up on her obvious offers if this was just to fill some sort of physical need, wouldn't he?

"Do you think it's possible to know someone for years but never really see them?" he asked, his voice low.

I swallowed. "I think so."

His hands rubbed circles along my spine, raising goosebumps everywhere. He leaned his forehead against mine. "But..." He sighed. "Getting mixed up with me is probably the last thing you want."

He was worried I didn't want to get mixed up with him? "It's not." I looked straight into his eyes, so he'd know I meant what I was saying.

"But what about your dad?"

"What about him?" My dad didn't get to control everything in my life. He didn't get to control my heart. I'd had a hard-enough time controlling it over the past couple of years when I tried to force it away from Noah.

But my heart wanted what it wanted. It wanted Noah.

"I don't have the perfect history, Lexi." He spoke in a husky voice. "I have a past."

I curled a strand of his shaggy hair around my finger. "It doesn't matter."

It was almost as if those words released a barrier between us, because when he kissed me again, it was different somehow. It changed and deepened and made all my thoughts disappear.

His hands traveled down my sides until he gripped my waist in his hands, pulling me even closer to him. We were already so close, but I loved how he didn't seem to want any space between us because I didn't want any space, either.

"Hey Noah, your phone keeps vibrating, you might want to get it." Easton's voice drifted up the stairs.

Noah pulled back from me and yelled back to Easton, "I'll get it in a minute." Then he turned to me with a smile and spoke in a quieter voice. "I'm a little busy right now."

I could have died from the suggestive look on his face. But he didn't give me a chance to do anything because a second later, he was kissing me again. This time his lips were rougher, hungrier, and I worried that I wouldn't be able to keep up with him.

I pulled back. "Wait, don't you need to get your phone?" I asked, needing a moment to catch my breath.

He shook his head. "My mom's probably just calling to make sure I'm not sleeping in my car again. I'll get it when I'm done with you."

He tightened his grip on my waist once more, and before I knew it, I was sitting on the end of the counter amidst all my baking mess. I gasped. "Noah, what are you...?" I let my question hang in the air, looking down so he'd know I was talking about suddenly being on the counter.

His gaze softened. "Just think of it as one of your step stools."

30

NOAH

WHAT WAS I DOING? I must have been crazy to kiss Lexi in the middle of her kitchen, right where her dad or Easton could have walked in on us. But my brain seemed to have left me the moment my lips had touched Lexi's again, because all I could think about was how I wanted to kiss her forever and never stop.

This was crazy. I had never even considered kissing my best friend's sister a week ago, but now that was all I wanted to do with my time. I wanted to hold her close and spend every waking moment with her, talk to her, laugh with her, get to know her better, and yes, kiss her. Especially kissing her.

But she was two years younger than me. And I knew she wasn't experienced with guys...at all. But that kind of made the pull I had for her even stronger. She was sweet and innocent, untainted from the hard realities of the world. And I wanted some of her sweetness to rub off on me. Having Lexi in my life was making things so much more manageable.

But I had no idea how I was going to break the news to her brother that I was falling for his little sister. What would Easton say? Would he even let me finish my sentence before he punched me in the face and told me to keep my hands off his sister?

And what about Mr. Stevens?

I pushed the thoughts away. I didn't want to think about them right now. I could figure that all out later. For now, I would just enjoy this moment and let Lexi's sweet lips continue to cast the calming spell over my mind.

I lost all sense of time and space, but when I felt her legs wrap around my waist, I knew it was time for me to say goodnight.

"I should probably go home." I pulled away from her slightly, letting my forehead rest against hers as I tried to catch my breath. I couldn't trust myself to keep her sweet and innocent if she was going to do things like that. My brain was still too hardwired as a hormonal guy.

"Already?" she asked, having no idea what she was doing to me.

I nodded. "I don't want to push things too far."

"You don't have to worry about that with me, Noah," she whispered.

"I know I don't have to worry about you...but you should probably be worried about me." I found her hand and rubbed my finger across her purity ring. "I know my limits, and you don't want me trying to find reasons to sneak into your bedroom again tonight."

Her eyes went wide like she couldn't imagine I would be tempted to do something like that with her. It was kind of sweet how she was.

"You wouldn't do that."

I gave her a look over, letting my eyes slowly run up and down her body, taking in just how good she looked in her dress tonight. "You don't want to take your chances on me, Lexi. When I want something badly enough, I find ways to get it."

Now she looked scared. Which was good. She was playing in a new ballpark now. She'd officially entered the world of guys, and the one she was with now was still trying to learn how to be a good one.

But when she continued to look at me with anxiety in those big hazel eyes of hers, I knew I needed to say something more.

I drew in a deep breath. "I don't mean to scare you too much, but I just want you to understand how certain things affect me."

"And kissing you like that is bad?"

I shook my head and gave her a half-smile. "Kissing me like that is *very* good. But wrapping your legs around me while we're kissing like *that*... Well, let's just say that I only have so much self-control."

She gulped. "I'll try to remember."

"Walk me to the door?" I asked.

"Sure." She slid off the counter.

We took a few steps before she stopped. "Oh, wait. I found your shirt in my closet earlier. Let me grab it for you real quick."

31

LEXI

MY LEGS WOBBLED the whole way back to my room. I still couldn't believe what Noah had said—that I had the ability to tempt him to cross those lines. It was mind-boggling. But I was glad he'd told me, so I'd know how to be more careful. I had no idea what I was doing, and I didn't want to mess things up. Even though I wanted to date and kiss him—the guy my dad forbade me from hanging out with—I didn't want to cross that line. I wasn't going to be the girl who forgot all her plans, goals, and desires just because she was finally dating the guy she'd always liked.

I didn't really think Noah would do that, either, since he'd been the one to stop things. But it was still smart to be careful.

I walked into my room, flicking on the light before going to my closet. Noah stepped just inside the doorway like he wasn't sure he could come in.

"You don't have to wait there, Noah. It's not like you haven't been in here before."

"I just don't want to get you in trouble. I don't think your dad would be very happy to find me in here."

I waved my hand. "He told me I shouldn't expect him back until about midnight. We should be fine." I was just grabbing his shirt, anyway. It wasn't like he was going to be sleeping in my room again.

I opened my closet and looked around for his shirt. I was pretty sure I'd seen it in here earlier when I was trying to figure out exactly what to wear. I put my hands on my hips and frowned at the huge mess I'd made this evening.

"Your closet looks a little different than it did when I left this morning," Noah commented, coming to stand beside me. I tried not to feel too embarrassed about how it was totally obvious that I'd tried on about everything I owned before throwing it onto the carpet.

"Trying to look nice for someone today?" There was a smile in his voice.

I rolled my eyes. "Yeah, okay you caught me. I was trying to get you to notice me."

He laughed and leaned against the door frame to my closet. "Oh, you already had my attention." He touched the sleeve of my dress. "But this didn't hurt, either."

I felt a blush rise to my cheeks. I shook my head. What was I doing in here again? Oh yeah, finding his shirt. I lowered myself to my knees so that I could dig through the messy pile of clothes on the floor. A moment later, I spotted it. I grabbed the gray shirt then jumped back up.

I stood up too fast and felt lightheaded. Noah grabbed my arm again. "Does that happen every time you look for things on your closet floor?" he asked.

I gripped his waist to steady myself. "It only seems to happen when you're around."

He smiled. "As long as it's only when I'm around."

I found myself getting caught up in his eyes but decided I needed to stop. He'd already told me he was tempted to be with me, so it would probably be a good idea to stop finding ourselves in my closet from now on. It seemed to have some sort of magical pull for us when we were in it.

I handed him his shirt and stepped away. "Here you go. I think that's all you left here this morning."

"I guess I better leave you with something else then." He pulled me against him and kissed me one more time.

I let myself lean into him, still not believing this was real.

"What's going on here?" My dad's voice cut through the air.

Oh crap!

Oh crap, oh crap, oh crap!

I slowly turned to face my dad, knowing the guilt on my face would make him doubt anything I said next.

"It's not what it looks like, Dad," I hurried to say, stepping away from Noah, hoping that if I moved fast he'd have less time to imprint the image of me and Noah kissing in my closet into his mind.

"You need to get out of here now, Noah!" My dad stepped into my room, looking more threatening than I'd ever seen him before.

"I promise this is not what it looks like, Dad." I stood in front of Noah as if that would protect him from my dad. "I was just giving him back his shirt."

"His shirt?" My dad looked incredulous. "What in the world do you have his shirt for? What have you two been doing together?"

He stomped closer to Noah, and the look on his face had me worried about what he might do.

From what he'd just seen and heard, he probably thought his worst nightmare had come true.

"I promise I didn't do whatever it is you're thinking," Noah said.

"What I just saw was more than enough. You are never going

to step another foot in this house again. You hear me?" He gripped Noah's arm and yanked him away from me, catapulting him toward my door. "I warned you to stay away from my daughter, and this is what you do? I knew better than to let Easton be friends with you."

Noah glanced at me, his expression pained, before going into the hall with my dad on his heels.

I chased after them. "I was helping him out! If you would just listen, I could explain."

My dad looked over his shoulder at me. His face was red, and it looked like his vein was about to pop on his forehead because it was so pronounced right now. "Oh, I'll bet you were helping him out. I know exactly what kind of guy he is. This isn't the first time I've had my daughter taken advantage of by an older boy."

We were in the living room now. Noah grabbed his coat from the closet and shrugged into it like he couldn't get out of here fast enough.

"Is this why you had me fix your window last night? So you could sneak that...that..." He pointed at Noah like he couldn't even bring himself to say his name. "That boy into your room?"

"We didn't do anything. He just slept in my closet."

I clamped my mouth shut, and from the look Noah gave me I realized that I'd said too much.

My dad gritted his teeth. "You need to get out of here, Noah." He pointed to the door behind him. "Now!"

Noah looked like he was debating on whether to leave or not, but a moment later he sighed and put his hand on the door handle.

But before Noah could make his escape, Easton appeared at my side.

"What's going on here?" he asked Noah.

"I have to go," was all Noah said, not looking anyone in the eyes as he pulled the door open.

"Wait," Easton said, stepping past my dad and putting his hand on Noah's shoulder. "You forgot your phone. I looked at the screen and you missed a few calls from your sister."

Noah's eyes went wide as he took his phone. Panic rose to his face and he disappeared out the door.

Was something wrong with his sister?

I wanted to chase after him to find out.

"Don't even think about going after him." My dad shut the front door and blocked it.

"But I need to know if everything is okay," I pleaded.

"I think you need to be more worried about yourself than that boy. But if you can't, I'm not above getting a restraining order."

"What are you guys talking about?" Easton asked.

"I caught your sister kissing Noah in her room. Turns out he's been sleeping in her room."

"My closet, Dad! There's a huge difference there."

"You are so naive, Lexi! Can't you see that he was using you? It starts out with the closet, then once you're comfortable, it's your floor by the closet, and then pretty soon he's in your bed. Does that purity ring on your finger even mean anything anymore?"

"Of course it does, Dad. I didn't do anything wrong! I'm not Maddie!" I shouted. Why wouldn't he just listen to me?

He shook his head. "If I ever see that boy around you again, Yale is off. I will not pay one penny for your college. I paid my own way, and you can too. We had a deal. And if you break my trust, it's over."

Then he turned on his heel and went to his room, slamming the door and making the whole house shake.

I shoved my hands into my hair, resisting the urge to pull it all out. "Dad is ridiculous!" I huffed and dropped onto the loveseat in the living room.

"Noah was sleeping in your room?" Easton asked in a quiet voice from behind me and when I turned to glance up at him, he had a look on his face that made me think he felt betrayed somehow.

"Nothing happened."

He walked over to the couch and dropped down. "Was it real then? Were you sneaking around right in front of my face this whole time?"

I rolled my eyes. "It was all fake until today, Easton. We told you the truth. Noah just needed somewhere to stay since he got kicked out of his house."

"Wait... What?" Easton shook his head like he didn't think he'd heard me right. "Since when did Noah get kicked out of his house? And why the heck did he tell you and not me?"

I scooted forward on the loveseat and sighed. Telling Noah's secret was probably the only way to keep my dad from getting a restraining order on him. "His stepdad kicked him out on Saturday."

"He's been sleeping here since Saturday?"

I blew out a frustrated breath. "If you'll just let me talk, I can explain everything."

So I told him all about Noah getting kicked out and sleeping in his car and me finding him in there. "He just slept in my closet for two nights. I promise he didn't lay a finger on me. I'm still wearing my purity ring, see?" I hated that I had to say it.

"But why didn't he tell me?"

"He didn't want anyone to know. The only reason why he told me was because I found him. He probably would have stayed in his car in the freezing cold last night if I hadn't begged him to come over."

Realization dawned on his face. "Is that why you didn't want me looking in your closet?"

"Yes." I crossed my arms.

Easton shook his head. "I still can't believe he didn't tell me."

We were quiet for a while. But then he said, "Wait, you said it wasn't real until today. What happened today? I thought you broke up."

Oh man. My stupid mouth was ruining everything, wasn't it?

"Lexi..." he prodded when I didn't say anything.

I blinked my eyes shut, knowing I'd been caught. It wasn't like it mattered, anyway. There was pretty much no chance of Noah ever talking to me again after all the things my dad had said.

I opened my eyes again. "Turns out, Noah actually liked me."

"And what makes you think that?"

"Because he just told me." And the way he'd been kissing me had certainly made those words really believable, too.

Why did my dad have to find us and ruin everything?

Easton sat up straighter. "Don't let yourself get too attached to that thought, okay? I know how Noah is with girls. He loses interest fast."

Sharp pains stabbed at my heart. But I tried to force it away. "He dated Ashlyn for almost a year," I said. A whole year was not losing interest fast.

"Yes, but after her, it was a new girl every week."

I furrowed my brow. "How come I didn't know about this?"

"Because you don't go to our parties. You don't hang out with our crowd." He shrugged like it was obvious.

"I don't believe you. He started this whole fake dating thing because he wanted to get Raven off his back."

Easton stared at me like I was missing a screw in my head. "And he only did that because he'd already made out with her at a party and couldn't man up enough to tell her it was just physical. That's how Noah is with girls. That's how all guys are."

No. That couldn't be true. He'd just stopped me from wrapping my legs around him because he didn't want to do that anymore. Easton didn't know what he was talking about.

"You say *all* guys are like that? Why are you lumping yourself into that category?" Since when was Easton like 'all guys'?

He blinked and looked away as if he didn't like my question.

Was he that way?

When he finally turned back to me, he had a tortured look on his face.

What had he done?

"I'm not a saint, Lexi." He sighed heavily and glanced in the direction of Dad's bedroom as if to make sure he wasn't listening. "Haven't you noticed something has been missing on my left hand for a few months now?"

I looked at his ring finger. His purity ring wasn't there. But hadn't he just said that he'd lost it?

"You didn't lose it when we went camping?"

His eyes tightened, and I knew I'd hit a nerve. I didn't want to believe it. Easton couldn't have done *that*.

"I really don't want to talk about it with you." He brushed my question away, and I was grateful. I didn't want to know that about him if it was true.

He pressed his lips together and seemed to switch back to the topic at hand. "But like I said, guys are wired differently than girls, and I don't want you to think that things are different with Noah. I don't want to see you get hurt."

"You don't need to worry about me, Easton. I know what I'm doing."

"Don't be so naive, Lexi."

That was the second time I'd been called naive tonight. I hated that word.

"Noah said he didn't do that stuff with Ashlyn."

Easton covered his eyes with his hand for a moment before looking back at me with more annoyance than I felt I deserved. "That's because Ashlyn was special."

Translation: Ashlyn was special, and I would never be.

Tears sprung to my eyes, threatening to topple over. My own brother had pretty much just confirmed my biggest fear in this whole thing. I was not the kind of girl guys went after. I'd just been stupid enough to think Noah might make an exception for me after getting to know me better.

I blinked back tears, not wanting to cry in front of Easton and let him know that his words had hit their mark. "Thank you for imparting your brotherly wisdom on me." I swallowed down the lump rising in my throat as I stood to leave. "Now if you'll excuse me, I'm going to go to my room and find out how many cats I'll be allowed to live with when I'm forty and still haven't ever been asked out on a real date."

"Lexi, wait—" He stood.

I put my hand out to stop him. "I think you've said enough tonight."

32

NOAH

I LISTENED to the voicemails from Brielle on my way home, driving as fast as I dared on the slushy roads.

"Noah, I'm scared. Daddy's really mad right now. Please come home."

My heart banged against my rib cage as I pressed play on the next one. *Paul was mad.* Why did we have to live at the opposite end of our school zone?

"Noah, why aren't you answering? Daddy's really mad. He's yelling. Please come home."

My hands shook as I pressed the button to listen to her next and final message.

When her voice came through the recording, it wasn't shaking like it had been in the first two. She was full on crying now, and I could barely understand her through the sobs.

"Noah, I think Mommy's hurt really bad. Please hurry. Daddy went away and I'm scared."

I dropped my phone onto my seat, adrenaline coursing through my veins as I tried to prepare myself for the worst.

What had he done to her?

I PARKED my car haphazardly on the road, then jumped out and rushed into the house. When I got inside, the scene was one that I had been dreading. My mom lay crumpled on the ground, blood dripping from her mouth, looking so broken and bruised. Her eyes were swollen and purple.

"Are you okay, Mom?" I asked, rushing to her side and lifting her head onto my lap. Her eyes flickered open and she groaned.

I looked around for my sister, but she wasn't anywhere to be seen.

I yelled out. "Brielle? Are you up there?"

She appeared at the top of the stairs a moment later. She'd probably been hiding in my room like she always did when Paul was mad.

"Come downstairs right now and get in my car. We need to take Mom to the hospital." Brielle nodded and ran down the stairs in her kitten pajamas, her face as white as the snow outside.

I rushed back to my mom and went to scooped her up into my arms. But then she stopped me, saying, "I don't want to go to the hospital."

I went still, not sure I'd heard her right. "You need to see a doctor, Mom."

"But the police will start asking questions." Her voice was so quiet and raspy.

I sighed, pressing my hands into my knees as I knelt by her side, trying to figure out what I could say to make her finally see reason.

"Do you want this to keep happening, Mom? Because that drive home after listening to Brielle's messages was about the longest drive of my life. A huge part of me thought I was going to walk in on a murder scene. I can't do this anymore. I had to sleep in my freaking car for the last week because of that man.

You need to leave him. And you need to get checked right now."

And we needed to hurry. I had no idea what kind of damage had been done to her insides. I could only see the outside which was bad enough.

My mom breathed in a few raspy breaths, and after a long moment, she finally met my gaze again. "Okay."

My heart swelled in my chest with the first piece of hope I'd had for her in a long time. "Okay?"

She nodded slowly. "Yes. You can take me to the hospital."

"Thank you." It was all I could manage with the wave of emotions choking me. I scooped her back into my arms and gently stood.

"Can you please open the door, Brielle?"

She did as I said, and I was out on the porch a second later, sprinting down the icy sidewalk to my car. Brielle, thankfully, was right behind me, and I had her open the passenger side door so I could set my mom inside.

After buckling my mom in, I turned back to my sister, knowing I needed to look as calm as I could in that moment. If she could see how worried I was about Mom, she'd probably start bawling and I couldn't take care of her like that right now. I had to focus on my mom.

So I bent down on her level and took her shoulders in my hands. "I know I don't have a booster seat in my car, so sit in the middle. We have to hurry."

I sped all the way to the hospital, constantly checking my mom to make sure she was still breathing. She kept on gasping for air, and I worried one of her ribs may have punctured a lung.

We made it to the hospital five minutes later, thanks to the roads being empty enough for me to speed the whole way there. I cradled my mom in my arms as I ran to the emergency room doors, Brielle following closely behind.

The waiting area was empty and no one was at the desk. "Is anybody here?" I panted, having a hard time drawing in a good breath after my sprint. "Please! Someone! My mom needs help!"

The door behind the desk opened and a very startled-looking hospital worker stepped forward. But she soon smoothed her face, probably used to scenes like this.

"How can I help you?"

"My mom's been hurt. I just got home and found her on the floor. She's having a hard time breathing."

I had no idea what Paul had done to her, but if I was ever within ten feet of him again I might just kill him. I gritted my teeth as I imagined taking that smug face of his in my hands and beating the crap out of it.

"And what's the patient's name?" the lady at the counter asked.

"Seriously? You're asking me that stuff? She needs help right now!"

"It's hospital procedure, sir. I have already pushed the button and help should be here soon."

"Her name is Shelley Stavros. Her birthday is..." I tried to remember, but in my state of mind, it wasn't coming.

Brielle stepped forward, hugging my leg. "June eighth," she whispered.

"Her birthday is June eighth," I repeated louder so the receptionist could hear.

A moment later the doors behind her opened, and two nurses came through with a hospital bed on wheels.

The nurses then instructed me to lay my mom gently onto the bed. "Can you tell us what happened?" the male nurse with swept-back blond hair asked.

"I just got home from my friend's house and found my mom lying on the floor. My sister was home." I looked down at Brielle and spoke to her gently. "Can you tell the nice nurses what happened?"

She nodded, and when she spoke, it was with a shaky voice. "Daddy was mad. He hurt Mommy."

I couldn't help but notice the dark look the nurses gave each other before turning back to us. "Is your sister okay?"

"I-I think so." Then I turned to Brielle, realizing I had no idea what might have happened earlier this week while I'd been gone. Who knew what Paul had done while I'd been out of the way? "Are you okay, Brielle? Did your dad hurt you, too?"

She shook her head quickly, her eyes wide with fear. "I was hiding."

The nurses seemed to look my sister over for a moment before addressing me. "We'll take your mom back and check her out. It might be best if you stay out here with your sister."

I nodded and tried to draw in a deep breath. I had to be strong for Brielle. "Please take care of her." Everything needed to be okay.

The male nurse's eyes were sympathetic. "We'll do our best."

And then they disappeared with my mom through the doors.

"YOU CAN COME BACK and see her now." One of the nurses came out to get me and Brielle after one of the longest hours of my life. While they'd been helping my mom, another nurse had asked if she could talk to Brielle some more. She had a comforting countenance and Brielle had been able answer her questions without seeming too nervous.

And from what Brielle said, it sounded like she had truly been left untouched. Thank goodness for that, at least.

My mom was lying on the hospital bed when we came in.

She still didn't look good, but she did seem more comfortable and was breathing a little better now.

"Hi, sweetie." Mom's voice came out all raspy. She held out a hand and Brielle immediately ran to her side, wrapping her little arms around her.

My mom groaned at Brielle's not-so-gentle embrace, but after the look of pain crested over her features, she replaced it with a smile.

"You don't need to look so worried about me, Noah," my mom said, her sad eyes inspecting my face. "I'm going to be okay."

"You shouldn't even be here, Mom." I shook my head, feeling my throat constrict. "You need to leave him. You need to never go back to him again."

She pressed her dry lips together and nodded slowly, her eyes falling closed for a moment. "I know."

But where would we go?

I could only think of one option. And it would take a lot of pride-sucking to ask.

Once Brielle had had her long hug from Mom, she held her arms open for me.

I only attacked her with slightly less force than Brielle had. And before I knew it, I was sobbing. "I thought I was going to lose you, Mom," I said through my tears as the image of her broken body on the living room floor came to mind. "I thought for a few minutes that I was going to have to raise Brielle by myself."

My mom shushed me and patted the back of my head gently —the way she had done when I was a kid. "It's going to be okay, Noah. I'm okay. Just some bruising. A couple broken ribs. But everything is going to be okay."

THE HOSPITAL WANTED to keep my mom there overnight to monitor her—worried about some slight head trauma. They tried to tell me it was just a precaution, that they hadn't seen anything when they'd done the scan. I just hoped they were right.

But it was a safe place to stay, so I would try to be grateful for that, at least.

The police and CPS came in later and asked all kinds of questions. And as far as anyone knew, Paul was still roaming wherever he pleased. Which meant he could come home at any time, and who knew what he might do next.

I needed to find somewhere safe for us to stay until my mom was able to help me figure it out. So once Mom was asleep and Brielle was curled up on the chair next to her, I left the hospital to go to the only place I could think of.

The two-story brick home was dark when I got there, and I knew the inhabitants would probably be annoyed at me for coming there so late and waking up the whole household. But for once, I didn't care if they tried to send me away. I was going to do this. My mom needed me to do this.

So I knocked on the door and hoped I wouldn't have to ring the doorbell.

A light turned on in the house, and then another one in the hall. I heard the deadbolt turn, and a moment later, the door creaked open.

My mouth was dry and my hands were trembling as I tried to force some courage into my tired body to face the only person I had left who could help me.

"Noah?"

"Dad, I need your help."

33

LEXI

MY DAD TOOK the doors off my bedroom, and closet the next day with the words, "Privacy is a privilege." And then he told me I would be volunteering to help Mrs. Vincenzo from down the street with her newborn twins for the next week to remind me of how much work babies really are.

"I was there for Grant, Dad. I remember things with him pretty clearly."

My dad just shrugged. "It's always good to have a refresher. Maybe I should recommend the same punishment to Noah's parents."

"Oh my heck, Dad! You saw us kiss one time. We were not making a baby." Just saying that last sentence made me squirm. I hated that I even had to say that to my dad.

"Kissing in your bedroom is where it all starts."

"The door was open."

"Yes, but it was not open those two nights Noah slept in your closet."

I sighed. He had me there.

My dad leaned my now free-standing doors against the wall in the hall then looked back at me. "Tell me this, Lexi. If you had walked in on Easton and a girl kissing in his room, and then found out that she'd been sleeping in there, what would you think?"

I cast my gaze down, digging a toe into the carpet. "I'd maybe worry about what was going on." Especially after what Easton had hinted about yesterday.

Dad smiled and nodded like I was finally getting his point. "Exactly."

"But nothing was going on. I'd barely had my first kiss."

"That's how it all starts, Lexi. One thing leads to another and another—you start to get more comfortable, and then before you know it, you're telling me that I'm going to be a grandpa again."

I shook my head, feeling the anger flare inside of me.

"When are you ever going to see that I'm not my sister? This is the first time I've ever broken the rules. I get straight A's in school. I babysit Grant for free to help Maddie out. I have good friends. I don't do drugs." I sighed. When was I ever going to stop being punished for things I hadn't even done? "I was really just trying to help Noah out. You can talk to Mr. Taylor. He can tell you that Noah was sleeping in his car."

My dad grunted. "I already did."

"You did?"

"I spoke to Mr. Taylor last night and he told me about Noah's family situation."

"So you understand why I had to do what I did, right?"

"You should have just told me he needed a place to stay in the first place, Lexi." He sighed heavily, his blue eyes more tired-looking than they should have been for this early in the day. I really was stressing him out. "As it is, I don't feel like I can trust you anymore."

"But—" I wanted to argue with him that I was totally trustworthy. Then I remembered all the lying and sneaking around I'd done over the past week, and I knew it was far from the truth.

How had I even gotten here? I barely recognized myself anymore.

I looked down and finally said, "I understand."

"Look, Lexi, I know I haven't exactly made things easy on you, either." When I looked up, there was more gentleness in my dad's eyes than I'd seen in a while. "I've been letting my fears over what your sister did in high school rule the way I've been parenting you. And I know that isn't fair. Yes, you are both my daughters, but you're two very different girls. And maybe if I hadn't been so strict with Maddie, she might not have pushed so hard against my rules."

I nodded, though I didn't know if I fully understood him.

"What I'm trying to say is, yes, what you did was wrong and you will be punished for sneaking around." He gestured to the doors behind him. "But I also don't want to push you away. If we can set up some rules, then I think we might be able to find a common ground to stand on."

"I think setting up some reasonable rules would be nice." Emphasis on reasonable. I knew who I was dealing with here.

But if there was even a chance that he'd ever let me see Noah again, I was willing to listen.

That is, if Noah still wants to see me after last night.

I'd tried to call and text him several times already, but all I got was his voicemail and a bunch of silence.

"I'm going to take some time to think this over. Let's talk again tomorrow, okay?" My dad lifted the doors again and started walking down the hall.

That conversation had gone surprisingly well. Maybe my dad wasn't a tyrant after all.

But just before he turned the corner, he swiveled back and said, "But I'm still serious about you volunteering at the Vincenzo's. You can't be too careful these days."

I'D HOPED that Noah was maybe just busy doing things with his family all day on Saturday to respond to my messages, but when I still hadn't heard back from him on Sunday, I started to get worried.

Maybe my dad had really scared him off for good.

Or maybe Easton was right, and I had just been one of Noah's weekend flings.

I tried to keep myself busy doing all the homework I'd neglected this week while hanging out with Noah. But I could only distract myself so much.

By the time Sunday evening rolled around, I was desperate. Was he okay? When I looked at the messages I'd sent him, they still just showed up as "sent" and not "read." Had he gotten in an accident on the way home from my house?

I knocked on Easton's door, even though I was still really mad at him for what he'd said.

"Have you heard from Noah since Friday?" I asked.

"No." He looked up from his Physics book. "But doesn't he talk to you more these days, anyway?"

I rolled my eyes. "Stop being such a drama queen, Easton."

"Well, instead of asking to sleep in his best friend's room while he was homeless, he snuck into my sister's closet. I'd say that warrants a little drama."

I wanted to kick him. He was so moody these days.

"Can you text him and see if he's okay? I just want to make sure he didn't get in a car accident or something."

Easton sighed in annoyance, like I was asking him to re-arrange the planets or something. "Fine. I'll text him."

"Thank you."

34

NOAH

"CAN you please pass the rolls, Noah?" Tracey, my stepmom, asked Sunday evening as we all sat around the big dining room table. Dad, Tracey, Mom, Mason, Paige, Brielle, and me. It was one of the weirdest family dynamics you could probably get, but strangely, over the past two days, I'd never felt more at home.

It had taken me a lot of humility to show up at my dad's house late Friday night, and I'd been ninety percent sure that he'd send me away. Instead, he'd welcomed me into his home with open arms and we had one of the best conversations we'd ever had in years.

I wasn't going to pretend like things were perfect between us, but we had finally broken down the wall of miscommunication and promised to try harder to have a better relationship. And the fact that he and Tracey had opened their house to my mom, Brielle, and me wasn't hurting my feelings toward them, either.

"Is it okay if I sleep in Paige's room tonight, Mom?" Brielle asked with her mouth full of roast beef.

My mom looked briefly to Tracey as if to ask whether that

was okay. Tracey gave her a nod of approval and my mom turned back to Brielle. "I think that sounds like fun. But make sure you don't stay awake all night because you still have school tomorrow."

Brielle groaned. "Can't I stay home?"

My mom gave her a small smile. "I think it will be good to get things back to normal."

Brielle pouted in her seat, but she said, "Okay." It only took her a few seconds, though, to start chatting excitedly to Paige about all the fun things they were going to do for their "sleepover" tonight, and it was fun to see Brielle happy amidst all the crazy that was happening in our family.

The police had found Paul when he'd gone home early Saturday morning and he was now in their custody. I had no idea what the law would be able to do with him, but my mom was finally pressing charges and realizing she deserved to be treated with respect and love. And though I hated that she had to come to the realization this way, I was just glad we were finally going to be able to put the pain and abuse in the past. My mom's body still had a lot of healing to do, but the doctors had a positive outlook for her and doubted there'd be any residual effects from Friday night.

After dinner, I went up to the room that I currently called my own and finally turned on my phone. I had decided to take a break from the rest of the world over the past couple of days, needing to focus on my family. But if Brielle was going to school tomorrow, it probably meant my mom would expect me to go there as well. And it would be good to find out if Mr. Stevens was going to get a restraining order put on me before I tried to approach either of his children again.

I hated the thought of not being able to spend time with Lexi or Easton again, but after seeing how mad their dad had been on

Friday night, I wouldn't put it past him to take away their college funding if they ever came within ten feet of me.

My phone powered up, and after a few seconds, it started chiming like crazy. By the time it had finished loading all my missed phone calls and text messages, it showed that I'd missed three phone calls from Lexi and twelve text messages from her.

I opened my text folder and read what she'd written me.

Lexi: **Was everything okay with your sister?**

Lexi: **My dad is so stupid. Don't listen to any of those horrible things he said to you.**

Lexi: **I'm going to call you.**

Lexi: **Why aren't you answering?**

Lexi: **Did I do something wrong?**

Lexi: **I'm really sorry, Noah.**

Lexi: **Do you hate me now?**

Lexi: **Me and my dad don't share the same feelings about you.**

Lexi: **Am I just fooling myself with you? Was it really a fling like Easton said?**

Lexi: **Am I really that bad of a kisser?**

Lexi: **Are you okay?**

Lexi: **I understand if you don't want to talk to me anymore. But please just let me know that you made it home okay. I'm worried about you.**

A text from Easton came through just as I finished reading Lexi's texts.

Easton: **Is everything okay? Lexi's worried. She's starting to think you either hate her or that you died in a car accident.**

I laughed. Lexi was awesome.

Noah: **Tell her I'm okay now. Just been dealing with family stuff.**

Easton: **Anything I can help with?**

Noah: **We're okay now. Staying with my dad for a while.**

35

LEXI

EASTON STEPPED into my room a few minutes later. "Noah is alive."

I sighed, relieved that he was okay. "Did he say anything else?"

"He said he's dealing with some family stuff right now. When I asked if he needed anything, he said he didn't."

I nodded. "Thanks for texting him."

Easton nodded then sulked back down the hall.

Noah was okay. But for some reason, he wasn't responding back to me. I tried not to be too sad about it. Easton must've been right after all. I was just a convenient target for Noah to make-out with when he wanted something to distract him, nothing more.

I tried not to feel my heart ripping apart inside of me at the thought; instead, I decided I might as well go to bed and not sit here waiting for nothing.

I was washing my face when my phone beeped. When I checked the screen, my heart stuttered in my chest.

It was a message from Noah.

Noah: **Meet me outside by your window.**

I WALKED out into the dining room as calmly as I could. My dad was sitting at the kitchen table going through some paperwork.

"Did you check the mail today?" I asked him, hoping that he hadn't.

He frowned and shook his head. "It's Sunday. They don't deliver the mail on Sunday."

"Actually, they do now. I'm just going to go check it."

"Expecting a package?" My dad narrowed his gaze and I worried I might have tipped him off.

I shrugged and tried to keep my face neutral and unconcerned. I knew I shouldn't be sneaking around, especially after our conversation yesterday. But I just needed a few minutes with Noah to talk about things before my dad was hovering over us.

That was to say, if this conversation went well...

"Juliette was going to send me something. And I could use a little fresh air, anyway."

My dad nodded and pointed to the counter. "My keys are right there."

"Thanks."

I walked as calmly as I could to the entryway and put on my coat, though I wanted to hurry. Once out the front door, I peeked into the lit living room windows to make sure Dad wasn't watching me from the slits in the blinds. The window was empty, so I sprinted to the side of the house where Noah had told me to meet him.

I'd just turned the corner when a hand shot out in the moonlight, grabbing me and pushing me against the side of the house.

I almost screamed before I saw it was just Noah. And before I knew what was happening, he was pressing his body against mine and kissing me like he hadn't seen me in years. My breath came in short bursts as I met his lips with the same enthusiasm.

I broke away and gasped for air. "I guess this means you don't hate me then?"

He shook his head. "Never." And then he kissed me again. We kissed for a minute longer before eventually pulling away, both of our chests heaving from the passion and the cold night air.

He cleared his throat. "Sorry I didn't text or call you back. I figured it would be better for me to do this in person."

I grinned. "I don't think that greeting would've been nearly the same through the phone."

"Definitely not." His eyes sparkled in the moonlight, and I loved that I was the reason for this vibrancy in him. "So are you grounded for life?"

"Well, I don't have any doors in my room right now. And I have to volunteer to help with the twins down the road for the next week."

"Wow, your dad doesn't mess around, does he?"

I shook my head. "Nope."

"Do you want me to talk to him? Tell him why you let me sleep in your room?"

"He already knows. He called your dad Friday night."

"So does that mean you already know what happened?

I furrowed my brow. "No? Did something bad happen?"

His expression darkened, and I didn't know if I wanted to hear the answer. Then he said, "Paul apparently didn't get the promotion and took it out on my mom."

"He did? Is she okay? What happened?"

He covered his eyes for a brief moment before looking back at me. "It was pretty bad. I had to rush her to the emergency room and she had a few broken ribs and bruises all over."

"Is she going to be okay?" No wonder he hadn't called or texted me back. It sounded like he'd been through way more than anyone should ever have to go through in just one night. First, my dad kicked him out of my house, and then he went home to find that? How was he even standing upright this minute? I'd probably be crumpled up in a ball on the floor if that had happened to me.

"Things will be okay and she's pressing charges this time. We're actually staying at my dad's house right now. It's kind of weird having us all under the same roof."

"I bet."

He shrugged. "I mean, my mom hated my dad about as much as I did for what he did to us. Hated Tracey too. But it seems like this whole experience has actually been good in a way. Don't get me wrong, it was terrible that this happened to my mom, and I wish it never had, but the dynamics of my family are better than they've been since before the divorce."

I touched his arm, rubbing the soft leather of his letterman jacket. "That's good that you and your family are doing better. I hope things continue to improve."

He nodded. "Me too." Then he looked to the side. "Anyway, I better let you get back in there. I don't want to get you in any more trouble than I already have."

"Actually, do you have a minute?"

He looked wary. "Yeah, why?"

I slipped my hand into his and squeezed it. "I had a good conversation with my dad yesterday, and I think it might be a good idea for us both to go talk to him right now."

He swallowed. "You do?"

I smiled, hoping to reassure him. "He's not as mad as he was on Friday, I promise."

"I would hope not, because I kind of saw my life flash before my eyes when he dragged me out of your room."

"Me too," I agreed. "Anyway, sneaking around is probably about the worst thing that I can do right now if I want my dad to ever trust me again. So how about we go talk to him together and see if we can convince him to let us hang out without it feeling wrong?"

"You promise he's not going to come after me with his shotgun?"

I smiled. "It's locked in the safe. You'll have a full minute's warning before you're in danger."

"How reassuring," he said, dryly.

"Well, I don't want to give you any false hope." I winked then pulled him to the front of the house.

36

NOAH

I NEARLY CRAPPED my pants when Lexi first dragged me into her kitchen to talk with her dad. I'd always been afraid of the man but walking into the house holding his daughter's hand was probably the scariest thing I'd ever done in my life.

"Dad, can we talk to you?" Lexi asked.

I didn't miss the grimace on Mr. Stevens' face when he saw me, but he smoothed his expression and said, "Sure."

My legs wobbled as we took the two seats across from him.

"In honor of being upfront and transparent in everything I do, I wanted you to know that I didn't go to get the mail. I went to get Noah."

Mr. Stevens' eyes narrowed. "Sneaking around again already?"

Lexi smiled, and I had no idea how she was so calm right now. I was practically shaking in my snow boots.

"Well, I wanted to find out if he was going to dump me or not first." She shot me a quick smile.

I give her hand a brief squeeze then addressed her dad. "I promise I have the best intentions where your daughter is concerned. And I know I'm probably the last person you want to see right now, but I just wanted to start off by asking for your forgiveness."

I had been ready to sputter all kinds of apologies that I'd practiced over the past two days, but Mr. Stevens nodded and said, "It's okay, Noah. And I'm sorry for my behavior the other night. I've had time to cool down, and your dad called me again last night to give me all of the facts."

"He did?" I asked.

He nodded. "I was too quick to judge and I'm sorry for that. It seems that I have not quite reached perfection yet, either."

A small laugh escaped Lexi's lips. She covered her mouth with her hand. I was worried he'd get mad at her for being disrespectful or something, but when I glanced at him, his eyes crinkled at the corners—he was indeed joking.

"Does that mean I have permission to spend time with Noah again?" Lexi asked.

My heart pounded as I waited for Mr. Stevens' answer. I hadn't really expected her to just come out and ask right here and now—I figured we'd slow our way into it. But apparently, Lexi was the kind of girl to jump in with both feet and keep running.

"You can see each other only during school hours for the next week. Once you have finished your service to Mrs. Vincenzo, we'll take things slowly."

"Can Noah drive me to school?"

Mr. Stevens shook his head. "You will ride with Easton to and from school for the next week."

"Are we ever going to be together without a chaperone?"

"Once you've proven yourself trustworthy again, then most likely yes."

Lexi slumped back in her chair and groaned.

I cleared my throat. "I'm sure you have certain rules that will help us prove trustworthy again."

Mr. Stevens smiled and nodded. A smile was good, right? He'd probably been curating some sort of list for many years in preparation for a day like this.

He turned to Lexi with a stern expression. "My first rule is that Noah is not allowed inside our house unless either Easton or myself are home."

Lexi and I both nodded obediently. He raised a second finger in the air. "The next rule is that you, Noah, will, under no circumstances, ever enter her bedroom. And if you ever defile my daughter in any way, I will not hesitate to turn you in to the police. You're eighteen and Lexi is still a minor, so I hope I'm not being stupid in allowing this in the first place."

I gulped and felt the blood drain from my face. "I completely understand. I wouldn't want to do that to Lexi anyway." He was not messing around.

He raised his eyebrows. "That's good to hear, son."

He then told us about her curfew and other embarrassing things, like how there would be no kissing in cars or while lying down.

Once he was done, he looked at me with a gaze that made me think he might somehow be able to see into my brain. "Do you think you can abide by those rules?"

"Yes," I said. "Those sound very reasonable."

Lexi reached for my hand under the table. "I'm kind of mortified right now. But yes, I'll follow those rules."

Her dad smiled, appeased. "Great, because believe it or not, I'm kind of looking forward to paying for you to go to Yale."

"ARE you sure you're still interested in dating me after all of that?" Lexi followed me out onto the front porch after our awkward conversation with her dad.

I rubbed behind my neck. "I don't know. That's a lot of rules."

Her eyes went wide before she stared down at her shoes. "I understand. My dad *is* pretty paranoid."

I lifted her chin in my hands, forcing her to look me in the eyes. "I was just joking, Lexi. Do I *like* all those rules? No." I most definitely didn't like them all. "But do I understand them? Yes."

"I really do understand if you want to back out now. I mean, I probably wouldn't want to worry about so many rules, and I can't believe my dad threatened to call the police on you if something were to happen. Which it's not. Not that you would even want it to in the first place." She was speaking so quickly I could barely understand her.

I put my finger on her lips to quiet her down. "Lexi. It's okay. I want to date you. Your dad could add another ten rules to the list, and I would still want to be with you."

She narrowed her eyes like she wasn't sure she believed me. "But it might be way easier with someone else..."

I laughed. "Stop trying to talk me out of it, Lexi. You're stuck with me. I don't want to be with anyone else. As crazy as it may seem to anyone on the outside, I kind of really dig the whole nerdy vibe you've got going on."

"You do?" she asked.

I smiled and stepped closer. "I totally do."

"Good." She smiled back.

"Now get over here and give me a kiss before I go home. It sounds like this might be our last moment alone for a while."

She closed the gap between us, and I gave her a kiss that told her just how much I wanted to stick around with her.

37

LEXI

NOAH WAS WAITING for me at the front of the school the next morning.

Easton stepped up beside me and spoke in a low voice. "Looks like your *boyfriend* is waiting for you." He was still a little touchy over the fact that he really did have to share his best friend with me now, but I figured he'd get over it eventually. Maybe if things didn't work out between him and Mercedes we could try a double date with Juliette sometime. I had definitely noticed some sparks between them before she left, and he had acted really depressed those first couple of weeks she was gone.

Easton made it through the door, and he and Noah briefly nodded to each other. And that was it—no conversation, no hellos, just Easton heading inside the building.

"That was weird," I commented, nodding toward my brother's retreating back.

Noah shrugged. "It's okay. We'll figure things out soon, I'm sure." Then he held his hand out for me to take. "You ready to face everyone on our first official day as boyfriend and girlfriend?"

I took his hand and smiled. "I've been waiting for this day for longer than you probably know."

He grinned. "Now how long is that exactly?"

I shook my head, not believing I was actually okay talking about my long-time crush on him. "Pretty much since you played Go-Fish with me that one day in middle school."

He squeezed my hand and led me further inside. "You mean the day that Easton wouldn't let you play that train game and you went off and cried on the staircase?"

I blushed, remembering how ridiculous he must have thought I was back then. But then I realized something else. "You actually remember?"

He smiled. "Of course. I mean, I don't just play Go-Fish with anyone."

"Well, I'm glad I made your list even back then." We arrived at my locker.

"Me too." He looked back at me and winked. Then he leaned his shoulder against the locker beside mine. "So, this is probably your last chance to back out of dating me before you see Harrison in band."

"And why would I want to stop dating you because I'll be seeing Harrison?" I cocked an eyebrow.

He scratched a spot on his cheek. "I think I overheard that Justin Banks is coming out with a new movie soon, and I know how you feel about watching his movies with Harrison."

I whacked him in the arm.

"Ow." He rubbed the spot where I'd smacked him, but the smile on his face was huge.

"So does that mean you're not interested in Harrison, or are you just not into the Justin Banks movie?"

"How about neither."

"Neither? Really?"

"Yes. We both know which impossible crush I was trying to forget about when I decided to chase Harrison to that last movie."

"Who?" He tried to look innocent as he stepped closer, his intoxicating cologne making it hard for me to remember how to talk for a moment. "Who were you trying to forget, sweet Lexi?" He ran his thumb slowly across my jawline.

I blinked my eyes shut for a moment before getting lost in his gaze again. "You know it was always you, Noah."

He smiled at me softly. "Thanks for being patient enough to let me figure out that you were always the one for me, too."

WANT to read a **bonus epilogue** from Lexi's point of view set six years in the future? Snag it here: https://BookHip.com/ LHSTCTH

Read the next book in the series!
Easton and Juliette's Story

They broke the rules. He broke her heart.
Does their love deserve a second chance?

Grab your copy today!

STAY CONNECTED!

I hope you enjoyed IT WAS ALWAYS YOU! If you haven't already, please sign up for my newsletter so you can stay up to date on my latest book news. https://subscribepage.com/judycorry

Join the Corry Crew on Facebook: https://www.facebook.com/groups/judycorrycrew/

Follow me on Instagram: @judycorry

Also By Judy Corry

Eden Falls Academy Series:

The Charade (Ava and Carter)

The Facade (Cambrielle and Mack)

The Ruse (Elyse and Asher)

The Confidant (Scarlett and Hunter)

The Confession (Kiara and Nash)

Kings of Eden Falls:

Hide Away With You (Addie and Evan)

Rich and Famous Series:

Assisting My Brother's Best Friend (Kate and Drew)

Hollywood and Ivy (Ivy and Justin)

Her Football Star Ex (Emerson and Vincent)

Friend Zone to End Zone (Arianna and Cole)

Stolen Kisses from a Rock Star (Maya and Landon)

Ridgewater High Series:

When We Began (Cassie and Liam)

Meet Me There (Ashlyn and Luke)

Don't Forget Me (Eliana and Jess)

It Was Always You (Lexi and Noah)

My Second Chance (Juliette and Easton)

My Mistletoe Mix-Up (Raven and Logan)

Forever Yours (Alyssa and Jace)

Standalones:

Protect My Heart (Emma and Arie)

Kissing The Boy Next Door (Lauren and Wes)

EXCERPT FROM MY SECOND CHANCE

I gripped my carry-on as I walked into the waiting area of the Syracuse airport, hoping it would somehow give me the strength I needed to face everyone again after my semester abroad in Paris.

I scanned around for my best friend, knowing my mom wouldn't be there since she had to meet with a congressman this afternoon. It only took me a moment to find Lexi, with her short frame, long dark hair, and glasses, standing in the middle of the waiting crowd. And it only took a heart-pounding second for me to realize that she hadn't come alone. She was flanked by her new boyfriend, Noah, and her older brother, Easton.

Why had Easton come?

My heart was stupid enough to skip a beat when he met my gaze. He was still as gorgeous as he'd been months before. His light-brown hair was combed to the side in the trendy way he'd started wearing it last year. And even from twenty feet away, his blue eyes could still pierce me.

I forced my gaze back to his sister and corrected my body's stupid reaction to seeing Easton after all these months. He probably wasn't even here for me. Lexi had complained the last time we'd spoken about how she and Noah were not allowed to be alone until they were deemed trustworthy by her father. Apparently, sneaking your brother's best friend into your closet to keep him from freezing in his car was not the selfless act Lexi thought it should be in her overprotective father's eyes. So, Easton was probably just their chaperone for the twenty-minute drive from Ridgewater.

"Juliette! I can't believe you're finally back." Lexi squealed as I reached her, attacking me with her hug.

"It's good to be home again," I said, returning her embrace. I had missed my best friend so much—had needed our video chats over the past few months more than she could ever know.

We pulled away, and I eyed her boyfriend. "Good to see you again, Noah. I hear congratulations are in order."

"Congratulations for what?" He narrowed his brown eyes at me.

I smiled. "Congratulations on finally seeing your best friend's little sister for the rockstar that she is."

He gave me a half smile and pulled Lexi close to his side. She was practically a midget next to his tall frame. "I hear you played a role in getting Lexi to make me see what I should have noticed all along."

I grinned. "Oh yeah. She had to—how do you put it? Make you want what you couldn't have."

He laughed. "Well, it most definitely worked."

I knew Easton was next in line for me to greet. He was also last, which meant I couldn't just quickly say hi and move on to the next person. So I put off what was sure to be an uncomfortable greeting a moment longer by asking Lexi, "Did Noah drive you here, or did your dad make Easton chaperone you guys?"

Lexi smiled. "Well, since I finished my babysitting punishment for the Vincenzo twins yesterday, Dad figured I was trustworthy—at least for another month or two."

Her dad was funny like that. But I'd probably be the same way if I'd become a grandpa at thirty-seven, thanks to Lexi's older sister. Everyone at school knew all about his rules for his children, and they knew better than to do anything to cross his path.

Which was exactly why I didn't know whether I'd be welcomed at his house anymore. I had no idea if Easton had told anyone yet.

"And of course we made Easton come along," Lexi said, breaking me away from my thoughts. "Since it wouldn't be the same without the four of us together."

I couldn't put off facing Easton any longer, so I turned toward him and smiled awkwardly. His hands were stuffed in his front pockets and he looked as uncomfortable as I felt.

Had he told anyone? Or was our secret summer fling still in fact a secret?

Easton cleared his throat. "Hi, Juliette."

"Hi," I barely managed to say, my mouth having gone dry.

"Come on, Easton," Lexi prodded. "You can give her a hug. I doubt Mercedes will freak out about that."

My heart plummeted into my stomach at the reminder that he had found a new girlfriend while I'd been away. What I'd seen on social media was true; he and Mercedes really were a thing.

Easton and I met each other's gaze for a second before he stepped forward and opened his arms. I leaned in for a quick hug, forcing myself not think about how perfectly I fit into his arms. My body felt warm, like it was finally home now that I'd hugged him.

But my body had been having a lot of strange things going on with it since the last time I saw him, so I decided to ignore the pull I had for him and stepped back before he could notice what was different about me. Tucking some of my grayish-blonde dyed hair behind my ear, I said, "It's good to see you again, Easton."

He nodded, his gaze briefly seeming to take me in. "Good to see you, too." The way he said those five little words made my heart thump harder than it had in months. Because he actually sounded sincere.

Could he have changed his mind about what he'd said to me the last time we were together?

I wanted to search his eyes, to try to figure out what he meant, but Lexi's voice cut through the air.

"How about we grab your luggage and get back on the road? I'm sure you're jet-lagged."

I *was* exhausted after the long flight. "Yeah, let's get going."

The boys led the way to the luggage carousel while Lexi walked beside me. "If you're not too tired, maybe we can stop by Emrie's for hot chocolate and take advantage of Easton's employee discount before taking you home."

I had to work hard to keep my eyes from glancing to Easton's back at the mention of Emrie's. Lexi had been busy babysitting her nephew over the summer, so she had no idea just how much time I had spent with Easton at his work. What had started off as innocent—me going there to beat the summer heat, requesting samples of every single flavor of ice cream on the menu just to annoy Easton before inevitably choosing my favorite, Rocky Road —had turned into a chance to get some of his undivided attention and flirt with him as he worked.

I swallowed the lump in my throat as the memories and everything that had happened because of them rushed to my mind. I needed to get a grip on myself, or there was no way I'd make it through the next few months with my secret still intact. I forced a smile on my lips. "Yeah, I'd love to go there."

We ordered our hot chocolate, which was the perfect thing to have on such a cold December day. Noah, Lexi, and I went to sit in a booth while Easton made us our drinks. He wasn't on duty, which made me think he was using it as an excuse to keep some distance between us for a little longer.

Easton stepped up to our booth a minute later with our drinks on a tray. He handed us our cups, and I noticed he was extra careful not to brush fingers with me in the exchange. He returned the tray behind the counter, and when he came back, he hesitated at the end of the table, like he wasn't sure if he should take the seat beside me.

So different from last summer when we'd talked and laughed and sat close in this very booth. He'd reach for my hand under the table, and we'd just sit and smile bashfully at each other, so giddy with our secret forbidden romance. Then when he finally got off work, I'd meet him at the back of the building and we'd make out against the wall for thirty minutes before going back to his house and pretending like nothing was going on.

It had been a great summer. I thought I'd found my person.

Until I made the stupidest decision I'd ever made and snuck into his tent at his family's end-of-summer camp-out.

I knew what happened after was wrong, and I regretted it almost as soon as it was over—when my brain wasn't so foggy— but I'd been delusional enough to hope that at least some part of him had cared about me like I'd cared about him. I'd given him something I'd never given anyone else before, and it had been agonizing to have him tell me that there was no "fixing things" and going back. That being with me was the biggest mistake of his life.

I should have seen it coming, especially with his family and their purity rings. But I'd been delusional enough to think he might say I was worth it.

I was so stupid.

"'Take a seat," Lexi said to Easton after taking a sip from her hot chocolate. "Juliette was telling us about how pretty the lights are on the Eiffel Tower at night."

Easton met my gaze with an unsure expression. I scooted closer to the wall and pasted on a smile. We'd kept our relationship a secret from everyone last summer; there was no sense in letting anyone in on the truth now.

"Go ahead and sit, Easton." I forced as much cheeriness into my voice as I could muster. "I promise I won't bite."

He only hesitated for a second longer before lowering himself into the booth. I was immediately met with the scent that I'd come to know as his. He had always smelled so good, and I had to force away the memories his scent evoked.

"So how was Paris?" Easton asked, his Adam's apple bobbing with the question.

I wiped my sweaty palms along my black leggings. "It was fabulous. Just what I needed and I'm going to miss it." I had needed to escape from this town, this country, after the way things had ended between us. An ocean separating me from my humiliation was just what the doctor ordered.

"What was your favorite part about Paris?" Lexi asked, her eyes bright with excitement.

As I thought over my answer, I took a quick sip of my hot chocolate. It was delicious. Creamy-chocolatey with just the right amount of raspberry flavor. Easton was actually really good at his job...but that was a given since he was good at everything: Looking way too cute in his dorky work hat. Kissing me until I couldn't catch my breath. Breaking my heart.

I pushed those thoughts away. "My favorite part was probably the food. I could eat crêpes every day and never tire of them."

Lexi's expression brightened. "Well, that's good, because my dad talked about making them for Sunday brunch tomorrow. Do you think your mom would be okay letting you come?"

"What time?" I hedged.

Lexi looked at Easton. "Do you remember what time Dad said Maddie and Grant would be over?"

Maddie was their older sister. Grant was Maddie's cute little boy who had just turned two.

Easton glanced at me. "I think brunch is at eleven."

"Will that work?" Lexi asked.

I watched Easton cautiously, wondering how he felt about me coming over to his house.

Then an even scarier thought occurred to me. How would his dad feel?

Had Easton told him?

I eyed his hands on the table. He wasn't wearing his purity ring.

My heart pounded. Was this some sort of trap? Was his dad's invitation to come over for crêpes just a ploy to get me into his house, so he could lecture me about how I'd seduced his son into losing his purity ring?

"I don't know..." I said.

Think of a good excuse, Juliette. Come on, you used to be so good at lying.

"My dad has been practicing making crêpes all week," Easton said, noticing my hesitation. He'd always been so good at picking up on my mood—which was exactly why I had to be super careful around him now.

I looked at him. I wanted to ask him if his dad knew, just to make sure I wasn't about to walk into Drill Sergeant Stevens's disciplinary action meeting.

He gave me a slight nod. I sighed and turned back to Lexi with a smile. "I'm sure my mom will be busy, so yeah, I'd love to come."

"Yay!" Lexi bounced in her seat.

And Easton seemed to visibly relax at my response. Was it

possible he wanted me to come, too?

When I got home, I took off my coat for the first time since landing and hung it in the closet by the front door. I caught a glimpse of myself in the mirror. How was I still standing? I looked like a zombie right now.

I inspected my reflection a little longer, smoothing down the fabric of my shirt. My belly hadn't popped out yet, but I was definitely looking pudgy around the middle. And if what I'd read online was true, I wouldn't be able to blame my thickening midsection on France's endless pastries much longer. The truth would become too obvious to ignore.

"Welcome home, sweetie." My mom stepped into the room and gave me a hug. "I'm so sorry I couldn't be at the airport to pick you up myself. I would have much rather been with you instead of talking to that stuffy congressman."

But of course, as Ridgewater's first female mayor, my mom had to bend over backwards to do her job. Which meant, sacrifices always needed to be made.

I knew she was doing her best, so instead of being annoyed at her job like I used to do, I wrapped my arms around her waist. I'd missed her so much over the past few months.

She held me for a few seconds before stepping back, her gaze taking me in and resting on my midsection briefly.

"You look really good," she said with a soft smile on her lips.

I nodded. "Thanks."

Then I just stood there uncomfortably, hoping she'd be the one to broach the awkward topic first.

She glanced at my stomach again. "I ordered takeout from the Chinese place on Elm. How about we catch up while we eat?"

I nodded and followed her into the kitchen. The house hadn't changed a bit in three and a half months. The kitchen was as bright and immaculately kept as ever—probably not such a hard thing to do since Mom had been alone at home and she barely cooked as it was. Cooking took time, and my mom never had enough of that.

I sat at the rectangular kitchen table in front of the bay window while my mom grabbed our takeout containers from the counter. She filled two glasses with water from the fridge then sat down across from me.

"I made you an appointment with Dr. Gunthrie for Monday morning at ten." She opened her box of stir-fry.

I nodded. "Okay."

"I figured you'd want to go in the morning when it was less likely for kids from school to see you at the hospital. She's a great OB-GYN and has promised that her staff will be extra discreet in your case."

Of course my mom would be worried about people being discreet about my pregnancy. It was an election year, and the last thing she wanted was a big scandal.

Mom continued, "And then I arranged with Grandma Irene for you to go live with her after Christmas. She's more than happy to have your company for the next few months."

I nodded as I twirled my fork in my food container, not feeling hungry after all.

"And I also have everything set up for you to start online school as soon as you'd like. You aren't showing yet, so you could still go to school for the next week before Christmas break and I doubt anyone will know you're pregnant. But if you want to just start it now, I think that's okay, too." She twisted some chow mein noodles onto her fork and looked me in the eye for the first time since sitting down. "Which would you prefer?"

I cleared my throat. "I guess I might as well just start with the online school thing. Doesn't make much sense to start here when I'll be gone again after Christmas break."

She blew on her hot noodles. "Sounds like a great idea. You can relax, spend time with your friends for the next couple of weeks, and then be gone before things become too obvious."

My cheeks heated up as she scrutinized me again.

"How far along did you say you were?"

"I think I'm eighteen weeks."

I had debated on whether I should lie to my mom, telling her that I'd gotten pregnant after I'd been in Paris for a few weeks. But since she'd be present at my doctor's appointments and would therefore hear the correct date while there, I decided to just make myself look even worse by telling her that I'd gotten pregnant right off the bat in a foreign country.

I hadn't dared tell her who the real father was, because then she'd make me tell him about the baby.

And I most definitely couldn't do that.

"Eighteen weeks," she said thoughtfully. "I think that's about the time I started wearing maternity clothes when I was pregnant with you."

"Yeah?"

She nodded and dug her fork into her takeout box again. "We'll have to buy maternity clothes before you go to Grandma's. If you can keep wearing your regular clothes a few weeks longer, I'm sure no one will suspect anything."

And there it was. Proof that I was a huge embarrassment to my mother.

"Sure."

I didn't know whether to be happy or sad that my mom was so determined to keep this baby a secret.

Mom eyed my untouched food. "You're not hungry?"

I pushed the container away and shook my head. "Not really. I'm pretty tired, actually."

"I bet you're jet-lagged. How about you go up and get some rest? We can talk about Paris tomorrow."

I nodded and gave her what was sure to be a tired smile. "Thanks." Then I stood and walked out of the kitchen and into the entryway.

My mom must have realized I was heading for my luggage because she called out, her voice drifting down the hall. "I can get those for you later. You shouldn't be doing a lot of heavy lifting right now."

I looked back toward the kitchen. "Thanks." Then I stepped closer to the staircase just off the entryway. I'd always imagined walking down these steps toward my prom date, wearing one of the super cute prom dresses they sold at the dress shop on main street. Or possibly one that I designed and sewed for myself.

I'd never pictured the dress being a maternity gown.

Why had I snuck into Easton's tent that night?

I gripped the railing and plodded up the gray-carpeted stairs to my room.

My room was just as I'd left it. My bed was neatly made with its white ruffled comforter. My sewing machine sat on my desk with the half-sewn red dress I'd started making last summer as my first attempt at designing my own clothes. And the photo of me and Easton at the lake was still safely hidden at the back of my sock drawer.

It was a sad reminder of how my life used to be. A life that was completely different from my new reality.

I got ready for bed quickly, and then lay down, pulling the covers tight around my shoulders. As I lay there, I felt the little fluttery kicks from inside me—different from the butterflies I had when I saw Easton today.

I ran a hand over my belly, but I still wasn't able to feel the kicks from the outside. Should I tell Easton about the baby?

I had no idea how to even begin that conversation. He'd

already freaked out on me about what we'd done. Losing his college money was a big deal. How could I tell him that I was carrying his baby?

Or *should* I tell him? I squeezed my eyes shut and tried to calm my breathing that went frantic every time I let myself think about my situation. The decision on whether to tell him or not had plagued me ever since I'd taken the pregnancy tests—well, after I'd decided not to throw myself in front of a train.

Telling him would only make him feel like I'd ruined his life even more. I knew his family. His sister had gotten pregnant in high school and had kept the baby. Would he feel obligated to do the same as his sister Maddie? He was a loyal guy. But that would totally derail his future. He had his whole life planned out. He was going to be a dentist, and that would take years of schooling. He couldn't have a baby to worry about while he did it all. That wasn't fair to him.

And I didn't need to give him another reason to hate me any more than he already did.

I just needed to stick with the plan my mom and I had come up with. Go away. Have the baby. Place the baby up for adoption with someone who could give him or her a stable environment—like two grownup parents who were ready for a kid.

Then I could come back home. Easton wouldn't ever have to know.

CHAPTER TWO

To say I slept badly would be an understatement, but I forced myself out of bed anyway, knowing I needed to put on a happy face. My plan was to go to the Stevens's house and pretend like Easton and I were never anything besides Lexi's best friend and Lexi's brother—two people who had known each other since we were kids but had never had a reason to care what the other was up to, or who they may or may not be dating.

If I could pretend, then maybe I'd have a chance at keeping my pregnancy a secret.

Mom was already gone when I came downstairs. She'd left a note on the counter.

Went to the office for a few hours, be back in time for dinner. I promise we'll spend the night together and you can tell me all about Paris.

I grabbed the house key from the hook by the garage, stuffing it in the front pocket of my jeans—which I had to leave unbuttoned at the top and fastened with a hair elastic—then grabbed my coat to walk to their house at the end of the street.

"Come on in. The crêpes are almost ready," Lexi said, beckoning me into her house a few minutes later. I looked around the living room. It was still the same as it had always been. Overstuffed furniture. Photos of Lexi and her family on the walls. It was a strange contrast from my house. You'd think that a home run by a man would have the less homey feeling out of the two, but my home was all straight clean lines with perfectly designed decor that matched—more like an extension of my mom's office instead of a home.

Lexi led me into the kitchen where her dad was flipping crêpes in a pan.

"Welcome back to the United States, Juliette," he said.

I swallowed and nodded. "Thanks. It's good to be back." I studied him for a moment longer just to see if he seemed tense at my presence. If he was, I couldn't tell. I sighed with relief. Hopefully, that meant Easton hadn't told him anything.

"Have a seat in the dining room. Breakfast will be ready in a couple of minutes," Mr. Stevens said over his shoulder as he cooked. "You'll have to tell us everything about Paris over breakfast."

"Sure," I said.

Lexi led me into their formal dining room, and I took my seat next to her at the already set table, grateful that Easton wasn't around yet.

"Now that we're alone, I want the real details on Paris," Lexi said, her eyes sparkling with excitement, like I had some sort of juicy gossip to tell.

Sadly for her and me, there wasn't anything really exciting that I could tell her that we hadn't already talked about over our video chats—aside from the fact that I'd taken a pregnancy test and it had come back positive.

But even though I was dying to confide in someone besides my mom, and have them assure me that everything would be okay, I couldn't tell Lexi. She was Easton's sister, and I couldn't risk him finding out.

Plus, she was asking about exciting events in Paris. The events that had caused my most life-altering news had happened here in New York and not there, anyway.

"What do you want to know?" I asked her.

"I don't know...everything. But mostly I want to know about all the boys who I'm sure were heartbroken when you left."

Of course Easton had to walk into the dining room with Grant's high chair just as Lexi mentioned boys.

But maybe this was good. It would help me plant some seeds in their minds if I was forced to use Plan B to explain why I was getting fat. If for some reason things fell through with me going to Grandma Irene's house, my plan was to tell everyone that a guy from Paris was the father of my baby. That way, Easton would be off the hook and he wouldn't have to hate me even more.

Easton set Grant's chair next to the spot where his dad usually sat for their family meals with Maddie. I eyed him as I formulated my next sentences in my head. I could tell he was listening for my answer, even if he pretended not to be.

"The boys there were just as amazing as we imagined. And their accents are to die for," I said.

Lexi's eyebrows lifted. "I knew there had to be more than just the one guy. Evan, right? The one you said—"

"The one that I said was super hot and had lips like an angel," I interrupted Lexi before she could finish. I had told her over video chat about how Evan was more like a stand-in to make someone jealous. Lexi just didn't know that it was Easton who I was trying to make jealous with that manufactured photo.

Easton's jaw tensed, and I didn't know whether to feel guilty or happy that my plan to make him jealous had possibly worked a little after all.

"So you kissed a lot of guys then?" Easton asked, his eyes tight as he took the seat across from mine.

I shrugged, hoping to come across that I wasn't nervous he was asking me about this. "When in France..." I gave my shoulder-length hair a flip with my hand for extra effect.

"I figured you'd have guys falling at your feet in Paris. Good for you."

That wasn't the reaction I'd expected at all. Based on the things he'd said the last time we were together, I'd almost expected him to call me a slut or something.

Except he didn't. He almost seemed sad that I was talking about kissing other guys.

But this shouldn't be happening, anyway. He was dating Mercedes Atkins, the town preacher's daughter. Easton was supposed to hate me for showing up at his tent that night.

Mr. Stevens set a plate of crêpes on the table at that moment, effectively bringing our conversation to a halt. He took his seat at the head of the table, unfolding his napkin and setting it on his lap.

"While we wait for Maddie and Grant to join us, why don't you tell us about all the wonderful places you went to visit?" Mr. Stevens said to me.

Easton eyed me from across the table, and I couldn't read what was in his expression, but he said, "Yes, I would love to hear what you've been up to."

What was he thinking about? I couldn't get a good read on him at all.

I sighed, giving up on analyzing his every facial expression for the moment, and finally said, "I'd love to hear what you've been up to as well."

"What's going on with you and Easton? Did something happen that I don't know about?" Lexi asked after breakfast. We were sitting on her bed in her room that didn't have any doors on it at all. No bedroom door. No closet door. Not even a bathroom door.

"What's with the lack of doors?"

Lexi sighed. "My dad is teaching me a lesson about how privacy is a privilege." She waved her hand. "The whole Noah-sleeping-in-my-closet thing made him do it."

"Wow, did he catch you two making out in your room or something?"

She shook her head and leaned back against the pillows by her headboard. "No, I think it was because of me talking about how Noah had left his shirt there that morning. That really set him off."

I laughed. That would do it. I'd probably freak out on her if I saw and heard that, too.

And her dad would for sure never allow me in his house again if he found out about Easton and me. In fact, he'd probably ban Lexi from being my friend anymore.

Yikes. Why hadn't I been thinking more clearly months ago? He *really* couldn't find out.

"So you still didn't answer my question. Why are you and Easton acting so weird around each other?"

I shrugged. "Must be the awkwardness of not seeing each other for a few months. I'm always a little weird around people I haven't seen for a long time."

"Makes sense." She pursed her lips thoughtfully. "Wanna hear something weird?"

"Sure." I'd love to talk about anything that didn't involve Easton and me.

She grinned. "I had the craziest thought last week about how cool it would be if you and Easton got together."

"You did?" I asked cautiously.

"Yeah." She sat up straighter. "I mean, Easton and Noah are best friends. You and I are best friends. It would just be kind of perfect."

"Except for the fact that he's dating Mercedes Atkins right now." *Little Miss Perfect.*

She shrugged. "He was asking about you last week."

"He was?" I knew it was stupid to hope that he had missed me, but I still did.

"He even talked about going skateboarding at the indoor skate park in Syracuse. That's something we've only ever done with you."

"Yeah?" Not that it would be smart for me to get on a skateboard anytime soon. My balance was not the same as it used to be.

Lexi's grin was huge, like she'd just done some sort of matchmaking between me and her non-single brother. "We should totally arrange it. I mean, I wouldn't mind giving Noah some private lessons." She bit her lip at the thought.

I shook my head and jumped at the chance to talk about her and Noah instead of Easton and me. "This is so weird."

"You think Noah and me together is weird?"

I laughed. "No. I think you two are super adorable. It's just...when I left, you were the one who'd never kissed a guy, and I was the one who kissed too many. It's just so strange how the tables have turned."

"Well, I'm sure you'll have a new boyfriend in no time. You've never had trouble finding one before."

I forced a smile on my face. "You're probably right."

"So when do you need to be home?" Lexi asked.

"I can hang for a few hours."

"Wanna help me get my skateboard ready so we can go next week?"

"Sure."

Lexi jumped off her bed and grabbed her skateboard from her closet. She looked over her shoulder. "Just wait for me by the kitchen table, I think I have my skateboard tools in here somewhere." She proceeded to rummage through the mess in her closet, and I couldn't help but wonder how in the world tall Noah Taylor was ever able to fit in that clutter for two nights.

I left her room figuring it might be a while. I might as well grab a glass of water while I waited.

I turned the corner at the end of the hall and stumbled when I saw Easton sitting at the kitchen table with a math textbook open and his mechanical pencil scratching numbers onto a sheet of paper. Did he hear us talking about him? Lexi's room wasn't that far from the kitchen.

He looked up from his homework, and my face grew hot.

Say something, Juliette. Don't just stand there and stare at his gorgeous face.

I cleared my throat. "D-do you have work tonight?" Maybe if I started a normal conversation, things wouldn't be as awkward as they'd been during brunch.

He gave me a confused expression. "No. Why?"

I shrugged. "Oh, I just figured you must have work since you usually like to wait until the last minute to do all your weekend homework."

"Oh, no," Lexi said, coming up behind me and making me jump. She propped her skateboard against the wall. "This is the *new* Easton. Ever since he started dating Mercedes, he's on this whole overachiever kind of thing. I really think he's trying to impress her."

Oh, it was for Mercedes.

Who names their daughter after a car, anyway?

Easton set his pencil down. "Um, I'm actually just trying to get a scholarship. I still have a few more to apply for, and every grade counts."

"Don't you know dad's going to pay..." Lexi trailed off. And when I glanced at her, her eyes had gone wide like she'd said something she hadn't meant to say.

Did she know then? Did Mr. Stevens know too and, true to his word, had cut off Easton's tuition fund because he'd lost his purity ring?

I swallowed, feeling the air in the room change.

"Um, never mind." Lexi laughed awkwardly, and I didn't miss the frustrated look Easton gave her. "I, um, do you still have my skateboard tool kit? Juliette and I were thinking it might be fun to go boarding together next week."

Easton looked relieved that she had changed the subject. "I-it's just on my dresser. I can get it if you want."

"I can grab it real quick." Lexi left the kitchen, her footsteps thumping on the stairs.

Once we were alone, I stepped closer to Easton and lowered my voice to a whisper. "Does she know?"

"Shh." Easton glanced around, probably to make sure his dad wasn't within hearing range. "Of course I haven't told her."

"Okay."

There was a long pause as we both tried to think of something to say.

He closed his notebook and looked around again. "I said something last week about not misplacing my purity ring. But she doesn't know anything more."

"That's probably good." I released the breath I'd been holding. "Does your dad know, though? Is that why you need the scholarships?"

His eyes hardened. "I haven't told him yet, either. As far as he knows, I misplaced my ring while we were camping. I-it's not exactly a conversation I'm excited to have."

I cast my gaze down. "I know. I'm sorry."

"Are you?" He sounded like he didn't believe me.

I looked up to meet his eyes. "Of course I am. We both know it was wrong. If I could take it back I would." My life would be a heck of a lot simpler if I didn't have to read all those pregnancy articles online.

"Me too."

I knew those words shouldn't have hurt, since I'd just said the same thing, but I felt my heart shatter all over again.

"I found it." Lexi entered the kitchen, holding her tool kit in her hands. "Can you make room for us to work at the table, Easton?"

He closed his textbook and stacked his notebook on top. "I'm actually done for now. The kitchen is all yours."

Then he picked up his things and left the room.

Want to find out what happens next? Read more from My Second Chance here: https://authorjudycorry.com/products/my-second-chance .

ABOUT THE AUTHOR

Judy Corry is the Amazon Top 12 and USA Today Bestselling Author of Contemporary and YA Romance. She writes romance because she can't get enough of the feeling of falling in love. She's known for writing heart-pounding kisses, endearing characters, and hard-won happily ever afters.

She lives in Southern Utah with the boy who took her to Prom, their four awesome kids, and two dogs. She's addicted to love stories, dark chocolate and chai lattes.

Printed in Great Britain
by Amazon